The Desert Run

Gregg Dunnett

For Alba and Rafa
You are my whole world

Now go and tidy your room

PART ONE

Chapter One

THREE CARS IN front the men wait for us, dressed in their uniforms and high-visibility jackets. They look serious. Suspicious. I've got the engine running—all the cars in the queue have—but the engine doesn't idle smoothly in Ben's van, so I have to keep revving it. I can see one of the uniforms keeps glancing at us, like that's annoying him.

"Don't rev it so hard," Ben says, getting a bit nervous now. "Don't draw attention to us."

I can't bring myself to look over at him. My best friend in the world, who's just knifed me in the back.

The brake lights on the car in front go off, as the queue crawls one place forward. I have no choice but to follow. What else am I going to do, reverse back onto the ferry? Even if I wanted to, there's a solid line of traffic blocking us off, and concrete barriers tight up against us on either side. We could make a run for it, just open the doors and leg it, but what good would that do? They'd probably catch us before we got out of the port, and even if not, how long can you last on the run? So our van tinkles as I move forward, from the bottles of wine and beer in the back. If only that was the problem.

This isn't the way we planned it. We researched this border crossing, and the plan was to drive straight in. Wave our passports and smile. We were counting on this one being a breeze.

But even so, it's not the fact that we're about to be busted with a hundred kilos of drugs that's worrying me. It's what Ben's just told me that's still ringing in my head. It's thrown me, it's like I don't care any more. It's like I don't even want to get home. Just to spite him, I give the engine a big rev.

"Easy," Ben says, anxiety spreading into his voice now.

I almost can't bring myself to answer him. I trusted him, and this is how he repays me? But I can't talk about that, so I go with the obvious problem. The one I barely even care about.

"We're gonna get caught and go to prison. And you know what Ben?"

He looks across at me.

"What?"

"It's all your fault."

I stare at him, and I see confusion and hurt in his eyes, and it's what I was hoping for. It makes me feel just a little bit better. But then he blinks it away and I see his confidence come back, but it's an effort.

"Jesus, Jake, what's got into you? Have a little faith. They're not going to find it. You did a good job."

For some reason this snaps me right back into the present. They really are searching every car, which really does mean we're in big trouble. A sudden hope flares up in my brain like a match striking: Can I blame all this on Ben? Just blurt it all out to the customs guy when he leans down to tell me to get out of the van? It was Ben's idea, so surely that makes him more guilty than me? But no. That's never going to wash. He might have come up with it, but I'm sitting right here in the van with him. I'm in this just as much as he is.

The car in front moves forward another place. Just one more car in front of them. We're close enough now to watch how this works. The customs officer, the same one who looked pissed off at me for revving the engine, beckons the car at the front of the queue into one of the bays where they do the searches. He goes round to the driver and taps on the window. I guess he tells the driver to get out because the door opens, and a man steps out. They walk together to the boot, and the driver opens it. It's a big car, a Volvo, and I can see little heads in the back, kids. Then the customs guy starts poking around. The driver leans in like he's trying to help, and he gets told off. He puts his hands up like they're gonna shoot him or something. Then they both calm down, and the customs guy points to the wall, and the man goes and stands and watches from there.

Then they get the dog, a spaniel or something. Another officer has it on a lead, and its little tail is doing circles, it's so excited. It jumps into the boot of the car and sticks its nose down. Tasting the smells coming out of the bags. Tasting the air in the car. Tasting with its nose, thousands of times more powerful than any human nose. I get a horrible feeling in my gut, like I've been punched. We sort of planned for a dog, but we didn't *really*. We were more messing about then. Don't make the mistake of thinking we were any good at this. This was our first time bringing dope in. We were making it up as we went along.

Tasting the air in the car.

I suddenly think of something. We might have the dope well hidden now, but a week ago, we just had it loosely piled up in the back of the van. We didn't think of that, did we?

And now I know we're going to get caught. There's just no way around it. And forget what I said earlier, I do care. I care about what's going to happen to me, I care about what my Dad is gonna think. I feel my heart rate soar as I watch. I feel dizzy, like I'm about to pass out. My stomach feels like someone keeps punching me there, over and over again. I can't believe I've put myself in this position. What the hell are they doing with a dog?

"Jake mate, calm down," Ben's voice cuts through my panic. "We planned for this. We didn't expect it, but we planned for it."

The words sound faraway, but they pull me back. Back into the van, back to the horrible reality.

"They're doing proper checks. We counted on them not doing proper checks." Suddenly I'm back to trusting Ben will sort it all out. I can hear it in my voice.

"Mate, you did a good job hiding it. They're not going to find it. Relax."

I look across at Ben. Right now, I don't know if I despise him or if he's my only hope. But the thought of all that dope loosely piled in the back of the van crashes back in. My head starts to shake, it doesn't feel like it's me controlling it, it's this simple, unfortunate fact. My head shakes even more.

"You're wrong Ben. We fucked up. There's no way that dog's not going to know we moved the drugs in the van."

And Ben suddenly gets it too. I see his face drop, his mouth fall open, as if to speak, but no words come out. We had all the dope just piled in here. Rubbing against the seats. No way the dog's gonna miss it.

Oops.

* * *

Just then, the customs guy walks two steps toward us, calling us forward again. It's our turn. I don't move. I can't move. He comes closer, looking pissed off that I'm holding him up. There's nothing else I can do. I slip the clutch, and the van crawls forward.

CHAPTER TWO

I GREW UP in Crawley, a commuter town south of London. We lived in an ordinary three bedroom house with a view of the railway lines. I went to the ordinary school down the road where I had ordinary friends, and when I wasn't at school, studying hard like the good little boy I was, I rode my bike or watched TV. Ordinary things.

But somehow, something happened to divert me from my ordinary path through life. This is that story. How I came to be sitting there that day, about to get busted for the large quantity of illegal drugs we had hidden in our van. And it all started when I went to university. When I met Ben.

* * *

It was just Dad and me who drove down there that day, in his maroon Rover, to drop me off at my new halls of residence. The University of Brighton looked huge and daunting. Around us rose the rolling South Down hills, the same hills that end so abruptly at the white cliffs of Dover. I was eighteen years old, and Mum didn't come because she was no longer with us.

My mum was a teacher. She taught French and German in secondary school, although not the one I went to because they thought that might be difficult for me. When I was sixteen she found a lump in her breast which turned out to be a kind of cancer. At the hospital none of the doctors were worried at first, the survival rates for the type of cancer she had were really good. Literally *no one* died from it. It was like they were pleased she had it so they had someone they could definitely cure. So she'd be given her treatment, and everything would go really well, and they'd do tests to confirm it was beaten, but then the tests would reveal it had popped up somewhere else. And the doctors would tell us how unusual this was, and they'd give her a new treatment, and run new tests. But it would pop up again, like a bubble in a sticker that you can't smooth out. And gradually the doctor's smiles became less genuine, more fixed. We tried to stay positive even then, as a family. But that bloody bubble kept popping up, and then more of them until the cancer was all the way through her. And then, once the doctors weren't smiling at all any more, she died.

* * *

I don't know whether Dad or I felt the most lonely or scared on the day he dropped me at university. He helped me carry all my bags into my room and unpack the few possessions I'd taken from the house I grew up in, then he looked around for something else to do, but there wasn't anything. Eventually, he had to go. We hugged. He turned his face away so I wouldn't see how close he was to losing it. And then he walked out, and I went to my new window and waited to see him returning to his car. Doing his best to pretend his heart wasn't being crushed for the second time in a year. I thought he wasn't going to turn and look but he did, just as he reached the car. He raised his hand to wave, as if he would see me later that evening, instead of pushing me out of his life and onto whatever path I would stumble down. Then he unlocked the car and climbed in, and I watched him drive away. Moments later, this guy stood in my doorway and waved a joint, asking if I wanted to smoke it with him.

I didn't want to, but I thought about what Dad had told me on the drive down. How I had to stay open-minded and be positive. How I had to make friends and live my life, not spend my time resenting how Mum had been taken away.

I looked at this guy, this kid really. He was a little shorter than me, with cropped, dark hair. He looked smart, not like the dope heads I'd known at school who would never have made it to university.

"Yeah, OK," I said.

"Cool." He walked in and sat down.

"I'm Ben," he said.

"Jake."

We leaned in closer and shook hands. My first handshake as a real student.

"I'm in the room next door," Ben said. "Was that your dad here before?"

I nodded.

"Pretty awesome to get away from them isn't it? Parents I mean."

Ben didn't wait for an answer. He put the joint between his lips and held up a silver Zippo lighter between his thumb and two fingers. He squeezed it and gave a flick with his wrist so that a bright orange flame danced from the top. He took the joint from his mouth and rolled the tip under the flame until it glowed orange. Then he took a drag, and held the joint out to me, the tip pointed at the ceiling.

"I made mine promise they wouldn't stay more than five minutes." He exhaled a cloud of blue smoke. "Mum couldn't stop crying."

I didn't reply but took the joint and sucked on it gently, just taking the smoke into my mouth, not down into my chest. Then I took a second drag, this time taking it all the way in. I could feel the effects right away. A tingling sensation that spread throughout my body, like the ripples from a splash on the surface of a calm pond.

"Could your mum not face it? Coming down and seeing you off?" Ben asked.

I'd never had to explain it to anyone before. When I went back to school after she'd died, the teachers had already told everyone. All the kids knew not to talk about it.

"My mum died," I said. "A few months ago." My voice sounded

strange to me. I watched Ben to see how he'd react.

I found out soon enough how most people would mumble some sort of apology and change the subject, and never meet your gaze. But not Ben. He wasn't like that.

"Oh shit. I'm sorry dude," he said, keeping his dark eyes fixed on mine the whole time.

"So what happened?" he asked and he sat down on my bed.

I passed him back the joint and told him, as the tingling spread and deepened up and down my body.

* * *

It's funny how often the subject of parents comes up when you go to university. I guess it's because it's one of the big experiences that everyone is sharing; everyone's living away from their parents for the first time. Or maybe kids on the verge of being adults just still define themselves by their parents. Anyway, it came up a lot. And every time it did, it was awkward, but every time, Ben looked out for me. Just to check I was alright. He'd take over the conversation if he sensed I needed it. He'd give me a look that asked if I wanted to get out of there. He'd make up a reason if I did.

And in return, I took part in his crazy plans and schemes. Whatever they were, I always said yes. Mostly they involved going out and getting drunk. Chasing girls in the town's pubs and clubs, and at parties in student houses. But sometimes they were stranger schemes too. Once he noticed a building site where a digger had been left unlocked with the keys stashed under a seat, and we broke in after the pubs had closed and tried to dig a hole. We wanted to make a sandcastle but it was harder than it looked to operate all the levers. We ended up reversing it into a ditch and then we had to run away because we were laughing so much.

Another time we climbed a crane. There was a ladder all the way up, and it was surrounded by a steel mesh so you couldn't really fall, but even so it was pretty scary up at the top. There was a craze for doing it and I think Ben wanted to see if it did anything for him. We never did it again so I guess it didn't.

We smoked some of the time, but not that much. Sometimes we took other drugs too, but it wasn't ever about drugs, not for me, and certainly not for Ben. For him they were just a means to an end. And that end was *adventure*. That's what Ben was searching for. It was like he could never get enough, it was an itch he couldn't scratch.

* * *

But mostly we weren't particularly creative. Mostly we just drank. Testing the limits for how unhealthily the young human male can live before the body refuses to cooperate. And in doing that we weren't special or different from anyone else. Everyone was drinking really, it's just Ben happened to live next door to me, so I'd be the first person he called on to go down to the off-licence. I'd be the person he stumbled home with when it was finally time to go to bed. It was always Ben and me, and then the others who sometimes tagged along, and sometimes didn't.

* * *

After the misery of hanging out in hospital watching Mum slip away, it was a relief to be having fun, to be allowed to be young at last. And Ben was pretty good at drinking, at finding adventures. So we slotted together and we turned that first year into one long party, so that before it even seemed to really get going, the first year was over.

Ben didn't want the party to finish. He had a bit of money saved up from somewhere and he spent it on a camper van. Nothing too fancy but it went. A few of us drove it down the west coast of Europe that summer. We built fires on the beaches; we got drunk on red wine. We tried and failed to sleep with French girls, who wouldn't even talk to us. Some of us succeeded in sleeping with German girls, who are so much easier. We bought surfboards and learnt to surf in the fresh blue water of the Atlantic Ocean. It was fantastic. But Ben—being Ben—wanted to push things a bit further. He talked us all into taking the van further down and catching the ferry to Morocco. It was his van so the rest of us thought, why not? And that was where this whole idea was born.

* * *

It wasn't exactly hard to get dope in those little towns on the beaches of southwest France. You just had to hang around in the right bar, and sooner or later some French dude would ask if you wanted to score. Then you'd follow him outside, you'd hand over a twenty euro note, and in return, he'd quietly press into your hand a little block of sticky brown resin. You'd get enough for four people to get comfortably stoned for a couple of days. And it was useful to have it around the campfires, especially if there were any German girls around. But in Morocco... oh boy. In Morocco, it was even easier. In Morocco you just had to walk down the street and people would ask as they walked past, you'd hear them saying it under their breath: "*Hello, my friend, you want hashish*?" It was like everyone was selling it.

And if you showed *any* interest, that same twenty euro note would buy three or four times as much in Morocco as it would in France. And all you had to do was hesitate and the price would drop. It was good stuff too. The dope in Morocco was smoother, stronger, just nicer all round. And that was from a total stranger on the street. We talked a lot then about what deal you might get if you were prepared to buy in bulk. Not seriously, not at that point, but there's no doubt that the way we laughed about bringing some back planted the seed.

That summer, out in Morocco, we just bought a little for personal use, but we didn't take anything back to Spain. We didn't dare. We thought we'd be prime targets for the customs men in the port. Four young guys in a beat-up camper van. We joked about which of us was most likely to get the full body-cavity search. So when we drove off the ferry back into Europe, we were clean, but we still expected to get taken apart. But it didn't happen. They didn't even check us. Honestly, they couldn't have been less interested. And there were loads of other vans around us, and dodgy-looking cars, and none of them got checked either. Actually, we were quite pissed off about the whole thing because that meant we had to drive the whole way home, and we didn't have anything to smoke. When we tried to buy more, it was expensive again, and all we could get was the shit European stuff.

Chapter Three

AT THE TIME it felt like that summer would last forever, but when it did end, reality began to bite. We had to find somewhere new to live since the halls where Ben and I stayed in our first year weren't available to second year students. Ben and I ended up together, in a small flat near the seafront which we shared with a couple of other guys. It wasn't particularly special, and it was more than I could really afford by then, since I hadn't earned anything over the summer. But I had to live somewhere, so I got out a credit card to cover the deposit. Everyone was doing the same thing, spending our student loans as soon as they came in, and collecting credit cards to live off. At first it didn't even worry me, the little pile of debt I was growing didn't seem real. But sometimes I thought about how big it might grow with still two years left at university.

I'd always worked, Saturday jobs and that sort of thing, so got a job then, to try and help keep my debts down. I worked a few nights a week in a petrol station. It was on the main road just out of town and I had the nighttime shift, starting at ten and finishing at six in the morning. I figured it would be quiet enough that I could write my essays between customers coming in. I thought it might even be fun, me the ruler of my own little illuminated empire. A splash of light in the darkness, with as much chocolate as I could steal from the shelves. I got that wrong though. It wasn't fun. Any time I tried to work I got interrupted by drunk or stoned students looking for late night snacks, and you'd be amazed how many people just drive around all night. I couldn't even steal chocolate. I had CCTV pointed at me the whole time, and I knew my boss sometimes watched it. But the extra income helped, a bit. It didn't mean I was climbing out of debt, but it slowed the rate I was falling into it.

What with me working, and most of us getting a bit concerned about money, we didn't go out quite so much in the second year. We all had to work a bit harder at uni too. It meant a lot of nights we'd stay in at the flat, either working in our rooms, or more usually in the flat drinking, playing video games or just watching TV. And since none of us had really mastered cleaning in those days, the flat wasn't the nicest place to hang out. To be honest it wasn't even that nice when it was clean, but when the kitchen was filled with dirty plates and smelled of rotten food, and when you had to clear a space among the empty beer cans, pizza and take-away boxes to sit down in the lounge, it soon got boring. We'd all taken the piss out of the cleaning staff in the halls of residence, how we missed them now.

I think that's what prompted Ben to invite us to his parents' house, well that and them being away on holiday. The idea wasn't to have a party, not at first anyway, just for the four of us guys from the flat to spend a couple of days somewhere a bit more comfortable. A bit warmer and cleaner. I was up for it right away. The two of us were the closest friends out of the group by then, and I was keen to see where he'd grown up, but the others weren't too sure, I think they thought it was a bit, you know, gay—just four blokes going to his parents house. Then he mentioned that the house had a swimming pool with a sauna. Somehow it wasn't gay after that.

I guess looking back it was always going to grow into something bigger than we first planned, but it didn't start out that way.

His folks lived a forty minute drive away, up towards London. It wasn't that far from where I grew up, but whereas I was on an estate, his parents practically owned an estate, or that was the way Ben described it.

And when we got there I saw he wasn't exaggerating. The house was huge, set all alone in grounds and the only neighbours he had were screened by trees. It was like being on a film set or something. And around the back was the swimming pool house, in a giant greenhouse-like building with the sauna on one end. Ben showed us around and told us how his dad would sit in there naked.

By then the idea of it being just the four of us had grown a bit. There were five cars that made the trip up from uni, all filled with students. And you can probably guess what happened next. The house was perfect for a party, and there were enough of us there to make it worthwhile, so a few people went off to buy booze, while the rest of us stripped down and jumped in the pool, some of the girls just in their underwear. Ben was pretty careful though. He went around locking valuables away so that nothing would get damaged if things got a bit wild, and he told us all which rooms were out of bounds. But by then the guys with the booze had returned and we had the stereo on pretty loud, so not everyone listened to him.

I know what you're thinking, we trashed the house, but it didn't happen like that. Because we were so far away from the university, we didn't have the problem of more and more people turning up that we didn't know. And a few people brought some dope which calmed things down too. We spent hours in the pool, pissed and pushing each other in, and then things moved into what Ben called the sitting room, where someone had rigged his dad's expensive stereo system into a proper disco, and then most people started looking for somewhere to sleep, a few of them pairing up and claiming the bedrooms, the rest of us just crashing out on the loungers in the pool room.

But even if it wasn't *that* wild twenty five students will still make a bit of a mess, and when I stumbled into the kitchen the next day in search of painkillers and coffee, it didn't look great. But everyone was good about it. Once we sobered up a bit we organised ourselves into clear up parties. I went around collecting glasses and loading them in the dishwasher, tipping out the cigarette ends before they went in, and still demanding coffee from anyone who would listen. By mid afternoon the place was almost back to how it had been when we arrived, and a lot of people had already left, going back for afternoon lectures or whatever. Honestly, the place wasn't that bad. If Ben's dad had come back a few hours earlier he really would have had something to shout about.

I was the one who saw him first. I was out the front, carrying a black bag filled with empty bottles and looking for the recycling bin when I heard the crunch of a car pulling into the driveway. I looked up and saw right away it wasn't a student car. It was a big, silver Mercedes with an older couple at the wheel, staring at me. The guy driving parked right in the middle of the drive and got out like he'd already decided to be angry.

"Who the hell are you? And what are doing in my house?"

It was obvious it was Ben's dad, he even looked like Ben, just an older, angrier version. I felt like I was still floating on a little cloud of alcohol and dope, but I sensed my high was about to be punctured.

"I'm just a friend of Ben's," I replied, going red.

"I don't care who you are. I asked what you're doing in my house." He demanded again.

I felt like saying I wasn't *in* his house, just because he wound me up. But instead I just looked down at the bag I was carrying but didn't answer. This seemed to infuriate him more.

"What the hell has been going on here? Where is Ben?"

Ben's mum was out of the car now, and she tried to calm him down.

"David dear, I'm sure there's a reasonable explanation to this."

"Like hell there is. Our bloody son has thrown some wild party while he thought we were away. That's the explanation and it's far from reasonable," he said, brushing her hand off his shoulder. "And you know what? It really caps a shitty twenty-four hours." With this he seemed done with me. He strode away and barged through the front door.

I met his mum's eyes for a second.

"I'm sorry about that," she said, and smiled nicely. "David's just in a bad mood. He had an emergency at work so we had to cut the holiday short, and then we couldn't get any tickets so we had to fly back economy…" She looked hopefully at the house. "Is it a mess in there?" She frowned as if fearing the worst.

I thought as fast as I could, thankful that it was mostly all cleaned up.

"No, it wasn't—wild or anything."

"So the house is OK?"

"No, it's fine now. I mean it never was that bad but…" I stopped, realising I'd said too much.

"I'd better go in and have a look." She smiled again but didn't move, probably because I was sort of blocking her way with the bags.

"OK. Oh—erm," I said, because I was still a bit drunk. "Where do these go?"

She looked at me and I thought I saw her shake her head a little.

"Over by the bushes," she pointed to where the outside bins were hidden. And when I'd dumped the bottles she'd gone inside too.

I didn't want to follow her in, but I didn't have any choice, and it turned out I'd missed the worst of it by then anyway. Ben's dad had stomped around and glared at people, but there wasn't enough for him to be angry about so he went for a shower to freshen up before going off to work.

Most of us left right away but I stayed. I don't know why exactly. Maybe because I wanted to support Ben, or maybe because his mum was being nice to us by then, sitting in the kitchen drinking tea and telling us about their holiday in America.

I didn't know too much about what Ben's dad did, just that he worked in the city somewhere. But I also knew, from looking around the house the night before, that he sometimes worked from home as well. He had a study in the house. Ben had told us not to go in there, but somehow the door got opened and a few of us had looked inside. I'd even sat in his dad's chair, a big leather swivel affair behind a huge antique desk and I'd spun around until the walls of books and framed photographs had made me dizzy. So when Ben's dad had announced he had to go to work, I'd imagined he was going to get back into the Merc and drive into London somewhere. It turned out that was wrong. He meant he was going into his study to do whatever it was he had to do. And that turned out to be unfortunate.

It seemed like everything had calmed down. Ben, his mum and I were still in the kitchen, we were nearly laughing about the whole thing and getting ready to head back to university when his dad appeared in the doorway like a ghost. And from the way Ben and his mum went silent I understood something was wrong again.

"Ben, would you like to come with me please," he said, in this creepy-calm voice. We all looked at each other. "Margaret, I think you'd better come as well."

No one said anything but the expression on Ben's face said it all. He didn't know what this was about but it was bad.

"You," Ben's dad's voice rang out again in the silence and he pointed at me. "You too. I'm not prepared to leave you alone in this house."

We all got up and Ben's dad stepped back from the doorway to let us pass. I could feel his eyes on me as I walked past. It felt like they were pouring out pure hatred.

"Where…?" Ben began but his dad cut him off.

"Study."

We walked along the hallway single file and into the study. We lined up behind the desk like school kids sent to the headmaster, and I saw right away what the problem was. Ben's mum did too, judging by the way she gasped. I heard Ben mutter "Oh *fuck*" under his breath.

"Indeed," said his dad.

There, in the middle of that great big desk was Charlie's bong. An expensive glass one that he'd bought in Amsterdam, complete with stickers of weed leaves printed on it and filled with brown liquid. A few of us had used it the night before, but not for long because we ran out of dope. Clearly in the excitement of jumping in the swimming pool he'd forgotten it. And probably because the room had been technically out-of-bounds no one had been in there to check it was clean.

"Would you mind telling me what the hell that is on my desk?" Ben's dad said from the doorway, his voice still unpleasantly calm.

All I could hear was Ben breathing for a moment. I guess he was working out what to say.

"It looks like a bong," he said, with just a little defiance.

"A bong," his dad repeated, emphasising the word so much it sounded ridiculous. "A bong. And what is a bong doing in my study?"

"Look I'm sorry Dad," Ben stepped forward to pick it up, "I did tell people they couldn't come in here..."

"Don't touch it," his Dad snapped, and Ben froze.

"I couldn't find the key to lock it."

"I said don't touch it. It's evidence."

Ben pulled his arm back but tried a small laugh. "*Evidence*? What, you gonna call the police? It's just a bit of dope. It's nothing serious."

"Nothing serious?" his dad turned on him now and his voice had risen. "Nothing serious? You hold a *drugs party* in my office, and you tell me it's nothing serious?"

They glared at each other and I didn't know how this was going to end. I thought they might even start fighting.

"Look it wasn't a drugs party," Ben started, backing down. "It was just a few friends over. I know I shouldn't have done it, but I was really careful. Nothing got broken. I put all the photos away and everything..." He stopped.

"We just needed a change of scene." He said finally and hung his head, waiting for whatever punishment he was going to get.

I guess his dad realised that calling the bong evidence sounded stupid because he didn't go any further with that.

"Get rid of it," he said instead.

Ben gratefully grabbed it and held it by his side, out of his dad's view.

"Now get out. Get out of my office and get out of my house."

"Dad," Ben began but his dad just pointed at the door and Ben gave up. We started trooping out.

"I never expected much of you Benjamin, but I never thought I'd have to face this. There will be consequences for this Benjamin. Major consequences. You realise that don't you?"

Ben opened his mouth to say something, but after a moment he closed it again, and just nodded.

And with that we left.

Chapter Four

"YOUR DAD'S A right arsehole," I said on the drive back. I was trying to get Ben talking again, but it wasn't coming very naturally.

"Yeah. He can be." Ben said pushing the van up to seventy.

"What do you reckon he means by major consequences?"

"Nothing. He's just mouthing off," Ben replied then lapsed back into silence.

"I mean what's his problem?" I tried again. "The house was alright. You were really responsible..."

"Yeah," Ben said, "I was."

"So is he always like that?" I asked, and Ben took so long to answer I thought he hadn't heard, but then he did answer.

"He didn't used to be. Not before."

I didn't understand so I looked across at him, and at the same time he glanced back at me, uncertainty in his eyes. He sniffed, like he was fighting to hold back something.

"Before what?"

He paused again, but this time it was clear he was just settling himself before telling me something, so I just waited.

"Before Julian died." Ben took one hand from the wheel and ran it through his hair a couple of times. He didn't wait for me to ask who Julian was.

"My brother. He was five years older than me. He was at uni in

Cambridge when it happened."

I felt the strongest sense of deja vu. I remembered how Ben had handled himself when I'd told him about mum.

"What happened?" I said, as plainly as I could.

Ben glanced over at me uncertainly. Now he'd started this it was like he didn't want to finish it.

"Will you keep it to yourself?"

"Yeah. Of course I will."

Ben glanced at me again, I could see the uncertainty on his face.

"He killed himself."

"Oh shit!" I blurted out before I could stop myself. Then I slowed down.

"Why? What happened?"

Ben answered in a faraway voice. "We don't know. He was doing well there, everyone loved him. He just..."

I didn't say anything, I waited to see if he'd go on.

"His girlfriend found him. Sasha. He was supposed to meet her for a picnic or something and he didn't turn up. She went to his room, you know, got the porter and everything to check he was alright. They found him swinging from the light fitting. He hung himself with his belt."

"Why?" I said again, a moment later.

"He had... Issues. Depression, I suppose. But there was no note. There was no real reason for it, at least not that we know of."

For a while neither of us spoke and the only noise was the burr of the engine.

"Julian was always Dad's favourite, he was the clever one, good at sports and stuff. He was going to follow in Dad's footsteps, studying law and everything. But then he died and it was just me left. It all changed. Dad's never got over it. He's not always a total arsehole, but it's like he resents that I'm the one who survived."

"Shit," I said, stunned. "When did this happen?"

"About five years ago."

I thought about that, how I'd talked to him about what happened to me. "Why didn't you tell me?"

He sniffed again. "We don't talk about it. The family I mean."

"Yeah but…"

"I'm telling you now."

I kind of understood. Not fully, but enough.

"So that's why my dad's such an arsehole." Ben looked at me, and now he smiled.

"But he won't do anything. He just likes to shout a lot."

* * *

I found out a week later that Ben was wrong about that. He came into my room and started asking all these questions about what you had to do to apply for a student loan and all this stuff. It was obvious he wanted to talk some more, and when I asked him about it, he told me his dad had cut him off financially. Not completely, he was still paying the course fees, but he refused to pay for any living costs if Ben was going to spend his time drinking and taking drugs. So Ben had to start applying for the same loans and credit cards that the rest of us needed.

That second summer we didn't go away again. Ben wanted to, but there was just no way I could afford it, and this time he had a better understanding of that. We stayed in Brighton though. Ben couldn't face spending the summer with his dad, and since we had to pay for the flat during the summer months, I figured I might as well live there. I had another reason too.

By then my dad had met another woman. He worried at first I might think it was too soon after Mum, or that she was too young, but actually it was a relief, I didn't have to worry about him being on his own and getting lonely. She had two young kids, so the house didn't feel like home by then anyway. My room had even been repurposed as a nursery, with Peppa Pig wallpaper.

The only downside was that it meant Dad didn't have any spare cash, so I was even more reliant on the credit cards, borrowing against the next instalments of my student loan and working as many hours as I could. I still tried not to worry about it at that stage. But the debt was mounting up.

Chapter Five

IN THE END I got my degree. A 2:2—a Desmond, they called it, on account of Desmond Tutu, whoever he was. It's not a great degree, but I think realistically that was the best I could hope for while holding down full time hours at the petrol station. And it only cost me thirty-five thousand pounds.

Ben didn't do so well. He failed his final-year exams and had to stay in Brighton to resit the third year. I stayed too. Dad's new woman had pretty much taken over at home by then so I had nowhere else to go.

* * *

The two guys we'd shared the flat with did move out though, so we had to replace them. And since we were sick of the mess that boys made by then, we pretended that the landlord would only take girls. And that's how Anna and Julia came to move in. They were both in their second year. Anna was pretty but a little chubby with black curly hair. She liked to cook and was one of those OCD people who couldn't go to bed unless all the washing up was done, which was perfect. Julia was... Well, how to describe her? I suppose I have to as she's crucial to the story.

At first I didn't see Julia as pretty exactly, more striking, with her blond hair, her figure, and her attitude which showed in the way she held herself and the way she moved. It was odd though because everyone else seemed to rate her right away. Friends down the pub would ask if our 'fit flatmate' was coming out with us, and be disappointed if she wasn't.

Maybe I didn't fancy her at first because she intimidated me a bit, right from the beginning, or maybe because I knew I had no chance with a girl like her. Or even because I couldn't quite believe she'd moved in with us. Whatever the reason, it hardly mattered at the time because she wasn't single anyway. She was seeing a semi-professional footballer named Andy, who always thought he was going to be signed any day by a major team. Even Anna had a boyfriend. So Ben and I were reduced to hoping they would bring lots of hot single friends around. But that didn't happen either.

But while they moved in, my next trouble was I didn't know how long I could afford to live there with them. My 2:2 in economics and business studies wasn't the instant ticket to a well-paid job that the university had made it out to be. I applied for everything I could find. Hundreds of jobs. Mostly, I got ignored. Very occasionally, I'd get an email back saying they were looking for someone with more experience. But that happened so rarely it felt like something to celebrate. I'd clench my fist and think "Yes, I actually got a rejection."

It wasn't just me either. I didn't know anyone from my course who managed to get a decent job. There were a few who were working as interns for various companies, but they weren't getting paid, they were just doing it for the experience. And I couldn't do that, not while I was still working at the petrol station. It would mean giving up the only money I had coming in. I wouldn't be able to pay the rent, and then I'd have nowhere to live. All I could do was work, and keep applying for jobs and juggling my debts around in the hope that something came up before I ran out of credit.

* * *

So that was my life as a graduate. That was why I'd spent hours poring over textbooks, constructing brilliant and original arguments on macroeconomic theory. Why I'd memorised the philosophy of prominent economists throughout the ages, so I could sit in my swivel chair, watching people key in their pin code one after another, queuing up to pay their taxes to Big fucking Oil.

Chapter Six

THE START OF Ben's 'solution' came one night in February the year after I graduated. I got back from work after an eight-hour shift, during which I'd cleaned out the toilets three times, once because someone had thrown up in there, once because someone else had pissed all over the floor and then finally because someone had blocked it with paper and kept flushing it till it overflowed. When I got home, I pulled off my red polo shirt and threw it in the sink with washing-up liquid, then wriggled into a T-shirt and hoodie. I grabbed a couple of beers from the fridge and slumped down next to Ben on the sofa, where he was playing on his Xbox. I snapped open my beer, and a little of it spilt on some papers on the coffee table. And Ben told me off for it. Which was odd.

"Careful, mate, that's important."

"Not like you to be studying," I replied.

"I'm not studying."

I frowned and looked a bit more carefully at the papers where I'd put the beer down. It was just a load of numbers and columns.

"What's that, then?"

"It's an idea I've been working on."

I picked it up to take a better look. Alongside the numbers were a few words in Ben's neat handwriting.

"What idea?" I said, but he was concentrating on shooting people on his game; he'd run into a nest of Russian soldiers. I watched to let the murder and mayhem calm what was left of my mind after my shift. Explosions and blood were gently washing away all my thoughts, except maybe that I could handle a joint. Then Ben suddenly asked me, not taking his eyes from the screen.

"How much do you owe, Jake?"

I fought for the energy to answer. "What, overall, or just on the credit cards and overdraft?"

"Total. How much would you need just to start from zero?"

I blew out my cheeks. "I dunno. Thirty-five? Forty?"

"Forty thousand pounds?"

"Yeah. About that. Why, have you won the lottery?"

Again, Ben didn't answer right away. He changed the weapon he was using to a handheld rocket launcher and aimed it at a helicopter that was hovering over his position. A man was leaning out of it, firing a machine gun and screaming hysterically. Ben aimed at the tail and released the rocket, blowing the back of the helicopter off so that it started to spin around in a death spiral. We both watched as the man kept shooting, even though he was doomed, and seconds later, the screen erupted in yellows and oranges as the chopper exploded. A satisfying death.

"You know how much I pay for a teenth?" Ben went on. In case you're not familiar with the word, it means an eighteenth of an ounce of cannabis. The smallest amount that people normally buy.

"About a tenner?"

"Yeah. For resin. Sometimes fifteen if there's not much about."

I waited to see where this was going, but it didn't go anywhere.

"So?" I said eventually.

Ben didn't take his eyes off the game. "So. If you have one ounce of resin, in theory, that's worth about a hundred and twenty quid. Maybe a hundred and eighty. Do you remember how much we paid for an ounce in Morocco?"

It seemed a long time ago by then, but I still remembered.

"About twenty euros."

"Yeah, about that."

"Are you thinking of selling drugs, Ben?" I asked, beginning to smile.

For the first time he looked at me, a little bit irritated, and he ignored the question.

"Of course, wholesale prices are different. At least, I assume they are. They must be. Otherwise, why would anyone bother doing it?" He toggled the menu suddenly and hit pause on the game, then pointed at the paper I'd spilled my beer on.

"I reckon, wholesale, an ounce is really worth somewhere between sixty to ninety pounds for resin."

He was looking right at me then, and his dark eyes had taken on a look I knew by then. A look of excitement.

"You know that resin comes over in nine-ounce bars? Nine bars, they call them?" He looked at me until I shrugged and nodded.

"So?"

"They're about the same size as... as a big chocolate bar, you know, the family-sized bars. You're an economist. How much do you reckon they go for?"

I couldn't help myself. I did the maths.

"Five hundred quid?"

"Depends on the quality," Ben said, and I was annoyed that he'd changed the rules of the sum just as I worked it out.

"It can be as little as four hundred, or as much as a thousand."

I didn't know what to say, so I kept quiet, but he went on.

"And four nine bars sold together is what makes up a kilo. And what's a kilo worth?" Ben asked but answered the question himself. "Maybe two thousand. Two and a half."

"Why are you telling me this?" I asked once we'd sat in silence for a while.

"I'm just thinking that if we drove the van down to Morocco and filled it with hash, then we could clear all of our debts in one go."

Chapter Seven

BEN REACHED FOR his beer and tapped the top of the can three times with his fingernail. Slowly, he tugged on the ring pull, and we both listened to that strange noise of sucking and breaking metal. He took a delicate sip, then turned to look at me.

"Or more likely, we could end up in prison," I replied. "Or murdered and buried somewhere in the desert."

"Why? Why would that happen?" Ben asked, suddenly animated.

"Because..." I turned my hands palms up and shrugged. "Because that's always what happens when someone gets into smuggling drugs. They get sucked in more and more until they get caught by the FBI, or gunned down by Columbian drug lords."

"You've watched too many films, and you've believed what they've told you."

I looked right at him for a moment.

"Most of those films are true stories," I said, and this got him. He looked frustrated and turned away.

"Maybe, but they're only the true stories of the minority who get caught. The ones who don't get caught don't get to tell their stories." He stared at me again now, and I could see he was at least a little bit serious about this.

"Nor do the ones who get killed," I replied, staring right back at him.

Ben took a sip, allowing me to think I'd won the point, then he went on.

"No one seemed very interested in killing us when we were down there," he said. "As I remember it, they wanted to sell us as much dope as they could." He sniffed like this was a challenge—find an answer to that, Jake, and I couldn't, because that much was true.

"And we could have had the van packed to the roof with anything. And yet we drove straight through both sets of customs. Spain and Dover."

I couldn't really argue with that either, although I tried to.

"They might have had dogs that could smell it."

"But that's not a problem. You pack it in coffee. Just like in the films," Ben replied, getting animated again. "And anyway, did you see any dogs?" He knew I didn't because we talked about it on the way back that summer.

"But what would you do with it when you got it here?" I asked instead. "Are you going to start dealing from the flat? That's where the risk is."

"No."

"What, then? Put it on eBay? Send me off to sell it outside the nearest school?"

He ignored this.

"No, what we do is move it wholesale. And not here either. We let someone else worry about splitting it up and selling it on."

Ben was now stroking his chin like he was some kind of criminal mastermind, and I'd had enough. I took a big swig of my beer and was about to tell him about the day I'd had, and use that as justification that it was my turn on the game, but at that moment, the lights went off, and the TV set died.

"Shit, that was a new high score." I could hear Ben's voice in the dark.

"Didn't you charge the key?" I said. I was really pissed off then because it was definitely Ben's turn to top up the electric key. We'd had a bit of trouble keeping up to date with the electricity bill by then, and they'd put us on a meter, so we had to pay in advance via a card, which we topped up at the shop round the corner. And it always ran out just when you didn't want it to. Although I'm not sure I can think of a convenient time for all the lights and the fridge to turn off.

"It's not my turn, is it?" Ben said, and even in the gloom, I could see on his face he was trying it on. Our eyes had already adjusted to the sudden lack of illumination. There was a bit of light coming in from the street, and I didn't trust myself to answer him. He changed tack.

"I'm sorry, mate. I would have gone," he said a moment later. "Just I haven't got any cash. Can I borrow a bit till the end of the week?"

I reached for my wallet and pulled out a twenty. It was the last note I had, and I didn't get paid until the next Friday. On the plus side, at least it was Ben who would have to go out into the cold. And it was definitely my turn to shoot Russian soldiers.

CHAPTER EIGHT

UNLESS YOU'RE AN accountant, or maybe one of those people with an "I heart spreadsheets" mug that you keep on your desk at work, you're not going to be that interested in my finances. But if you know the basics, it'll help you understand why Ben's idea caught in my mind.

By then I owed thirty-four thousand pounds in student loans. I had three grand on one credit card, and another with two grand on it. I was constantly sinking right down to the limit of my thousand-pound overdraft. I also owed my dad about five grand, but neither of us really believed that was going to be paid back.

I was working full time by then. Although my contract didn't guarantee any hours, my boss liked me and I generally worked between thirty-five and forty hours a week. It was boring as hell, but it brought in about two hundred quid, after deductions. That was nearly enough to cover rent, bus fares, food, a little bit of money for beer, and most of the interest on my credit cards. Most of it.

So even though Ben's plan was ridiculous, it was tempting. Not tempting to actually do it—just tempting to think about. It was like those daydreams you have about winning the lottery. How you'd spend the money. That was all I was doing at that stage. Dreaming about what it would be like to wipe away all my financial worries at a stroke.

And actually, it was a simple enough plan. Ben still had his camper van. It was on its last legs, but it still ran. So maybe we *could* drive it down to Morocco, just like we had that other summer. Maybe we could find someone to sell us some dope, and maybe we could drive it all the way back, straight through the two sets of border checks, and sell the lot in one big deal?

Ben's figures had a fair few assumptions in them, but fundamentally, they held up. We made a spreadsheet in Excel. We scaled up what Ben typically paid for his teenths. We allowed twenty percent for whoever sold the dope to us, and another twenty percent to whoever we sold it on to. For the sake of the figures we ignored the possibility that they might shoot us rather than accept our commission rate. And based on that, we figured a kilo of Moroccan hashish would wholesale for a bit over a thousand pounds. That meant all we'd need to be debt free was about a hundred kilos. It was a nice round figure so it stuck.

But daydreaming wasn't going to get me out of my hole. So I went on filling in application form after application form, and I assumed Ben was getting on with his resits. Maybe I'd have noticed otherwise if I hadn't got distracted. But I'm pretty sure what happened next would have distracted anyone.

Chapter Nine

MY FRIENDS STILL asked about Julia all the time, and by then I'd realised that she was hot. But she still made me nervous, and with her having a boyfriend and everything, I tended to avoid her. I certainly wasn't expecting anything to happen between us. And I absolutely wasn't expecting what *did* happen to take place. I guess I was kind of innocent in those days.

It happened one evening, I was alone in the flat, waiting for a frozen pizza to cook and watching TV. A rare night off and this was what my life had come to. Oh, and I was cutting my toenails. I had the clippings from one foot balanced on the arm of the sofa, and I was leaning forward, halfway through the other foot, when I heard her calling softly from the doorway.

"Hi, Jake, what you up to?"

I froze. First in surprise, since I thought everyone was out, and then because of what I was doing—I don't know where you're supposed to cut your toenails but it's probably not on the sofa, not where everyone eats. Then finally because it was Julia, and that always got me on edge. So I tried to make out I was just sitting like that, leaning forward and holding onto my feet.

"Nothing, just watching telly," I said.

"On your own?" she replied. "Isn't Ben here?"

"No, he's gone out. He said he'd be back late."

"Oh."

I thought she'd go upstairs to her room. She usually did if it was just me around.

"It's just you and me, then," she said, in a voice I'd have to describe as playful.

And with that she came and sat at the other end of the sofa, pulling her bare feet up after her. Then she straightened her leg so that the tip of her toe began to tickle my side.

I didn't mean to but I tensed right up.

"Are you ticklish, Jake?" she said.

"No," I said, and twisted to escape her foot. I managed to sit back in the sofa too, in a slightly more normal position.

"OK." She stopped digging into my ribs and went back to watching me.

"What are you watching?" she asked.

"It's a Bourne film," I said. "The second one." I wondered if I could slip the clippings down the gap between the cushion and the side of the sofa. I know that's disgusting, but I wasn't thinking about leaving them there; it was just until she went upstairs.

"I like that one," she said. "Mind if I watch it with you?"

"No, course not," I said, and there was a little awkward silence. Or at least it was awkward for me.

"Not with Andy tonight?" I asked suddenly. And inwardly, I kicked myself for bringing him up, because the thought of watching a film with Julia was actually quite appealing, if I could just relax.

"Football practice," she said, making a face. "He's so boring."

I agreed but didn't know if I should say so, so I didn't say anything. Instead, I glanced at her, at her long hair which was all over one side, pulled in front of her body. I tried not to look usually; I didn't want to get caught perving at a flatmate. She looked good, let's just say you wouldn't have caught me running about in the mud if I could shag Julia instead.

We watched the film for a little while, about a minute maybe. Then she spoke again.

"Jake, can I ask you a question?"

"Yeah, course." Maybe she wasn't as much of a Bourne fan as she'd made out. That was cool, I'd seen it before anyway. But what she came out with really surprised me.

"What do you think of my boobs?" she asked.

I didn't think I could have heard her right.

"What?" I said.

"My boobs," she said again, very clearly this time, and putting her hands on the sides of her top so that the material was stretched tight over her chest. "Do you like them?"

"What?" I said again because—well, because what the hell else can you say to that?

"Do you think they're a bit small?" She was still pulling at the sides of her top, pointing her tits at me, and staring straight at me, like she was actually expecting an answer.

I still said nothing.

"Come on Jake, I'm thinking of having them done."

"Done? Like a..." Suddenly I realised what she was actually talking about. "Like a *boob job*?"

"Yeah," she said. "If you wanna call it that. What do you think though? Do you like them?"

"Well, I haven't really noticed," I said, which obviously wasn't true since she'd been living there for a couple of months by then and I'd thought about them plenty. I'd compared them to Anna's. There had been one time when she was walking back from the shower that I'd even managed to get a half-decent look at one of them because her towel didn't quite meet at the side. But I couldn't admit any of that to her.

She just gave me a funny laugh. "Yeah, right, Jake. All men notice."

I could feel my face going red. I was pleased the light wasn't on, so maybe she couldn't tell.

"But come on. Have a look now. What do you think? I really want to know." She turned so I could see them from the side, then turned again so that she was facing me again. Her face looked earnest, a little furrow of concentration on her brow, where I was trying to keep my eyes.

"Come on, they won't bite you, Jake," she said. And slowly, I let my eyes sink down to her chest.

"Well?"

To be honest, I couldn't see much. Even with her stretching her top behind her, mostly, I could just see the outline of her bra. I guess she realised this because suddenly, she leant forward and grabbed the bottom of her top and pulled it up quickly over her head. In a flash, I was looking at her flat belly, the bottom of her rib cage, and above that a white bra, with frilly lace at the edges.

But she still wasn't happy. Now, she reached behind and unclipped her bra in one swift movement, then let it drop onto the sofa between us. She flicked her hair and again posed herself for me to inspect.

"There. What do you think now?"

I was stunned into silence. Staring open-mouthed at her breasts as they swayed gently from side to side.

"Andy says they're too small." She screwed up her face. "Actually, he hasn't *said* they're too small, but I can see it's what he's thinking."

She began to fidget again, pushing her breasts from the side, then underneath, as if she were in her bedroom, or the bathroom, or wherever women go when they want to touch themselves up, instead of sitting across from me on the sofa in the living room.

And I didn't know what to think. I'd gone from cutting my toenails to staring at a naked pair of breasts in less than five minutes. I don't think the human brain can adapt that quickly. Not the male brain, anyway. I just stared at her, at how her nipples were hardening from a puffy softness to stand proud and erect. I could feel the effect it was having on me too. I tried to hide it with my arm, moving so that it draped over my lap.

"Well, come on," she said again. "What do you think?"

I'd seen a few pairs of breasts by then, for real I mean, not just online. Although mostly it had been either in the dark or I'd been drunk. But these were definitely the nicest pair I'd ever seen close up. You could argue they were a little on the small side, but they more than made up for that with their shape—how tight and pert they were, and with the rest of her body being so hot, and the way the longest strands of her hair were touching the tip of her left nipple. I thought they looked amazing, and given enough time, I might have been able to say all that. But she didn't give me time.

"What? Say it."

"They're nice," I said, feeling rushed.

"Just nice?"

She sounded deflated and puffed out her cheeks. It made her look cute which wasn't a word I'd associated with Julia previously.

"You'd like them more if they were bigger, wouldn't you? You can tell me."

I searched my brain for an answer, but nothing came.

"Come on, Jake, a handsome guy like you, you must have been with lots of girls. You must know what you like?"

I nodded.

"Do you want to touch them?" she asked a moment later, a smile coming back onto her face. I felt like she could read my mind. But I was confused too, I didn't know what the hell was really going on.

"Do you want to feel them?" She smiled and leaned closer to me on the sofa. Then she took my hand, the one that was covering my erection, and held it between both of hers.

"Cold hands," she said. Then she placed it over her right breast so that it cupped it. I could feel her chest moving as she breathed. I could feel the hard nub of her nipple against my palm.

"There." She still held my hand and pushed it firmly against her. "Do you like that?"

Again I couldn't answer. I just stared at her.

"Give me your other hand," she ordered, not laughing now.

I wanted to do what she said, but I had a problem. I still had the bloody toenail clippings in my other hand pressed into my palm. In the end I did the only thing I could and slipped them down the sofa, wiping my palm against the cushion as I pulled it back out to make sure they were all gone. Then I gave her my other hand and she placed it on her other breast. We were close together now, she was staring right into my eyes, I never dared to hold her gaze before.

"What do you think Jake?" She said.

I opened my mouth to answer but I didn't know what to say. I was thinking about how I had a packet of condoms in my room; I was wondering if I should suggest I go and get them. Or would it be better to suggest we both go upstairs, since it wouldn't have been cool for Anna or Ben to come back if we were going to do it right there in the lounge. But at the same time, I didn't want to move my hands from where they were, each cupping one of her breasts. I let my eyes drop down from her face, her belly, where her slim body disappeared into tight jeans. I wondered about trying to kiss her. Then there was a loud beeping sound from the kitchen.

"What's that?" she asked.

"Nothing," I replied. I decided to go for it. I squeezed her breasts a little and I leaned forward, aiming for her lips.

"No, seriously," she pulled back. "What's that noise?"

The tone of her voice cut through my brain. The playfulness was gone. She sounded totally matter-of-fact.

"It's just the oven timer," I said. "Don't worry. It'll go off in a minute."

She screwed up her face like this was crazy.

"No, it won't. It doesn't stop. And anyway, whatever you've got in there will burn."

"Don't worry," I said again. It wasn't like I'd been that hungry in the first place.

"Jake," she said now, giving me a look like I was behaving really strangely. I still had my hands planted on her breasts, but she leaned back now, making it awkward for me to stay holding onto them.

"You can't just leave it making that noise. Go on. Go and turn it off." And with that, she let herself fall back on the sofa. She made no effort to cover herself up, just lay there against the cushions, her hair fanned out around her head, the weight of her breasts now falling back against her chest. I looked at her in confusion for a moment, but she was right, the noise wasn't going to stop, and it was my pizza. So I pushed myself up, awkwardly to try and hide my erection. And I half-walked half-ran to the kitchen.

I turned the oven off and got myself a drink of water. I could see my reflection in the inside of the window. I looked startled, but I gave myself a wide eyed smile and whispered to myself that I was definitely going to get laid. I thought again about those condoms upstairs. I decided I should suggest we go upstairs. My room was tidy enough to do it in, or we could use hers. I'd read how girls often preferred to do it in their rooms; it made them feel more secure or something. I didn't think about Andy once, clearly she wasn't. I took a deep breath and walked back into the living room.

And Julia was gone. Her bra and top were no longer on the sofa. There was nothing to show what had just been happening. I panicked for a second, and then I realised. She'd had the same thought as me, that we couldn't go any further in the living room in case Ben or Anna came home. So I went upstairs, a little slowly now because I was nervous again for how I might find her.

I tried my room. I thought I might discover her naked, lying on my bed, beckoning me in with one hand while showing me her other rubbing between her legs. But the room was empty. I quickly grabbed the condoms from my drawer and went straight to her room, down the other corridor off the stairs. When I got there, the door was shut, and just because I still wasn't quite sure, I knocked.

"Yeah, what is it?" She called from inside. That wasn't what I expected.

"Um, shall I come in?"

"Why?"

I didn't know how to answer that, but just then the door opened, and Julia was standing there. She wasn't naked, or in her underwear. She was fully dressed, a loose black blouse covering her top. She was even putting her coat on. She looked at me pretty funny too, as if to ask what the hell I wanted. I shrank back across the hallway.

"Jake," she said, as if this was a surprise. "What do you want?"

I blinked a few times, trying to work out what was going on.

"I was just, um—" I began, not knowing how to finish this sentence. I still had the condoms in my hand. "I thought you wanted to know what I thought."

She frowned at me, like she had no idea what I was talking about. Then noticed what I was carrying.

"Oh that. Oh." She smiled. The sweetest smile. "Oh Jake. You thought… I don't think we're going to need those. I'm with Andy remember?"

She reached out and touched my hip and I dropped my head, but didn't turn away, not while she was touching me.

"He just texted, they've finished early, so he asked me to come round to his place."

I didn't say anything, there was nothing I could say.

"I really did just want your opinion. You don't mind do you?"

I shook my head, still looking down at my feet.

She gave a little half-laugh. "Look if I ever get fed up of being less important to Andy than his silly football games, you'll be the first to know, alright? I'll make it up to you."

She reached out and with her finger underneath my chin she lifted my head up. The look I saw on her face was what made me fall in love with her.

I nodded.

"OK." She gave me a smile, "I've got to go."

She pushed past me, I felt her body press momentarily against mine as she did so, then she was gone, gliding down the stairs in her loping, bouncing steps and straight out the door.

* * *

And for a very long time after that I found it hard to concentrate on applying for jobs, or working at the petrol station, or even to notice that all Ben seemed to talk about was his crazy drug smuggling idea. But if you'd seen how she looked that day with her top off. If you'd had your hands where mine were, I'm pretty sure it would have distracted you too.

Chapter Ten

TIME DIVIDED THAT evening. Like an axe splitting a log it separated into the 'before', when Julia was just a flatmate, and the 'after', when I saw almost everything through the prism of Julia, how wonderful she was, how wonderful she looked. I marvelled at how I could have lived with her for so long without seeing just how stunning she was. I must have been blind. And I felt sure that whatever had happened, would happen again, if I only made the right choices.

I wanted to tell Ben about Julia. I wanted to tell everyone. But especially Ben since he was my best friend. But I wasn't sure what to say. I suppose I could have just described what happened, but despite my euphoria it confused me, I came to think I perhaps hadn't handled it too well. And I certainly didn't want Julia to find out I'd been bragging about it, not if that might make her less keen to repeat it. So I didn't tell Ben, nor anyone else. Instead I hung around the flat as much as I could, hoping to bump into her when no one else was home.

But that didn't go so well. In the weeks after, Julia always seemed to be around Andy's. And even when she was at the flat, she'd be upstairs, doing her uni work. Every now and then, I'd hear her coming downstairs to the kitchen, and I'd jump up, suddenly needing to make a cup of tea or something, but it was always awkward in the kitchen. She'd be distant, apparently engrossed in thinking about her work, and then she'd disappear back up to her room, leaving me standing there, with the memory of how she'd looked that evening fading, no matter how hard I tried to fix it in my mind.

But while I filled my head with thoughts of Julia undressed, Ben was busy filling his with his plan. Although as far as he was concerned, it was our plan, not just his.

It was our 'meeting' that brought that home to me. That happened a few weeks later. It was my day off and I was hanging around the flat with Anna when Ben came in and suggested me and him go and get some air. He looked at Anna as he said so, and raised his eyebrows at me, like we had to talk, but not in front of her. Anna had already told me Julia was out for the day so it made no difference to me. I shrugged and followed him out.

* * *

We went to a café on the seafront. I queued up to get the drinks while Ben bagged a table right in the corner where we wouldn't be overheard. When I found him he had his laptop open, and was punching in the key for the wifi.

"I need to update you on progress, and maybe give you a few tasks," he said, not looking up at me, so I had to clear the space myself to put the tray down.

"OK. Progress on what exactly?" I had genuinely forgotten with everything that had been happening.

Now he looked up at me.

"Jake, I'm not going to say it out loud, am I?"

I thought for a second.

"Are you still going on about your dope plan?"

"Fuck's sake Jake. Keep your voice down." Ben glared at me and glanced around. "Yes, we're still very much looking at the plan. That's why I asked you here. To update you."

I shook my head and stirred sugar into my coffee.

"Alright. Whatever," I said.

"We need to properly think about all the issues we need to solve, then divide up responsibility for them. So that we're working together, but not wasting resources," Ben said. Or he said something like that. I wasn't really listening. Outside the window, a girl had just walked past, long hair blowing in the breeze. I thought she looked like Julia. A bit like her, anyway, same hair colour but not as good-looking. But then, no one was quite as beautiful as Julia. I couldn't help noticing how the breeze was blowing the girl's top against her chest, making it easy to get a sense of what her breasts were like. Smaller than Julia's, I thought. I really didn't know what she was worrying about.

"Jake, are you listening or what?" Ben interrupted me.

"Yeah, course I am," I said. I looked at him and smiled.

"Can you maybe focus a bit?"

"Sure."

"So I was saying, what are the actual problems we've got to sort out?"

Reluctantly, I turned my attention to what he was talking about.

"What?"

"What are the issues we've got to address?"

I could see what Ben was doing. He was approaching this just like we were taught in our course. We'd shared some topics and sat in the same café a year before when we'd been given the task of writing a marketing plan to launch a new brand of goat's cheese. *Go Goat,* we called it, with an idea for running adverts that featured a cartoon goat doing tricks on a skateboard. It's kind of fun when you get into it.

"Where do you want me to start? There's loads of issues."

"Start wherever you like. We'll write them all down and sort them one by one."

I took a big slurp of coffee and gave up. Ben was in one of his persistent moods. I'd known him long enough by then that I knew it was easier just to go along with it.

"OK. Money. We don't have any, so we can't afford to buy the dope in the first place."

I watched as Ben typed this into his laptop. Then he started a new line and wrote, "How do we get it?" Then he looked at me again. "Any ideas?"

I thought for a bit and decided to try a joke.

"Your dad?" I asked. "Could you explain what you want to do? Maybe ask for a loan?"

But Ben didn't seem to get it. He just shook his head. "Not directly. But there's a bit I can still get from him." He added notes saying "my dad" and "two thousand pounds," followed by a question mark.

"How about your dad?" he asked. "There anything there?"

I shook my head.

"You sure?"

"I'm pretty sure."

He frowned but added a second note: "Jake's dad. Zero." Then he took a sip of his coffee and inspected his work so far.

"Other means, then. How much in credit cards have you got access to?"

I didn't really like to think too hard about my financial situation, but I kind of knew where I was all the time. It hung over my head like a persistent black cloud.

"I'm a bit overdrawn, but I've got about fifteen hundred quid left on my credit cards."

This went into the file on the laptop.

"How about other credit cards? Can you get more?"

I hesitated at this question. Maybe because I'd seen how my answers went straight into his laptop. It was like just handing him the cash.

"Maybe," I said in the end.

"And that could be quite a bit, couldn't it?"

"Yeah, but I need that to live off until I get a proper job. I don't want to get more into debt." That second part was a stupid thing to say since it gave him an opening to launch into his lecture, now fairly familiar even if I hadn't paid much attention up until then.

"Jake, this whole idea isn't about getting more into debt. It's about getting out of debt altogether. It's about beginning our careers from zero, rather than half a mile back from the fucking start line. You know?"

I did know. Ben had explained this to me several times already and I didn't need to hear it again.

"So how much could you get?"

I thought for a moment.

"Maybe three grand?"

I watched as "Jake credit cards, five thousand" was added. No question mark this time.

"You can probably get the same," I said, as if that evened the score, but he just nodded and did something fancy with the cut and paste so that another line was added with his name.

"I've also got some money from my gran," he said.

And with that he added fifteen thousand to the total and sat back, looking pleased.

"OK, so that's, what? Nearly twenty five thousand. So money isn't really an issue, is it? Because we're going to make it all back, and a lot more." He looked pleased with himself. "So what else? How about where we're going to hide the gear?"

I was still a bit shocked Ben had fifteen grand he'd not told me about.

"I thought we were going to hide it in the van?" I said at last.

"Yeah, but where, exactly? It's got to be pretty good, just in case we do get stopped."

I didn't like the idea of that. What was the point of a daydream about drug smuggling where you imagined getting caught?

"Well, what did we decide before? When we were driving back the other time. In the seats, wasn't it?"

The word "seats" with another question mark went onto the file. But the expression on Ben's face told me he wasn't entirely satisfied with this.

"Don't you think it's a bit obvious? And how do we actually get it in there? And how much can we get in there?" He took another sip of coffee and watched out the window as a couple of surfers walked past.

"Inside the doors, then. Behind all the interior panels?" I tried.

Ben wrote this down too, but again without massive enthusiasm, and we both added a few more suggestions, mostly remembered from conversations we'd had the summer before. Only this time, now that I understood we were on some level seriously considering doing this, I agreed with his lack of enthusiasm. None of the ideas sounded quite as good as they had. Eventually, Ben moved us on.

"OK, maybe we'll come back to that. How about where we buy the gear from in the first place? I think it's important to get something in place before we actually get there. Have you got any ideas on that?"

"Me?" I asked. "No."

Ben frowned, disappointed.

"How about where we sell it on to?" I said. "I'd have thought that's more difficult."

"I've got that in hand."

"What do you mean?"

"I spoke to Danny. He's getting something sorted."

Danny was the guy Ben bought his dope from. A small-time, local drug dealer who sold mostly to students. But still, a drug dealer.

"You what?"

"I spoke to Danny."

I stared at him. "You actually spoke to Danny?"

"Yeah."

"Fuck, Ben, you actually asked a drug dealer questions about his suppliers?"

"I just said I did."

"But isn't that dangerous?" I had no idea Ben had taken things this far. Actually asking his dealer?

"It's only Danny." Ben looked like it was me who had just said something stupid. "Danny's alright."

I frowned and thought about that. I'd only met the guy on a couple of occasions, when I'd gone with Ben to buy some dope. We'd go in, make awkward small talk for as long as it took them to exchange cash for a cellophane-wrapped teenth, and then we'd get out of there. I'd always feel a frisson of excitement at being inside a dealer's house.

"Well, what did he say?"

"He said he can't handle it himself, but he's asked the guy who supplies him. Someone up north somewhere. And he came back saying if we could get that much dope into the country, then he'd take it off our hands, no problem. We've just got to get the gear in the first place."

I didn't think for a minute it could be as easy as that. But I decided to let that pass for now, and concentrate on the other problem.

"Well, OK, so can't Danny, or this other guy, put us in touch with someone in Morocco too? To buy the stuff, I mean?"

Ben shook his head.

"Nah. You see, most of the stuff here is grown here. In lofts and barns and stuff. It's why the quality isn't that good. But it's also why this is such a great plan. If we can get hold of some genuine Moroccan hash, everyone here will want it. It'll be easy for this guy to sell, so we'll get a good price. It's really just how we get it." Ben looked up and stared out the window. I didn't say anything. I didn't have any great ideas.

"Of course, we could just drive down there and hope for the best," Ben went on, he was talking to himself more than me by then. "It wasn't hard to buy it before. But it might take them a long time to come up with such a large amount. I'd far rather order it in advance so we're just picking it up."

But I'd had enough by then, it was too much to take in all at once.

"Ben," I interrupted him.

"What?"

"Are you really serious about this?"

"What do you mean?"

"I mean, why are we sitting here making spreadsheets and lists? It's crazy. We're not actually going to do this. You do know that?"

He looked at me and his face slowly set into a look I'd seen many times before. Like I'd just issued him a direct challenge. But then he softened. I think he realised that getting me to do this was a far bigger step than anything he'd ever talked me into before.

"You know why we're doing this don't you Jake? We're going to wipe away our debts. You're going to start your working life not owing tens of thousands to the government. And I'm going to be free of my dad. That's why."

I puffed out my cheeks. I still felt bad for him about his dad, and his brother.

"Look, that's all great. But it's mental. What happens if we get caught? We go to prison for our whole lives or something."

Ben didn't look at me this time. He stared at his computer instead.

"Ben, I just think you're spending too much time on this. You can't fail your course again; they'll kick you off this time. You've got to finish your degree. We've got to get jobs. That's how we clear our debts. That's how you stick it to your dad. Jobs. We've got to get serious about life."

Slowly, Ben closed the top of his computer. His face was set firm.

"I'm totally serious, Jake."

We sat in silence for a long while, and it was like we'd both agreed to drop the subject for the time being. Eventually, I started telling him about an application I'd just sent off. For a local job. He listened politely, even asked a couple of questions, and I thought I'd heard the last of his crazy plan. But just as we were getting up to leave the café, he brought it up again.

"Jake, I know you're not fully into this idea yet. But can you do me a favour? Can you work out how much money you could get hold of—just in case we work it out? Start applying for those credit cards or whatever. I'll look into the other issues." He gave me a sad smile and quietly slipped his laptop into his bag.

CHAPTER ELEVEN

I SHOULD TELL you a little about the application I just mentioned; it plays its part in this whole story. I was still applying for every job I had any chance with, and still mostly hearing nothing back. But every now and then, a job came along that I got excited about. And a few days earlier I'd come across a job I *really* liked the look of. It was a place on a graduate training scheme for a firm that sold services to other businesses. Nothing exciting, really, but that just happened to be what I did my final-year project on. I actually understood everything it talked about on the job description, and, when it came to filling in the form, I could make a pretty good case for why they should consider hiring me. When I emailed that one off, I knew I was such a good fit that I had a good feeling about it. It was strangely powerful, it was like I could sense something good was finally coming my way. Like my luck was turning.

Even so, I did what Ben asked with the money. Not because he'd asked, but because I had to. If I wanted to pay that month's rent, and buy any more food that month, I had to do it. Once again, I was mildly surprised at how willing reputable financial institutions were to lend more money to kids like me, with no obvious means to pay it back. I couldn't quite get the full five thousand that Ben had noted down, but for just filling in a few more forms, I had a piece of plastic worth four thousand pounds on its way to me in the post.

And just for a little while, I was optimistic that maybe a change was on the way. I just had to get that job, and I could turn things around. I'd be able to cover my monthly outgoings and start to make a dent in paying back the bigger loans I had hanging over me.

Two days later, when I was at work, my phone pinged with an email. Before I even looked, I knew it was about the job; I had that same feeling as before. And when I did look at the message header I saw I was right. I couldn't see what the email said, though, and for a long while, I didn't look. I kept serving customers, barely aware of what I was doing, my hands going through the motions, my brain whirring away behind my blank face.

I didn't want to open the email just in case it was another "no." All my anticipation and all my hopes would be dashed yet again. And then there was a gap in customers. All the pumps were empty—I had a few minutes to myself. I pressed the button to open the phone and took a couple of deep breaths before opening the email. I didn't need to read it all. I could see at once what it said. I had an interview. I fucking had an interview! My first in eight months of sending out hundreds and hundreds of applications. I made a fist and banged the desk, then again, so that the till shifted on the desk in front of me. I was finally getting out of this place. Then I remembered that my boss watched the CCTV of me sometimes. I had to fight the urge to stick one finger up at the camera, but I pulled myself together.

Then I read the email a bit more carefully. They wanted me to come for an interview the following Thursday. Now, I worked all day Thursdays. And the interview wasn't just for an hour: it was an all-day thing. That was a problem because I knew my boss wouldn't want to give me the time off. So I had to decide whether to try and book the day off, or just call in sick that morning. I thought about it for a while and in the end decided to tell my boss the truth. Sometimes, she could be decent about things. During the next lull in customers, I sent her a text explaining what had happened, and asking for the day off. Then I spent the rest of my shift with such a stupid grin on my face that people kept giving me funny looks.

Late that night, my boss wiped the grin away. She texted back to say I couldn't have next Thursday off. She was already short-staffed, and she couldn't cover it herself because she had to attend a course at the head office. She somehow implied with her text that she was the one who was being hard done by, having to reply to a text and turn me down. When I said she could be decent sometimes, I forgot to mention she could also be a real miserable bitch.

That left me with a dilemma. I could still text her and say I was sick on the day, but now she'd know that it was a lie. It probably wouldn't matter because I was one of the most reliable people she had, and I didn't think she'd fire me for it, but it would piss her off. Or I could stick to my honest route and just insist that I had to take the time off. It wasn't like she didn't know I was looking for other jobs. She couldn't force me to work there.

Ben was all for me telling her where to stick the job entirely, inasmuch as I had his attention. It was mostly still on his dope plan. I only talked to him about it at all because I hoped that maybe Julia would come into the room when we were discussing it. I wanted her to know that I had an interview for this amazing job. I wanted her to see that there was more to me than just a guy working in a petrol station and getting stoned. But that didn't happen, at least not yet.

In the end, I decided to be up front and honest. I told my boss I was really sorry, but I just couldn't work the next Thursday. She texted back:

Jake, you have REALLY LET ME DOWN. I thought better of you. I'll review rota and get back to you.

I got a second text later that night, presumably after she'd reviewed the rota. She said my hours for the next two and a half months had been reduced to zero. She hadn't fired me, I don't think she'd be allowed to do that for nothing, but she'd reduced my hours so I wouldn't get paid anything, so it amounted to the same thing. I stared at that text for ages, just stared at it. The thought of having no income, just like that, filled me with a kind of cold fear. But at the same time, there was this lifeline. There was this job. I was going to get it. I had to get it. Fuck the petrol station. Fuck my bitch of a boss. I was moving on up from there. I was destined for way better things.

And I put more effort into that interview than I had for anything I'd done for a long time. I bought a new suit. I had one already—Mum bought it for me when I was sixteen—but I'd bulked up a bit since then, and to be honest, Mum's taste had stopped right about the time she married Dad. By then, the new credit card had come through, so I used that to pay for it. It was a risk, but if I got the job, I'd need a few suits anyway. You have to speculate to accumulate, right?

Then there was the presentation I had to prepare. Fifteen minutes on the benefits of outsourcing for medium-sized organisations. Thrilling stuff, huh? Fortunately, Ben had been spending a fair bit of time with Danny, working up his plan, so we had a bit of dope lying around the flat which helped me get creative. And with no hours at the petrol station to get in the way, I had plenty of time to come up with something.

* * *

It was different getting to hang around the flat again. I hadn't done that since I was a student, and that was what finally got me some alone time with Julia. I'd taken to bringing my laptop downstairs to the living room rather than hiding up in my room. And one day, about lunchtime, she padded in. She was still in her pyjamas, an oversized Mickey Mouse t-shirt that I'd seen a couple of times before and imagined her pulling over her head many times more. She was carrying a bowl of cornflakes. She sat down at the table opposite me and crunched her spoon in.

"What you doing?" she asked.

I felt a tingle of anticipation. I was working on my presentation for a proper job that I had a real chance of getting. Like a serious person. And I'd been hoping for the chance to tell her that for a long time. I was about to go up a notch or two in her eyes. But I wanted to play it cool.

"I've got an interview next week. I've got to do this presentation," I said, as nonchalantly as I could. I knew she'd want to know more.

Julia munched her way through a few spoonfuls of cornflakes, and for a moment, I feared she wasn't going to ask anything more, but I held my nerve. Eventually, she took a break.

"What's the job?"

"Management trainee scheme," I said, a little too quickly, then slowed down.

"It's a local firm. It does outsourcing work, HR, employment law. I've been looking for something like this for a while."

She screwed up her face.

"Sounds exciting," she said. It was fairly clear she was being sarcastic. "I thought you had a job at that petrol station?"

"That's just until something better comes along," I said, trying not to sound hurt, and maybe she picked up that she'd been harsh, cos then she said:

"So you're going to be a corporate clone. Sign your life away before you've even lived it?" She had a faraway look in those pretty eyes. I found myself scrambling to explain.

"Well, it's kind of what I studied in my final year. It's kind of interesting when you get into it."

She gave a little half laugh.

"Well, the money's good, anyway."

She raised an eyebrow at this.

"Go on, then. What's good?"

I told her.

"Not that good."

"Well, no. Not that good right at the start. But it's an accelerated promotion scheme. In a few years, you're on good money," I began, but I stopped out of disappointment. She looked so bored.

She crunched her way through more cornflakes, but otherwise, we sat in silence. In some versions of my fantasy about this moment, she'd offer to help me with the presentation, laughing in wonder at how brilliant my slides were—before we stripped off and had sex. In other versions we just went straight for the sex. But I didn't dare suggest either route just now. It was harder in real life. Instead, I asked her what she wanted to do with jobs and stuff. That animated her a little bit.

"I want to travel. Explore. Do something exciting. I want to *do* something. Don't you ever feel like that?" She leant forward, and her eyes sparkled for the first time as she said that. Not that I was looking at her face. She wasn't wearing a bra and her thin t-shirt wasn't doing a very good job of containing her breasts. I forced myself to focus.

"Like a gap year or something?"

"Yeah. Or a gap five years. Just—" Suddenly, she swept a hand around the room. "There's a whole world out there, Jake, and you can do anything. Spend a year travelling round Asia. Go skiing in the Rockies. Don't you want to live before you settle?"

Even though this was Julia, and by then, I would have agreed with anything she said just to get her to spend five minutes with me, this still annoyed me a bit. Of course I wanted to go travelling. Who didn't? But that was only an option for the kids with rich parents. Kids like... well, like Ben and Julia.

"Yeah, well, we can't all do that," I said, a little petulantly, but I didn't elaborate, and we lapsed again into silence.

"You got any of Ben's dope?" she asked next, surprising me a little.

I thought for a minute. Clearly, I hadn't impressed her with my job interview, but maybe that was just a stupid fantasy anyway. I already knew she liked to have a few puffs on a joint. Maybe I could regain a little lost ground here by the two of us getting stoned together? Anna and Ben wouldn't be in for hours, and I still had plenty of time to finish my presentation. But a couple of relaxing joints, now, who knew where that could lead?

"Yeah, sure. Do you want me to roll you one up?"

She didn't seem to hear me; by then, she'd started looking at her phone, tapping out a message on the screen. The dope was sitting on the table along with the tobacco and the papers in Ben's little tin.

"I could join you, actually," I said casually. "I'm nearly done here anyway. I'll get rolling."

She was still working on her text, so I reached over for the cigarette papers and began to stick two together and sprinkle tobacco into the crease.

A minute later when she finished her eyes flicked up from the phone and to what I was doing.

"Oh no, it's alright, Jake, I'm just gonna nick a bit for later on."

I was already half way through making it, I couldn't really stop at that point, so I just carried on.

"I wanted to have a smoke later on with Andy. It might loosen him up a bit." She smiled at me, a smile that lit up her face. With that and the mention of Andy, my body and soul ached for her.

"I might just have one anyway," I said, hoping that would explain away what I was doing. "Are you sure you don't want some?" I said, hearing the desperation in my voice.

She didn't say anything for a moment, and I really thought she was going to say yes.

"No, you're alright. It doesn't really go with breakfast."

I looked at her now empty bowl of cornflakes. But I finished off making the joint anyway. When I sensed she was about to get up and leave, since I had nothing else to say, I risked asking her directly about what had happened between us.

"So, have you made any final decisions?" I asked, forcing chirpiness into my voice.

She looked at me now, confused.

"What decisions?"

"You know, about the..." I indicated her chest with my hand, but she didn't understand, or pretended not to.

"The what?"

"The, um... you know, your idea to..."

"To what, Jake? What are you talking about?"

"The boob job. Are you still thinking about it?"

Now she looked annoyed, or perhaps just bored.

"Oh, that." And slowly, a small smile finally came back to her face. "Yeah, I'm still thinking about it. Why? Are you keen to check out the final results?"

"Yeah, whatever," I said. "I'm always here if you need any help." I tried to hold her attention, to show her I was being witty and just a little bit suggestive. But all too soon, her eyes sank back down to her phone.

"Here you go," I was forced to say to get her attention even half focussed on me. I separated a generous amount of Ben's dope into a second bag and handed it to her.

"Thanks, Jake." I got another brief flash of smile, but then I lost her attention again, and a few moments later, she trailed back to the kitchen, leaving her empty bowl on the table.

I heard her going upstairs, and a while later, the front door shutting, presumably behind her. I finished rolling the joint I'd begun making for the two of us and lit it up. Even if that hadn't gone exactly to plan, I still had a few hours to kill.

CHAPTER TWELVE

THE NEXT THURSDAY rolled around soon enough, and I got up, had a shower, and got dressed in my new suit. Somehow, it didn't feel as smart as it had in the shop. It might have been nerves, or maybe it was something to do with the dope I'd smoked the night before.

I felt a bit awkward coming downstairs. I could hear there were people in the kitchen, running around, getting breakfast, and I still hoped it might be Julia, and she'd at least wish me luck or something. But when I got in there, it was only Ben and Anna. And all I got from Ben were raised eyebrows. But Anna was nice. She said I looked very smart, and she made me a cup of tea. When I had to go, she gave my tie a little straighten, which was ironic because I'd imagined Julia doing the exact same thing.

The office looked impressive from the outside: a big steel-and-glass building that stood out on the street. The entrance was through a revolving glass door. Inside, I found a shiny marble reception area, where a pretty girl took my name and pointed to a bank of seats along the wall. There were eight other people there, all staring at me. Most of them looked about as nervous as I was feeling, but the guy on the end seemed more relaxed. And the only free chair was next to him, so I went and sat down and nodded at him to say hello. There was a smell of cheap deodorant that I hoped wasn't me.

Ten minutes of silence later, a woman with a clipboard turned up. She spent a few minutes talking with the receptionist and glancing over at us, then walked over and told us all her name was Helen. I don't know if I imagined it, but she seemed to give a personal smile to the guy next to me, and he said hello back, using her name as if he'd known it already. Then she asked us all to follow her and we tried to look like we were used to walking through a working office in our stupid suits and smart shoes. We arrived in a large room where the desks had been pushed together to form a kind of board table. There were two more people here, middle-aged guys in suits that didn't disguise their bellies. Helen introduced them. The first one was the vice president of the company; the other was something to do with HR.

Then we all sat down and Helen explained that we were going to introduce ourselves in a fun way. Everyone was going to say an interesting fact about ourselves. The two guys smiled at her when she said this, and she busied herself writing names on big white stickers that were destined for our suit lapels.

We went around the room clockwise, which meant I was the fourth to speak. The girl who went first told us she had just graduated with a first-class degree from Newcastle, but that she actually lived in Surrey. Her interesting fact was she had a pony called Mr. Tumnus. She turned to the rest of us and explained that this was a character in C. S. Lewis's The Lion, the Witch and the Wardrobe. This got her more indulgent smiles from the suits at the front and blank stares of hatred from the rest of us. The second guy tried a different tack. He told us he was an Arsenal supporter, and this was met with a sharp intake of breath from the HR guy and a comment that he was a Tottenham season ticket holder, and that drew laughs around the room. I didn't hear the third guy say his piece because I was too busy panicking about what I was going to say. All I could think to say was totally inappropriate, like what Ben and I were planning, or what had happened with Julia. Then it was my turn. I opened my mouth to speak.

"Hi, everyone. My name's Jake. I just graduated from the University of Brighton with a degree in business and economics. And I..."

I stopped. I still hadn't thought of anything to say, so I had no choice but to go with whatever popped into my head next. And I knew it was crap before I said it, but it came out all the same.

"And I like to go rollerblading on the seafront to keep fit."

I think I'd been aiming for amused smiles, but instead I just got just slightly raised eyebrows from the suits, and a wave of discomfort that rolled around the room, bounced off the walls, and rolled back again. It was like everyone was embarrassed that someone had said something so totally shit. It wasn't even true. I'd never been rollerblading on the fucking seafront.

* * *

I didn't hear what the other people said. I was too busy trying to get my blushing face to calm down. By the time I had, Helen was into her explanation of what was going to happen next.

She called it the group activity. We had to pretend we worked for a made-up company called *Jupiter Bank* which had lost its market share to bigger international competition. She told us to imagine the senior management had asked us to come up with a list of options for strategies to help this fictional bank, which we knew nothing about, to recover its market share. Then, without really explaining what she meant by this, or anything which might be relevant, she pointed to a flip chart and a pack of different-coloured marker pens, and smiled and wished us luck.

It turned out she and the two other guys were going to sit and drink coffee and watch us. Slowly, we all stood up and walked over to the flip chart.

Although this was the first real assessment I'd been involved in, I'd heard about this sort of thing before, and I'd even done a practice one at uni. I knew what you were supposed to do: You had to make sure you were heard and got your point across, not just sit in the background. But you also had to demonstrate that you weren't too dominant and let other people have their say. Basically, you just had to show you weren't too shy to open your mouth, or an asshole. I opened my mouth to speak, but unfortunately, it turned out we did have an asshole in the group.

It was the guy who hadn't seemed nervous back in the reception. His name was Pete—it was stuck to his chest now—and just as I started talking, he interrupted me and started telling us what we already knew, what the woman had said. Then he picked up the pens and wrote "Jupiter Bank" on the top of the flip chart. He switched colours and added "Options for Senior Management" underneath. Then he stopped and looked at the rest of us.

While he was doing that, all the other interviewees had gathered around like he was the teacher and we were all students. I could sense that some of the others were anxious like I was. That we were giving him too big an opportunity to stand out.

"OK, everyone." Pete started afresh. "Welcome to the Jupiter Bank junior management ideas meeting!" He flashed a grin at the back of the room, where the observers were sipping their coffees and exchanging glances with each other.

"As you all know, the bank is having some issues, and we're here to come up with some killer strategies to fight back. So who has some ideas to kick things off?"

It was obvious what he was doing, he was planning to 'lead' the session and take all the credit, even if he didn't come up with any good ideas himself.

The girl with the pony came up with the first idea, something about opening more local branches, and Pete wrote it down. Then another guy, with thick glasses, said something about advertising in schools, which didn't make much sense, but Pete added it anyway. Then pony-girl said something else, and for a while, it was just the three of them, chatting about their ideas as if the rest of us weren't there at all, or were just there to make them look good. I knew I had to do something so I opened my mouth again to try and turn it around.

"Perhaps rather than all of us work in one group, we should divide up into two teams and brainstorm ideas separately?" I said, my voice cutting into their fun. "Then we can be sure that everyone will have an opportunity to speak." I glanced at the back as I said this, and sure enough, Helen and the HR guy both made notes on their clipboards. I smiled at Pete and enjoyed the pissed-off look that flashed across his smug face. He had no choice but to agree.

It was Pete though who divided us up into the two teams—his way of showing he was still in charge, and he put himself with pony-girl and glasses-guy, and another girl who hadn't said anything but was pretty—so he kind of had an A team and a B team. They got the flip chart and the pens; we got to huddle around a writing pad. But we came up with suggestions of our own. There was nothing spectacular, but that's not the point of these exercises, is it? They just wanted to see if we could handle ourselves in a professional manner. By the end of it, I was feeling a lot better about how this was going. I even began to enjoy myself. This was how it was going to be. Jake, the impressive young executive. Cutting a dashing figure as he strode up and down the boardroom, senior management watching him with wry smiles. This boy had potential. This boy was going places.

When the interviewers finished their coffee, or just got bored watching, they stopped it. And they'd obviously bought into my two-teams idea because Helen then asked us to present the two sets of ideas, and she said they would then say which team had won. We got to go first, and since the rest of my group looked at me expectantly, I stood up to present what we'd talked about. I looked at each of the interviewers in turn and cleared my throat.

I'm not pretending our ideas were anything remarkable; they weren't, but the point is it went well. I could see the interviewers were all listening, and making notes. They looked impressed. When I'd finished, I thanked them again and sat down.

Then Pete got to his feet and said what his team had done. They'd somehow gotten obsessed with this advertising-in-schools idea, and he was talking for ages about a competition where schoolkids drew pictures of what Jupiter Bank meant for them. He was speaking in the same confident voice he'd had all morning, but it was bullshit. And it was obvious the interviewers didn't really get the relevance, and then when Pete actually held up some examples of what the kids might draw—pretend kids' drawings that his group had done, it was just embarrassing. And then the vice president guy, who up to that point hadn't spoken all morning, said he was going to announce the winner.

He stood up and stretched out his stomach, and I got myself ready to accept the win magnanimously.

"Thank you all for your hard work so far this morning," the VP said. "On behalf of the panel, I can say it's been absolutely fascinating." He looked at the others to make sure they were nodding in agreement.

"And I have to say I've seen a lot of this type of exercise, and it's very rare that a really genuinely good idea comes up. But this time, we really think it has. An idea I think we may even consider taking forward." He paused again, and gave a fat smile, building up the suspense. My mind ran through the few ideas we'd had, wondering which one had so caught his attention, none of them seemed that good to me.

"But I'd like to first of all thank..." The vice president stopped and stared blankly at me.

"The rollerblade guy—I'm sorry, I can't read your name from here—for some good ideas," he flashed a half-hearted smile at me but then looked away.

"But the clear winner is Peter's group and his frankly excellent suggestion of involving local schoolchildren. Because we both get the kids involved and interested in banking while they're young—and we get the parents involved. It's a really great idea. Thank you, Peter." He started clapping, and then we all had to do the same. Giving Peter a jolly good round of applause.

We broke for lunch. Sandwiches cut into triangles and half Scotch eggs. I didn't put too many on my plate but watched as Pete took a massive pile and wandered over to the vice president, and began chatting like they were old friends. After a while, I realised I wasn't the only one watching. Mo, one of the other candidates from my 'B' team was watching too.

"Cocky wanker."

"Excuse me?"

"That guy. Peter. Cocky fucking wanker." He spoke quietly so I was the only one who could hear him. "You do realise this whole thing is a set-up don't you? They had to hold the interview, but he's already been given the job."

I looked at Mo with suspicion. "Why do you say that?"

"It's fucking obvious, man. And I'm sorry to disappoint you, since you're trying so hard." Mo took a bite of a sandwich, and while he was chewing, I thought about what he was saying. It did seem to explain how confident Pete was.

"But why would they do that? I mean, surely they're looking for the best candidate?"

"I dunno. Maybe his dad goes to the same golf club? Maybe he's gay and they're fucking each other? You wait. The VP guy is supposed to be in on all our individual interviews this afternoon. I bet you he doesn't even bother with the rest of us." Mo stopped and took another bite.

"But why would they bother with the interviews if they already know they want him?"

Mo looked at me like I was a bit slow.

"It's the law, innit? They have to show they're equal opportunity employers. Why do you think I'm here?"

Now I frowned at him, not following.

"Dark skin? Foreign-sounding name? I tick the ethnic minority box. Oh, yeah. I get a lot of lunches like this. No job offers, though. That all you're eating?"

"What?"

"You might as well have a decent lunch is all. Since that's all you're getting out of this."

Behind Mo, I noticed Helen was standing alone, balancing a plate of sandwiches and looking about for somewhere to stand and eat them. I wasn't prepared to give up yet on this job, so I excused myself from Mo and went and asked her some of my pre-prepared questions about the company. Soon, a couple of the other candidates joined us, and we spent the rest of the lunch competing to try and ask the most intelligent questions. I nearly forgot what Mo had said. But at one point I did notice that Pete and the VP both seemed to have disappeared.

The afternoon was set aside for the individual interviews and presentations. We were given half-hour time slots each, and told we could go away and come back in time for our slot if we wanted. The first to go in was Pete. I was last, so I went out for a walk to go through my presentation a few more times in my head. I came back at quarter to five, ready for my interview at last, and sweated for ten minutes until I got called in. Inside, there was a desk with three chairs, Helen was in one, the HR guy in another.

"I'm afraid Mr Oliver has been called away," she said, meaning the VP. "Something very urgent has come up which needs his immediate attention. But if you'd like to give us your presentation now that would be great." She smiled at me like she really didn't know this was all a giant waste of our time.

I still gave it my best shot. The presentation, and then the questions that followed. But I knew, and I realised Helen knew too. And the HR guy who kept looking at his watch like he'd had a really hard day doing fuck all. We all knew there was never any job in the first place. For them I was just an interesting day with free sandwiches for lunch. For me I'd thrown away my fragile grip on getting by for nothing.

Chapter Thirteen

"HEY MATE, YOU look like you need to get pissed!"

This was right after I'd finished the interview. I was walking down the street, trying to decide whether I should keep walking all the way home or wait for a bus which I probably couldn't afford now. I turned around, and it was Mo, standing there.

"I saw you from the window," he explained, pointing to the pub I'd just walked past. "I'm drowning my sorrows. You wanna join me for one?" I guessed he wanted to tell me he'd been right all along, but that was OK with me. I wasn't in a hurry to get back to the flat and face my messed up life. I followed Mo back into the pub and sat down in a little window booth while he went to the bar.

"So, how many did you get for your interview?" he asked, putting a pint of Stella in front of each of us.

"Just the woman and the HR guy."

"Told you, man."

I didn't reply at first.

"You never know," I said at last. "They might not just give it to Pete."

"I love your optimism. I've signed up for the company blog. Just so I can see it announced in a few weeks that Peter whatever his name has joined the management training scheme."

Neither of us spoke for a while. I still hadn't touched my pint.

"You know, I pretty much lost my job to come to this interview?"

"What job?"

"Petrol station attendant."

"That sucks."

I didn't know if he meant my losing the job sucked, or just the job itself. I didn't bother trying to clarify.

"Say, do you really like rollerblading on the seafront? I can't see you doing that."

I smiled weakly. "No. I just couldn't think of anything else to say. It was either that or say I like to get stoned and play Call of Duty on the Xbox."

Mo laughed. "I wish you had, would've been funny."

We both drank from our pints. I was clearly playing catch-up since Mo already had two empty glasses in front of him. Maybe it was this, or maybe he was just a really easy guy to talk to, but suddenly I thought how odd it was that I'd just mentioned getting stoned to a stranger. I never did that. I never brought up the subject of drugs. It wasn't just that it was illegal. It was that some people disapproved, and you never could tell with people at first. But with Mo I'd just come out and said it. And he seemed totally cool with it. But it got me thinking in the background of whatever we were talking about. I guess that's part of what happened next.

"So, you live around here?" I said a while later. It must have been a while because there were quite a few empty pint glasses on the table now. By then, an idea had started to form in my mind. A crazy idea, but I couldn't shake it.

"Nah. I'm down from London. I've got an off-peak ticket, so I've got to hang around a bit." I nodded. Whenever I got the train home to see Dad I did the same thing to save money.

"And where are you from? Originally, I mean." I know you're not meant to ask questions like that, but like I say, I had this idea.

"London."

"No, like your parents and that?"

Mo looked at me like he was wondering if he'd misjudged me.

"Morocco. Well, my mum's Moroccan. Dad's from south London."

I knew it. You could tell from his features. He looked just like the people we'd seen out there the summer before.

"Cool. So what, were you born there or over here?"

"I was born there. We lived there until I was twelve. Then Dad moved us to the UK."

"That must be weird," I said, and when he didn't answer, I went on.

"So, do you still have friends out there? Family? People you keep in touch with?"

"Yeah. Some. Why are you so interested?" He was looking at me like I'd annoyed him, but he wasn't really sure what to make of me. I decided to roll back a bit.

"Sorry, I don't mean to pry. It's just I went to Morocco the other summer, on holiday."

"Oh, right." This satisfied him a little, so I pressed on.

"Must be annoying, huh? Living somewhere with such great dope when you're too young to smoke it, and then moving here?" I gave him a big smile to show I didn't mean anything by this, I was just making conversation. But all the same, I saw the curious look on his face go deeper.

"Yeah, I guess," he said slowly. "I mean you can still get it here if you want to. It doesn't really bother me either way. I'm not really into it."

"Oh, me neither," I said quickly, then added as casually as I could. "Listen. This is going to sound a bit weird, but..." I paused, just long enough to question whether I was mad to bring this up, but not long enough to stop completely.

"A mate of mine has this crazy idea that he's going to drive down to Morocco and buy a load of dope to bring back. I was wondering if you might know, you know, where to go, how someone would get hold of it in the first place?"

"Fucking hell, Jake, what kind of a question is that?"

I panicked. I couldn't believe the words had actually come out of my mouth.

"I'm sorry. I shouldn't have asked. I'm just... You know, I've got this mate who's always going on about it. I thought if you grew up there, maybe you'd know someone..." It was the beer talking. That and the release of the pressure from the interview.

"You say some fucking random stuff don't you?" He laughed at me and I felt an idiot. But rather than continue to be annoyed, Mo seemed suddenly interested. He leaned forward so we wouldn't be overheard.

"So how much does he want to bring back?"

I looked back at Mo. All the suspicion from his face had gone. He was smiling now, enjoying the turn of the conversation.

"Come on? How much?" he said again.

"I don't know, exactly. He's got this idea to bring in enough to pay off all our debts, maybe a hundred kilos."

Mo whistled and leaned back again in his chair.

"He'll never do it," I said quickly. "But I was just wondering, you know." I shut up, feeling suddenly stupid, Mo looked thoughtful.

"It's easy enough to get a little bit," he said, a moment later. "But I don't know about a big load like that. Don't you know anyone there who can help you?"

"No. That's the thing. How do we... my mate, I mean, how does he know who to trust? That's why it's such a crazy idea."

And then, just like that, Mo solved the problem.

"I reckon my cousin could sort him out. He lives near Marrakech. He knows people who... You'd have to give him a cut or whatever. But that's OK, isn't it?"

I blinked a couple of times before answering this. Through the fuzz of the beer, this was actually happening.

"Yeah, I guess so." And for a moment, I wasn't listening to Mo anymore. I suddenly realised that this was it. The good feeling I'd had all along about that stupid job, it hadn't been about the job at all. It was this.

This contact with Mo had been the good fortune I'd sensed. I felt a little sick at the implication.

"I'll text him now. See what he says." Mo leaned to one side to dig his phone from the pocket of his suit trousers. He keyed in a code and popped open his messenger screen. I couldn't read the screen from where I was sitting, but I could see they sent lots of messages back and forth.

"Woah , what are you going to say?" I asked, suddenly nervous.

Mo shrugged. "I'll just ask him. It's alright. It's WhatsApp, it's encryted innit?"

I sat back and watched as Mo typed something into the message box and added a smiley face at the end. Then he hit send, and I imagined who might be about to receive it.

"So, what's he like, your cousin?" I asked.

"He's alright. We grew up together, before I moved over here. He's a motorbike mechanic, you know, scooters and that. You must have seen them everywhere?"

I had. I tried to imagine a young Moroccan man reaching for his phone in a filthy street garage somewhere, perhaps wiping his greasy hands on a rag before picking it up. I saw a workshop, nothing more than a front room, really, open to the traffic on one side, a few tools lying around a dismantled scooter, a radio blaring Arabic music. A topless calendar on the wall, the face of the model veiled. Mo's phone screen lit up. A reply was here already and this time I saw it. Just one word.

"What?!"

Mo frowned and his fingers bashed out another message. This time I leant in so I could see.

"Just asking! Do you know anyone who could help?"

There was no delay this time.

"Probably, but it's a stupid idea."

Mo shrugged at me and texted back.

"I'm not doing it. Asking for a friend. Would be a cut for you, though."

A minute of silence later, and then:

"How much do you want?"

Mo looked at me for confirmation, and I shrugged.

"Go for it," I said. "A hundred kilos."

The corners of Mo's eyes crinkled with the fun of it.

"That's a lot of fucking dope!" He said. He typed it in, though.

"What?" came back again pretty quickly, then a second message.

"You serious about this?"

"I'm seriously asking," Mo typed back.

There was a longer pause this time. I tried to image Mo's cousin thinking hard before he replied.

"OK. I can probably sort something."

Mo looked at me with a huge grin. "Come on, mate. You definitely owe me another drink for that."

I slipped off my stool, floated unsteadily to the bar and got our fifth pints in. Or it might have been sixth by then.

Chapter Fourteen

I GOT TO the flat just after midnight, still in my suit and pissed as hell. And if I'd started drinking to forget my sorrows, it certainly worked. I'd forgotten all about the interview, and with the booze, I'd forgotten all the reasons I thought Ben's dope plan was ridiculous. Now it was a great idea, and best of all, I was suddenly the one who made it all possible. Just like that, I had a contact, thousands of miles away, who could actually set us up with the dope.

I knocked on Ben's door. It was one in the morning by then and even through my drunkenness, I realised he was asleep. But I had to tell him the news, right then, so I kept knocking until he opened it, standing there with a towel wrapped around his waist. Looking sleepy and annoyed.

"Ben," I slurred. "I've got a contact to get the dope!"

He stared at me, and either he was swaying slightly—along with the whole doorway—or more likely I was.

"Who?"

"I met a guy. He's called Mo. He grew up in Morocco, and his cousin knows people who can get it. They can get as much as we need."

At this, Ben stepped outside his door and pulled it closed behind him.

"What are you talking about?" He asked.

"I met a guy. At the interview."

"What? How did you get talking about that at a job interview?"

"It was in the pub afterwards." I beamed triumphantly. I had to put my hand on his doorframe to stay standing. Ben stared at me. I could see he was still angry about me waking him up, but also that he was interested. I knew he would be.

"We need to talk about this in the morning."

"No no no no. It's alright. I can show you him. Mo texted me a photo. He's called Ahmed. He fixes motorbikes. You remember we saw them everywhere when we were there? We can have a joint as well." I'd already scouted around downstairs for Ben's stash, but he'd taken it upstairs with him, and now I tried to push past into his room.

"No, mate." He blocked me with his body. "Let's look tomorrow."

I shook my head and tried to say it was alright, we should look now, but he blocked my entrance into his room again. I didn't understand, I kept trying to push past.

"Jake."

"Come on, mate. Let's have a smoke, and I'll show you."

"Jake... I'm not alone."

Even in my drunken state, this caused me to pause.

"What?"

"I've got someone in there."

"What? Like a girl?"

"Yeah, like a girl. So we'll talk about this tomorrow?"

"Oh, right." I felt deflated but not defeated. "Can I just get a joint, then?"

"Fucking hell, Jake." Ben shook his head in annoyance. But he sorted me out. He told me to wait in the hallway and he went back into his room to get his stash. As the door opened, I saw the end of his bed: there was a pair of feet there half poking out the end of his duvet. I tried to crane my neck to see higher up the legs, but then Ben came back, plastic bag in hand.

"Who is it?" I asked, grinning and pointing. "Anyone I know?"

"No. Now fuck off, will you? We'll talk about this in the morning."

And then, just as I was I stumbling away down the hall he called me back.

"Jake!"

I turned round.

"Yeah?"

"Well done mate. Nice one." He gave me a grin and then retreated back into his room, pulling the door firmly shut behind him.

* * *

The next morning, I woke up feeling cold, clammy, dehydrated and needing a piss—pretty much my standard hangover. I staggered between the bathroom and my bed a few times, and by midmorning, I felt OK to get up. I came downstairs and found Ben sitting, looking on the Internet. He was alone; I was too late to get a look at the girl he'd pulled.

"Dude," he said as I walked in. "You were pretty far gone last night!"

I ignored this and dropped into a chair beside him.

"Yeah, sorry. I didn't know you had someone in there."

Ben waved this away with his hand.

"That's alright. You did me a favour. After you woke me up, we had another go." He grinned at me again and moved the conversation on. "So, come on. Tell me about this contact you've made."

I told Ben all about what had happened. In the relative harshness of the morning after, it sounded a bit less brilliant to me, but Ben seemed impressed. More than impressed, really. He thought it was fantastic. And the more we talked it through, the more plausible it all became to me too.

* * *

The summer we went to Morocco on holiday, we'd been terrified that when we bought any dope from the guys on the streets, we'd actually be buying from an undercover cop, out to catch tourists. We had a guidebook that said this could happen, and that if it did, you could be facing ten years in prison. Everyone we talked to said this was bullshit, that the chances of getting caught were tiny, but the idea of ten years in prison does kind of play on the mind. But using Mo's cousin, and the chance way it had come about, Ben decided it almost totally got around the problem of being unlucky and trying to buy from undercover cops.

"It's the randomness of it that's so awesome," he said, after I'd been through it several times.

"Yeah," I agreed, not really believing it again, now I was sober.

"There's no way this guy can be working undercover. It just wouldn't make sense. Working in a motorbike garage, waiting for his cousin to text him because some random English guy wants some help buying a hundred kilos of dope. It's totally random."

"Yeah," I agreed again.

"You know the police, the customs guards, they're all looking for patterns. That's how they catch people. But there's no pattern here. It's just random. Mate, you're a genius!"

And hungover or not, whether I particularly liked the overall idea or not, it's nice to be told you're a genius.

"Yeah," I said again, a little more forcefully.

* * *

Ben didn't love everything about the deal I'd made. For example he wasn't keen on the price that I'd agreed to a little later on that night. So from that point on both Mo and I dropped out of the negotiations and they became exclusively between Ben and Mo's cousin Ahmed. And then Ben told me he hadn't been sitting around doing nothing either.

Chapter Fifteen

THAT SUMMER IN Europe, we'd all bought ourselves surfboards. We hardly ever used them back in Brighton because the waves were never up to much, but we still had the boards. I kept mine in the corner of the lounge, partly because my room was small, and partly because I thought it made us look cool. Actually it worked too. When Julia and Anna came to look round, this was before they moved in, Julia mentioned the board and sounded impressed. She wanted to live in a surfer's flat.

But Ben actually did use his board occasionally. And that afternoon, he told me how, a few days previously, he'd gone for a surf and left his board leaning against a wall while he was getting changed out of his wetsuit. And then how a gust of wind had blown it over and knocked a big dent in the side. He told me how he took it to a local surf shop where they repair boards and got talking with the repair guy, who showed him another board that he'd just finished fixing. Apparently, it had been snapped clean in half. But here's the point. According to Ben, you couldn't tell from looking at it. The guy had just finished the repair, the paint was nearly dry, and it just looked like a normal board. Like nothing had happened to it.

Can you see where this is going? I could, the minute Ben told me that part.

And he knew I knew, because instead of telling me anything else, he got me to follow him upstairs to his room. He said he wanted to show me the other reason he wouldn't let me into his room the night before.

His room was its normal mess, I tried not to look at the bed with the duvet screwed up, I didn't want to see any stains or used condoms lying on the floor. Instead I looked at the other end, where he had a bay window that had a view of the sea. His surfboard was propped up there, between the back of a chair and his chest of drawers. It was upside down, the fins pointing at the ceiling, and it looked like a patient undergoing an operation, one that wasn't going well. Ben had peeled off a large section of the skin from the board and hacked out a hole from the foam inside. But he'd done it in a really messy way. He hadn't taped off the area he was working on from the rest of the board, and he'd hacked at it. In fact, there wasn't a neat edge anywhere in sight, and the rest of the board, the carpet, the chest of drawers—it was all covered in bits of foam and fibreglass, pots of chemicals, and the tools he'd used, mostly knives from the kitchen downstairs. And as I went over for a closer look, the smell hit me, cloying fumes like smouldering plastic. He'd opened the window, but it still stank.

"Jesus, Ben. What have you been doing?"

He tried to look confident and in control, but I think he wasn't exactly sure of himself.

"It's just a test. You can get it all neat again afterward. I wanted to see how much space you could make in there."

I went for a closer look. Now I could see there were actually two holes. The one he was currently working on was on one side of the wooden stringer that ran the length of the board. He'd already tried to repair a smaller hole on the other side. But he'd done a terrible job. When I touched it, the chemicals were still sticky, and through the cloudy gloop, I could see there was something inside the board.

"What's that?"

"Sugar. A half-kilo bag. I thought that'd be about the right weight and size."

I gingerly pressed down harder on the repair, and felt how underneath the stickiness, it was set hard.

"You're smuggling sugar in your surfboard?"

Ben's smile became a notch more confident.

"I reckon I can get a full kilo in the other side."

"Yeah, but you've fucked your board up. It looks a total disaster. No one's going to be fooled by that."

Ben's confidence faded away again.

"Yeah. Well, it's a bit harder than it looks to fix it up again afterward. But I'll get the hang of it. The guy in the surf shop showed me."

I didn't say anything. I was already examining the mess to work out what you'd need to do to sort it out.

"Actually, I was kind of wondering if this might be something you were better at," Ben said, as he watched me.

Now, Ben might be shit with his hands, but I'm not. I told you Mum was a teacher, but I didn't say what my dad does. He repairs and makes furniture. He has a little workshop in the garden where he goes every day and builds tables and chairs and cabinets, or puts old ones back together again. For years when I was growing up, I was going to be exactly like him. I spent hours with him in that shed, cutting the wood for him, filling holes, sanding, painting. I could do it all. I could knock up a set of chairs, side tables, or even a full cabinet with all the joints properly dovetailed.

And now I was thinking how you could fix Ben's surfboard the same way. Ben had bought a surfboard repair kit from the shop: a little bottle of epoxy resin and another of hardener. For small holes, that was all you needed to repair the tough outer skin of a board. For bigger holes, you'd need to bridge the gap, and if you needed strength, you could glass in some fibreglass mat. I ran my fingers over Ben's catastrophic attempt again. There were parts where the bag of sugar wasn't lying flat, when you sanded this, all the sugar would fall out. And judging by the mess on the carpet, he'd already realised that.

"You need to dig the hole deeper, then sand it properly," I said. "Have you got a sander?"

Ben pointed to a cheap power tool lying on the floor.

"Yeah, I bought one. But it's a bit harder to use than I thought." He shifted his weight awkwardly, waiting for what I was going to say next.

But I was already lifting the board up. I could feel at once it was heavier than normal. I checked the deck on the top; it didn't look any different from that side. I put it back down the right way up and leaned my weight on it, gently at first, to see if what he had done meant it was likely to snap in two. Maybe it flexed a little more than it should. It was hard to say.

"How much did you say you put in here?"

"Half a kilo, but the other hole's bigger. I can get more in there." Now, Ben came up to the board and showed me how he could fit two half-kilo bags roughly side by side in the second hole he'd cut out. This one was already a little bit neater so I ignored it and started prodding the first again.

"This is the hole you've finished is it?"

"Alright I know it's not great. Do you reckon you can have a crack at it?"

We rolled up a joint, and I got to work while Ben tidied up the mess. I calculated that if I cut enough chambers in the bottom of Ben's surfboard, I could make a hiding place big enough to put two, maybe even three kilos of sugar—if we packed it tightly enough. Then we could cover it up, using exactly the same techniques that he'd already used—only this time doing the job properly. It would take a bit of work to sand it all flat, since the epoxy they use to fix boards is pretty tough. But that would be useful too, since once it was all smooth and painted again, we should end up with something that was strong. You could probably even surf on it still. And there was a bonus. We also figured that whatever was inside would be totally sealed. Airtight, so in theory, there was no chance of sniffer dogs finding it.

Ben had used up most of the epoxy that came with the repair kits, and he didn't have any brushes or anything. If I was going to do this, I was going to do it properly, so once we'd finished smoking we went down to B&Q and I picked up all the stuff I thought I'd need. I bought a big pack of epoxy resin and hardener, fibreglass matting, a little power saw with a tiny rotating blade, craft knives, masking tape, some spray paints, and a decent sander with lots of different grades of sanding pads. Ben was paying, so I didn't skimp like I normally would. I even bought disposable gloves and face masks for the smell, and that gave me a brilliant idea. There was a giant pet superstore next door, and we went in and searched around in the dog section for the smelliest, most disgusting treats you could get. We settled on half-cooked bits of cows and pigs—ears and snouts, chopped into pieces and covered in a sticky, horrible residue. We took it all home, rolled up another joint, and kept going. Or I did. Ben just watched and made excited noises.

I decided to start over completely with Ben's repair. Partly because it was easier, and partly to make a point. I hacked out everything he'd done and widened and deepened both holes with the circular saw. I smoothed around the edges of both until they were nice and neat. I was in my element, doing this. Nicely stoned and kind of enjoying how much dust and crap was going all over Ben's room. I emptied the disgusting dog treats into freezer bags and packed them carefully into the holes, then covered that with greaseproof paper. I cut sections of fibreglass matting to fit the missing parts of the board's skin, and then taped off the area where I was working with newspaper so that even if I did spill something, it wouldn't go everywhere. This was a proper operation now. Only then, when I was totally happy I had everything ready, did I begin to mix up my epoxy. I used Ben's little drugs scales to weigh out the right amount of resin to hardener, stirred it for five full minutes, and then painted it on. I laid the fibreglass matting over the repair and used the tip of the brush to wet it out. Finally, when I was happy with that, I wrapped the whole thing with cling film and went off to clean up my tools. I told

Ben to hoover up and roll another joint.

It took me three days until I was happy with Ben's board. I worked in stages, building up the repair, first with the epoxy, then simple filler, and sanding in between. And then when it was all perfectly smooth, painting it. It was a shame I had to paint it though because the skin on surfboards is normally left unpainted, so you can see the foam, but I didn't have a choice if I wanted to hide what was glassed inside. But I did a good job with the paint, several layers, with a light sanding between each, so that when I was finished the board looked pretty fucking good.

The next stage was to test it.

* * *

We took Ben's board for a walk down to the bit of the seafront where they still allow dogs to play. We set the board down on the edge of a green area where the dog owners all hang out with plastic bags stretched over their hands. And we waited.

The first dog we saw was a doberman puppy, young enough that it wanted to come up to everyone and say hello. We grabbed it by the collar and tried to direct its excited licks and sniffs to Ben's board but it wasn't interested, clearly it wasn't picking up the scent of the dog treats and eventually its owner managed to get it to move away, at least onto the next people it wanted to greet. Next there was a Labrador. That looked like it might take a piss on the board, but had no interest beyond that. We pretended to dog after dog that we wanted to scratch their ears or play ball and to each one we nudged the treat-filled surfboard close enough that they couldn't have missed the smell if it was there, but there was nothing. Not a flicker of interest. Just the odd yelp when we tried too hard. After about an hour, and probably twenty dogs, we gave up. Either the dogs of Brighton had crap noses, or there simply wasn't anything to smell through several layers of beautifully applied epoxy resin, filler, and paint. I was all for returning home for a celebratory joint, but Ben wanted to do another test.

* * *

When he said what it was I was nervous at first. I persuaded him at least not to return to the same surf shop where he'd had his board professionally repaired a few weeks earlier. Instead, we went to another surf shop. At first, we left the board in Ben's van and spent a few minutes browsing the rack of new boards, and when the owner came over and asked if he could help, Ben asked casually if he'd take an old board in part exchange.

"That depends," the guy said, looking at us like he wasn't expecting a sale here, but that this might just swing it. "If it's in decent nick, I might."

"I've got it outside," Ben said. "Shall I go and get it?"

The guy shrugged and said OK, so Ben went and got it.

I hung around at the back of the shop, pretending to be interested in the t-shirts while the guy picked up Ben's board and had a look. He checked around the nose and tail, then gave the fins a flex to see if they were solid. He clocked the paint on the underside and frowned at it, then gave the board a tap with his fingers in different areas. Then he looked at Ben, as if trying to gauge how low a price he could get away with.

"It's not the sort of board that's easy to sell," he said, rubbing his chin and beard.

Ben looked disappointed, not nervous like I was, just disappointed. "Why not? Is there anything wrong with it?"

"It's had a repair here." The guy tapped the painted bottom. "It's well done, but even so. And it feels a bit heavy, might have a bit of water in it."

I didn't like how this was going. I willed Ben to grab it back off him and get the hell out of the shop, but he didn't.

"Yeah, it feels a bit heavy surfing it. That's why I want to trade it in," Ben said, as easy as you like. "But I need to get rid of it before I can get a new board." He ran his finger down the rail of the new surfboard he'd been looking at, and the shop guy looked thoughtful. I don't suppose they sold many boards a day; he couldn't really turn it down. He glanced at Ben again, and made a decision.

"I can give you fifty. And I'm going to struggle to sell it for that."

Now, Ben started stroking his chin. "The new board's three fifty, right?" He stopped and turned to me as if thinking aloud. "There's that other surf shop, isn't there. We could go and check that out." He stopped again, then turned back to the shop guy. "Look, if you can make it a hundred, I'll shake on the deal right now. I can't really be bothered to check out the other shop." The two of them stared at each other, the board lying on the carpet between them.

"Seventy-five is as high as I can go."

"I can't go below a hundred. It's a shame as I really like the look of that new board." Ben reached down to pick up his old board, and I breathed a sigh of relief. It didn't seem a good idea to me to sell a board filled with dog treats. But the guy stopped him.

"Eighty."

"Eighty-five."

"Alright. Eighty-five."

Ben beamed, and they started to talk about the extras you need with a surfboard. I got a moment while the shop owner was out the back finding a deckpad to talk to Ben without the shop guy hearing.

"Mate, you can't actually sell it. It's got two kilos of dog treats inside it."

"So it's no good to me, is it? I still need a board for surfing." He turned away, but I grabbed his arm.

"But what if it snaps? What if someone finds them?" I hissed, then shut up as the sales guy came walking back. He was carrying the new board Ben had selected and placed it carefully down in front of the counter.

"Yeah, well, they can feed their dogs, can't they?" Ben replied at normal volume raising a quizzical look from the salesman. I had to get out the shop I was giggling so much by then, and moments later Ben walked out with the new surfboard under his arm.

I still wonder what happened to his old board, and if anyone ever found it was filled with dog food.

Chapter Sixteen

AS PLEASED AS we both were with how the surfboard experiment had gone, it still took a bit of work until we had the problem dialled. Although we'd successfully hidden two kilos of dog treats in Ben's surfboard, and I'd turned his bedroom into a fibreglass factory in the process, we still had a problem with volume. You see, surfboards are quite small. I hadn't used all the potential available space in Ben's board, and the dog treats I'd used were probably a bit bulkier than the cannabis resin we were planning to smuggle for real. But even so, even if we each took a board, and I filled both to capacity, it was hard to see how we were going to get much beyond six kilos through in total. We'd need to take hundreds of boards if it was going to be worthwhile. We needed bigger surfboards.

But fortunately, you can get bigger surfboards. Ben's was what they call a shortboard, about six foot long, but you can also get longboards, up to about ten foot in length, and with quite a lot more space inside to work with. But even better than that, there was a new type of board that had come out in the last few years that was perfect for our needs. You'll have seen celebrities using them, wobbling around in the Caribbean. They're called Stand-up paddleboards and they're huge, not just longer, but also substantially wider and thicker. They were perfectly suited, it turned out, for smuggling banned substances across national borders. And if that's not good enough, there was more. Whenever you see people who are into stand-up paddleboarding (and since Brighton is full of idiots who'll do anything if a celebrity tells them it's cool, there were plenty), they often have at least two boards on their car and sometimes even more than that. We realised that we wouldn't look out of place with two stand-up paddleboards each. Plenty of room, in theory, for the full hundred kilos. And absolutely best of all, almost all stand-up boards came painted white on the bottom. Easy to colour match, easy to disguise any repairs. They're not even that expensive, we bought our first one secondhand on eBay for three hundred quid.

Over the next couple of weeks, I chopped it up just like I had the surfboard. And actually, it was even better than we'd hoped. Surfboards come with the wooden stringer that divides the two halves front to back. Stand-up boards don't—they're just filled with standard polystyrene—so you can hollow out a single, much bigger space. We'd run out of dog treats by then, so just to piss Ben off, I glassed both the pillows from his bed into his new board.

And while I was doing that, Ben got back on eBay and bought three more boards.

Chapter Seventeen

IT TOOK TWO weeks before I finally heard about the job—my dream job, as I'd thought of it for a while. The email they sent me read like a copy-and-paste affair, and I remembered what Mo had said, about keeping an eye on the news section of the company's website. I logged on and, sure enough, there was a photograph of Pete, and a short announcement saying how thrilled everyone was that he'd accepted the offer.

I could tell you I didn't care by then, but it wouldn't be true. I stared at the screen for a long while, at Pete's smug smiling face, and it hurt. Somehow, it reminded me of when Mum died: it was a moment when the reality of life showed too clearly through the cracks. It wasn't fair, not the random underlay of life, where good people were picked out to die from cancer and bad people lived to be a hundred. Nor the overlay of life, society—where politicians went on and on about equality and how if you work hard, you can make something of yourself, and then they voted through a massive hike in student fees or got caught hiding millions in tax havens.

I looked from the laptop screen in Ben's room to the paddleboard I was still working on. I'm not trying to draw too direct a line, I'm not saying I agreed to smuggle drugs because this firm didn't give me a job, or because I'd lost my hours on the petrol station job. That would be too simplistic. That's not it. But it wasn't unrelated either.

But if I'm really honest, it was mostly about Julia. I'd fallen for her so hard by then I'd built up a whole false reality based around us and how we were going to get together. Impressing her with my sensible job hadn't worked so now I was trying the opposite, wowing her by becoming an exciting, daring international drugs smuggler.

Of course I wasn't really telling her anything at all. In reality we lived together but we didn't even talk. Nonetheless she commanded my attention. If she was home, I was always alert to where she was in the flat. My pulse would quicken when she walked into the room; I'd stop whatever I was doing. I'd try not to look, but my eyes followed her as if drawn by some irresistible force. I took a thousand mental photographs of the back of her head. I thought it was love. It felt like love. The most powerful, physical form of love I'd ever experienced. It hurt that we weren't together, but it was an easy pain to like, it distracted me from reality, it gave me something to feel that was at least about her.

I couldn't tell her, of course I couldn't tell her. Ben and I had agreed we wouldn't tell anyone, except those who had to know. But I think I always knew I'd crumble in the end.

* * *

It happened late one night. Ben and Anna had gone to bed, and I was about to, when I heard the front door, and Julia came in. She'd been out with Andy, and I'd assumed she'd stay over at his place. I listened in case he was with her, but all I heard was her in the kitchen, making a drink. So instead of going to bed, I waited in the lounge, hoping she'd come in.

She did, with a mug of coffee, blowing steam off the top, then she sat down. Not next to me this time. In the armchair, at the opposite end of the sofa.

"Hi Jake," she said. "You're up late."

"Yeah. I'm just working on something," I replied, surprising myself. Suddenly I sensed this was where my fantasy became reality. Earlier Ben and I had been writing a list of stuff we needed to take and I quickly grabbed it from the table, along with a pen.

"Another job interview?"

"No. Something else." I gave a half pause. "Something a bit more interesting."

She went back to her coffee, and I fought back the urge to fill the silence.

"Well, go on," she said when she'd taken her sip. "Is it a secret?" She gave a little roll of her eyes, as if telling me she knew what I was doing.

"It's just a list. You know, for the trip me and Ben are going on."

"Oh, your holiday?" We'd told them we were going away, we couldn't just disappear.

"What if I told you it's not just a holiday?"

"What?" She blew again on her coffee, as if that was more interesting than what I was saying.

"This trip. What if I told you it was something else?"

Her face didn't exactly light up, but I had her attention. But she misinterpreted me.

"What, like it's travelling or something? Jake, you're only going away for two weeks. Proper travelling is at least six months. Or maybe a year." There was a magazine on the table, and I saw her eye go to it. She was about to pick it up; then I'd lose her in celebrities and their vacant lives.

I shouldn't do this, I thought. I knew I shouldn't do this. Ben would kill me. No. Ben would understand.

"That's not what I'm saying," I said, aiming for a sly tone of intrigue in my voice. "What I mean is there might be another purpose to this trip."

Those lovely grey eyes came back to me, and widened slightly.

"Like what?"

"Well, you know we're going to Morocco, don't you?"

"Yes," she said slowly.

"And you know we're taking those new stand-up paddleboards that Ben's got in his room?"

A little pause here from Julia, then:

"I haven't seen them..."

"But you know he has them? I heard you talking with him about them the other week."

"Yes..."

"Well, let's just say when we come back from Morocco, those boards might be a little heavier."

She looked like I'd gone too far. She put her coffee down and wrapped her arms around herself.

"Jake, what are you talking about?"

I didn't answer, but Ben's box was on the table in front of me, and very deliberately, I opened it. I pointed at the little block of hashish inside, and watched her face as her eyes followed my finger.

"What are you talking about, Jake?" she said again.

I shook my head.

"I've already said too much." I gave a short, half-hearted laugh, and watched her face. It was like she tried to hide that she understood.

"Are you telling me what I think you're telling me?" she said, swallowing carefully.

I nodded very deliberately, and then, as if I were pretending we might have people spying on us, or bugging the room. "I've no idea what you think I'm telling you."

"Are you telling me you're planning to smuggle drugs back from Morocco?" She said it harshly, there was none of the smile or delighted laugh I'd hoped for. But before I could frame an answer, try and bring things back on track, she softened on her own. I couldn't read this girl. I was blinded by how I felt for her.

"Jake, Jake, Jake. You do surprise me. What a dark horse." And there it was, the smile I'd known was there all along. She tilted her beautiful head on one side and watched me.

"We've already got this guy we're going to buy it from…" I began, but she put her finger to her lips.

"Shhh…" She shook her head. "It's better you don't tell me," she said.

"Better you don't tell anyone."

Neither of us spoke for a moment but our eyes were locked together. But having told her I suddenly felt stupid.

"It's just a one off. Just to clear our debts, and—you know, grab a bit of adventure."

"No Jake. I don't want to hear it."

I felt deflated again. How come I always got it wrong with this girl? I sat in silence for a minute thinking if there was a way to restart the conversation with something else, but before I had regained enough composure to try, she set her coffee cup down, still nearly full.

"I'm pretty tired. I think I'm going to go to bed," she said, and I just nodded my head and watched her get up and walk to the door.

"Maybe you can tell me all about it when you get safely back?" She smiled one last time and disappeared, leaving me alone. Wishing there was something I could do or say that would make her talk to me and love me back.

* * *

I suppose it wasn't much to sustain my obsession, but I was used to existing off scraps. So it was plenty to keep me distracted from the madness of what I was doing with Ben.

Chapter Eighteen

BY THEN BEN was exchanging regular messages with Mo's cousin Ahmed. I didn't play a big part in what he called the "negotiations." I was happy enough making sure my epoxy cured properly and my surfaces were sanded perfectly smooth. But sometimes, Ben would give me updates, when he wanted a break from sitting with his laptop and his phone beeping every few minutes as another flurry of messages went back and forth.

And it took a lot of work. He was using an app with encryption software built in, so in theory, he could talk freely, but Ben was worried that just using encryption might flag up the messages they were sending on some government database. He did as much as he could using a set of invented code words. But then, Ahmed's English wasn't perfect, and there was another problem—we didn't really know what it was we wanted to buy.

When you buy a little bit of hash from a dealer, you basically buy what they've got. But when you want to buy in bulk, it's a bit different. You see, cannabis varies hugely in lots of ways. We first noticed that when we went to Morocco that summer. The colour can vary from a dark green to turd brown. The texture can vary, and most importantly, the effect it has on you can vary massively. And that's just solid; I'm not even talking about weed.

Think of it a bit like wine. Sure, you might think that people who claim to know the difference between a five-pound bottle and a twenty-pound bottle are just wankers—you're probably right. But the truth is, if you drink enough of it, you probably do start to notice the subtle little differences. It's the same with dope.

And just as with wine, you have to pay a lot more for the higher-quality product. But just try negotiating that with a guy who doesn't speak English that well, a thousand miles away, and using code words. That was why Ben was looking so stressed with the whole thing.

We knew by then we wanted hash, not grass. It lasts longer, it smells less, and most importantly, it packs down much smaller, so we could fit more of it in. But what type of hash? From Ahmed's texts, it seemed there were about a million different types of the stuff, and they all had wildly different prices.

Ben seemed to be stuck in a loop where Ahmed would suggest a type of hashish he could get us, and Ben would read all about it on the Internet and get some idea of what it should be worth here. Then Ahmed would give him a price that was probably more than we could sell it for here. Then Ben would go back to him and say we couldn't possibly pay even a tenth of that price, and Ahmed would sound all offended, and we wouldn't hear back from him for a few hours. But when he did come back to us, he'd tell us about a different type of hash we could have if that was what we were prepared to spend, and the whole thing would start again. He'd text us photos too; when we stripped off the encryption, there'd be these big, shiny blocks of sticky brown dope. In the background, I could see the workshop he had; it looked a lot like how I'd imagined it would. And all the dope he sent us looked a whole lot fresher and better than whatever we could get here.

Ben persevered, and he got there in the end.

CHAPTER NINETEEN

AND SO THE days ticked down. Ben booked the ferries, and we sorted the route we'd take. I handed Ben all the money I had access to, taking my debts to new heights. He put in more than me, but he was generous. We were partners, fifty-fifty.

These felt like significant milestones, but there always seemed room to back out. I'm not sure I really believed Ben's van would get all the way down to Morocco, or if it did, that anything would happen when we got there. There'd be no dope. We'd find out Ahmed was just stringing us along, or the crop would fail. We'd just end up having a holiday like we had the other time. We'd probably smoke a load of gear for a week and come home. And everything would go back to normal, whatever normal meant by that time.

Maybe that's denial. Maybe that was me sticking my head in the sand. Maybe that's how everyone gets themselves ready to do something stupid. Truth is I didn't even think about it much. There were plenty of practical things to keep me busy. I had to work out what equipment and material I'd need to open up and fix the paddleboards with the gear inside. There was the van to get ready, serviced, and packed up with sleeping bags and all the other stuff we'd need driving down and back. There was the issue of where we would stay to sort out. And when I wasn't busy with that, I had to fit in a lot of daydreaming about Julia.

* * *

One thing we didn't spend much time on was what we were going to do with the dope when we got it back to the UK. If I did ask him, Ben would always tell me it was sorted, but I didn't bring it up much. Like I say, I didn't really believe there ever would be any dope, so this didn't feel that important. If Ben said it was sorted, that was fine, one less thing for me to worry about.

The days passed. Other-worldly days spent in a lightly scented haze of dope smoke. I still had no hours at the petrol station. I'd stopped bothering with job applications by then too. Handing my money to Ben felt like handing over responsibility for the debt too. At some level I knew I'd have to face reality again after our 'holiday', but for a short while I was content to let it all be something I would worry about later.

They were days tainted only by my longing for Julia, a longing that was made worse by her knowing our secret, but refusing to talk about it. I made it bearable by living mostly in my fantasy world in which she loved me as much as I thought I loved her.

And then, suddenly, I discovered that all the days had ticked by. We had to pack up the van and drive to the port. We were off.

Chapter Twenty

FRANCE IS BIG. Really big.

We saved a bit of cash by taking the Dover-to-Calais route, but it added about five thousand miles to the distance. I'm exaggerating, of course, but in a van like Ben's, it really seemed like it. We had the boards strapped to the roof, two on each side, which meant we couldn't go much above sixty before the noise made us worry the whole lot might be ripped off. We took it in turns to drive, stopping only for refuelling, and to pay the tolls. That and those little coffees you get from the machines in service stations where everyone stands around, looking French.

We put ourselves back an hour getting lost around Paris, and then another hour when we hit Bordeaux in the rush hour, but slowly, we crawled southward through France. Our plan was to just keep at it, taking it in turns to sleep, but at three a.m., we gave up and both crawled in the back for a sleep, somewhere just shy of the Spanish border.

Spain's pretty big too, but the thing about driving long distances is you get into it. Spain's empty too. Apart from the cities, and for what seemed like hour after hour, we seemed to be the only people there at all, barrelling across the high plateau, vultures circling above us and a yellow, dusty landscape stretching all around forever. When we stopped to refuel, the petrol stations were dirtier, and we had to rely on the basic Spanish my mum taught me for what we needed. Mostly that meant pointing at sandwiches and holding out handfuls of euros. But by the time we approached Algeciras, in the southern tip of Spain, neither of us wanted to stop driving. It was like we were on some video game hell mission. Totally addicted to the objective of eating up mile after mile after mile.

* * *

The ferry across to Africa felt suitably Third World, compared to the slick Dover-Calais experience two days and two hundred cups of coffee before. And then arriving in Morocco was exactly how we'd remembered it two summers before. Noisy, dirty, chaotic. Hot. Just generally mad as hell.

That other summer, we'd fallen into an annoying tourist trap. We'd driven out of the port slowly, a big unfolded map clearly visible, making it obvious we'd just arrived. We stopped when a young guy stepped out in front of us, offering to help show us around. Somehow, he talked his way in, and then it took hours to get rid of him. He told us about his cousin in Manchester, or Leeds, or wherever we said we were from. We figured out in the end he just wanted to get us to his carpet shop. So this time, we kept the windows up and ignored the confident waving arms of the guys who prey on the newly arrived. We just followed the satnav until it led us out of town.

And driving in Morocco is a shock to the system, but with three days' solid travel behind us, we were basically driving machines. So the live cows strapped to the roofs, the mental overtaking, the driving at night with the lights off: we took it all in our stride. We enjoyed it.

We kept on the coast road all the way down to Casablanca, sleeping for a few hours again on a bluff overlooking the ocean. Next morning, we diverted inland toward Marrakesh, and then we were there. It's amazing how easy it is, really. You type a few letters and numbers in your GPS in England, and three days later, you arrive at exactly the right place in a whole new continent, right in the middle of nowhere.

* * *

The reason it had taken so long to find somewhere on Airbnb was we had very particular requirements. It had to have somewhere suitable for me to fix up the boards, and it had to be out of the way. We didn't want anyone wondering what we were up to. We didn't want to meet the owner either, picking up the key from under a rock suited us just fine. The one we found was perfect, owned by a French guy who ran it as a peaceful, out-of-the-way desert retreat. It was cheap too.

It looked like a small castle, square, with a little courtyard or garden in the middle that had a narrow opening to the sky. The walls were deep orange red, and the tops of the doors and windows were all pointed; I guess you call that Arabic style. That courtyard—I couldn't have hoped for a better workroom. It was totally hidden, and it felt deliciously cool, with plants growing everywhere, and even a little fountain in one corner so you had the sound of running water to work to.

Up above, there was a roof terrace, kind of like the ramparts of the castle, and the view from there was awesome. You could see the mountains on one side, and the haze from the city on the other. There were a few other buildings around us, but they were far enough away that no one would see what we were up to. Mostly, we were just surrounded by the beautiful garden. Oh, and the pool.

It was late in the afternoon by the time we arrived, unwashed after nearly four days driving in a van with no air con. We hadn't been too worried about the swimming pool when we booked, but now, it was just about the best thing in the whole place, twinkling blue against the orangey red of the landscape.

We didn't waste any time. We left the van door open, changed into our shorts, and just jumped right in. It felt amazing. Just to be there felt amazing. I couldn't help but think about Peter, the asshole guy from the interview. Where would he be now? Sitting in some office somewhere, worrying about spreadsheets and where the stationery cupboard was. And what was I doing? Floating in my own pool in the Moroccan desert, as the sunset lit up the mountains in more shades of red and gold than I even knew existed. I realised then I'd never wanted that job, not really, or not for the right reasons anyway. I still didn't know exactly what I did want, but it wasn't that.

I stayed in the pool that first night for ages. I floated on my back and watched the sky fade from blue to black. I watched the stars appear, one by one, until the whole of the heavens stretched out above me. A billion stars, the eternity of the infinite universe. The water warm and comfortable even though the night air by then was cool. What we were doing was finally beginning to feel real by then.

Chapter Twenty-One

WE COULDN'T GET a mobile signal at the house, but it had Wi-Fi, so it was just as easy to get in touch with Ahmed as it had been from home. Ben sent him a message that night, saying we'd arrived and Ahmed replied with the name of a café in the town nearby and a time for us to meet the next day. We ate the rest of the food we had in the van and went to bed. I began to sense then how nervous we both were. I think for different reasons. For Ben, there was so much riding on whether Ahmed was for real or not. I kind of hoped he wasn't. That way, we'd get out of actually going through with this, but neither of us would lose face. But even with our nerves we didn't stay awake for long that night; driving takes it out of you.

* * *

The town where we were meeting Ahmed was twenty kilometres away, on a road that cut through a scrubby desert landscape that stretched off to the horizon, flat and featureless in most directions, only the mountains to the north giving any shape to the land. We'd taken the boards off the roof; they were safely stashed in the house, but even so, we felt out of place on the road in Ben's van, among the trucks and pickups and the old-style Mercedes everywhere. But no one paid us much attention.

We left the house early, and we had no food, so we stopped along the way at a kind of truck stop restaurant. This wasn't a tourist area. We were the only westerners there, but apart from a few curious glances we were mostly ignored. For my part, I tried to ignore the dirt and grime everywhere. But I drew the line at drinking from the tin cup that we were given with our plates of food. I stuck to bottled water.

Ben and I weren't talking much. We were both properly nervous now, not even trying to hide it from each other, just trying to deal with it. I sometimes wonder, if either one of us had found the courage to say we didn't want to go through with it at that point, we might have given up. But it took less courage not to think and just to push on with the plan. Just to keep taking the baby steps toward a fate we'd put in place from the safety and distance of England.

We got to the town where Ahmed had arranged to meet us. It was closer to the mountains, so that they seemed to loom over the dusty buildings and dirty streets. As we drove through the outskirts, it seemed empty. Three-storey apartment blocks set well back from the road, many of them unfinished with steel rods poking out the roof, as if another floor had been planned but never delivered. But they were all lived in, with washing hanging from the windows. There were no gardens here, just a kind of hard-baked wasteland where goats wandered, and rubbish blew on the hot breeze. There were a few cars parked around, battered Renaults and Fiats, but they made Ben's van look good. As we got closer to the centre of town, still amazingly able to follow our GPS, it got busier. The road filled up with cars and motor scooters. Little gangs of kids stared at us as we drove past, and some waved. Most of them seemed to be wearing Manchester United football shirts, old ones with Eric Cantona on the back. Men in dirty robes watched us too. They sat outside cafés smoking shisha pipes, their faces the colour of leather, their dark eyes following as we drove past. Most of the women we saw were covered up, their faces and bodies hidden beneath the veils they wore.

Most of the signs were in two languages, the indecipherable Arabic script that we couldn't read a word of, and a second language that looked like French. And then a few names were written in bad English. Ahmed had sent us to a café called Happy Palms, and we found it just where the GPS said it would be. Ben rolled the van to a stop across the street, and we got out and crossed the road.

The café didn't look much different from some of the others we'd passed. Half of it was inside, the other outside, and there was little distinction between the two parts. There were large wooden containers filled with plants, so it felt almost like a garden but the leaves were dirty and dusty from the street. In one corner there was a charcoal burner glowing hot, and a few kids were busy ferrying hot coals and shisha pipes to groups of men who sat around small metal tables, drinking from tiny glasses and puffing out clouds of smoke. It actually smelt really nice, sweet and pungent. I looked at Ben to see what to do, but he seemed uncertain too. Then one of the kids came up to us and said something in rapid Arabic.

Neither of us knew what to do to. Ben was looking around as if he might spot Ahmed, but no one looked likely. In the end, I pointed to a table and asked the kid if we could sit there. He said something back that I didn't understand, and then beckoned us angrily to follow him and sit there. He said something else, and I shrugged and made a drinking motion with my hand.

"Tea," I said, until I thought the kid understood, and held up two fingers, one for each of us. He still looked confused, but an older guy shouted something to him. I guess he translated, and the kid shouted back, but then ran off. He didn't bring us anything though. He just hovered near the wall watching us, like he was hoping we'd go away so he didn't have to deal with us.

"Now what?" I said to Ben, who'd sat down opposite me.

"We wait until Ahmed turns up," Ben said. He was pale and drawn and I could see how much he wanted this to go well. Me, I hoped Ahmed would stand us up. I just wanted to get away from there.

Still the kid watched us and did nothing. The man who'd helped me with the order shouted something to us, but it was in Arabic, so we still didn't understand. I smiled back and tried my 'tea' mime again, but the guy kept shouting and then stared at us while we sat there, feeling about two thousand miles out of place.

Then Ahmed arrived.

"Hey guys! You must be Ben, and Jake, right? Welcome!" A young Moroccan man was walking toward us, his arms open. He was about our age, maybe a little older, dressed in tight jeans and a white shirt. Skinny, hair cropped short, and teeth already stained by something, coffee maybe or just a lack of cleaning. Ben stood up at once, and I did the same. Ahmed reached out his hand like an American rapper might, a fist pump instead of a handshake, his fingernails nearly black with grime.

"I can't believe you actually made it! You crazy crazy English boys!" Ahmed motioned us to sit. He looked around until he saw the kid and he shouted at him in Arabic for a minute until he finally scurried around bringing us various things, a shisha pipe for each of us, filled with sweet apple tobacco, and then mint tea, which Ahmed poured for us into small glasses. "You motherfucking crazy boys," Ahmed kept saying. It was like we'd known him for years.

And for me, it actually felt like meeting an old friend—I suppose he was one in a way. Ben had spent hours talking to him, discussing prices and stuff, and I'd played my part in that. What was a little weird was that they didn't seem to know what to say to each other now. I was doing most of the talking. Ahmed was asking question after question: How the journey had been. How we'd found the café; what we thought of Morocco, the tea, the town we were in now, where we were staying. I was cautious, though. We'd already agreed to not tell Ahmed where we were staying, nor any details about what we were planning on doing once we got hold of the dope. It just seemed a sensible precaution.

"So, you know my cousin Mo?" Ahmed said to me. I was drawing in a big breath of apple tobacco smoke, and I stopped, then blew out a big cloud before passing the pipe to Ahmed.

"Yeah, we met at a job interview," I replied.

"And you just ask him for somewhere to buy hashish?" He shook his head again in amazement. It was the first time he'd mentioned the subject of why we were meeting, and his voice dropped so that there was no danger of anyone nearby overhearing. Even so, I noticed Ben stiffen.

"Yeah," I said. I felt I should say something else, but there wasn't anything more to say.

Ahmed waited and then nodded, as if he understood.

"I have some here. For you to see the quality." Ahmed reached into the pocket of his denim jacket and pulled out a foil-wrapped rectangle. He placed it on the table, keeping it hidden with the palm of his hand until Ben put his hand over it too, and Ahmed took his away. Ben pulled the dope into his lap, but did nothing more, not even looking at it, his eyes roaming the café to see if anyone had noticed. If they had, no one cared.

"It's very good quality. When you asked for so much, I don't know at first if I can get it?" Ahmed said, smiling. "But for a friend of my cousin, I have to try. And in the end, I get it. Go have a look. Have a smell. Is good. Very, very good."

I watched Ben as he unwrapped it. He was keeping it under the table and out of sight, so it was only his face I could see. He put it up to his nose, still hidden in his hand, and he breathed in, then rewrapped it again. He pushed it into his jeans pocket then glanced at me. He gave a tiny nod.

"You take it away, you have a little smoke, you see if you like it. You see if Ahmed do a good job. Tomorrow, we do the deal, huh?" He flashed a huge smile at Ben.

"Where are we going to meet? We can't do it here," Ben said.

"No." Ahmed kept smiling and leaned forward to top up Ben's tea. "You stop out of town. You meet my friend there. He will bring the hashish. You will bring the money. No more than five minutes. There is no risk that way of people who don't understand, seeing." He leaned back again and reached into his pocket for a scrap of paper on which he'd drawn a map. He placed it on the table facing Ben and stabbed a finger where he'd drawn a black cross.

"Here. You take the road out of town and there is a car wreck. You turn here." The map was basic but clear enough—as far as we could see there were only two roads in and out of town, and we'd both seen the wreck as we drove in.

"You go up there and stop where there is an old truck. OK?"

We nodded, and Ben folded the map and put it in his pocket.

"Now, I am hungry," Ahmed said. "I want to show you that Moroccan food is the best in the world!" He shouted again at the kid waiting the tables and when he ran over Ahmed gave him a handful of dirhams, the notes so used and dirty the paper was almost falling to pieces.

"Come, come. Crazy English boys. Are you hungry?"

We had goat, cooked in a clay tagine pot, which we all sat around on carpets on the floor, dipping bread in to wipe up the sauce. I'd never had goat before; it's like lamb really, it's pretty good. We actually ran out of things to say quite quickly since there were so many topics that we couldn't discuss, and Ahmed seemed to understand this and didn't press to know more than we were comfortable telling him. The restaurant we were in was a little more private than the Happy Palm café, and at one point, Ben handed me the dope that Ahmed had given him, and I had a good look at it. It was soft and crumbly—the stuff we got back home was never such good quality. Never this fresh. I was excited. I was buzzing.

But along with the excitement there was also fear. The next bit, the part where we had to do the actual deal, was always the part I'd been most scared about. It just seemed likely that if anything was going to go wrong, it was here. And by "going wrong," I meant I thought there was a significant chance we were going to get shot. Or if not shot, then just robbed. Or failing that, then set up so that the police would descend on us and put us in a Moroccan jail for the next forty years. I liked Ahmed, I wanted to trust him, but there seemed no way to eliminate all the risk from this part.

And actually, despite his bravado he seemed a little nervous about it all too. I could see a tremor in his hands as he ate. I didn't know if that was a good sign or not. I didn't even know if it *was* a sign, for all I knew the guy just had shaky hands.

Either way I was glad when we finished and said our goodbyes. Ahmed left reminding us not to be late and there were more gangster style handshakes before he disappeared down a dusty side street. Then we made our way back to the van and drove slowly out of town, noting where we had to turn off the road the next day as we went back to the house.

When we arrived Ben rolled up a joint to test the dope, and we sat up on the roof terrace overlooking the mountains. It was good. It was better than good. We got so stoned we could hardly get downstairs.

Chapter Twenty-Two

THAT NIGHT, I dreamt of my death. We were waiting in Ben's van, by the side of the road where Ahmed had asked us to wait. No traffic, no noise, nothing in sight, just an empty horizon. Then, across the desert, we saw them coming. Three shiny black Range Rovers. Identical. Blacked-out windows, plumes of yellow dust flaring out behind them, roaring across the landscape toward us. I had the money at my feet, packed into a sports bag. Bundles of euro notes, counted and recounted so we were sure it was the correct amount. The cars came closer and closer. Even if we wanted to escape now, we could never outrun them, not in our shitty van. And then they were here. They circled us now, driving around and around so that we were like fish caught in a ever-shrinking net. Then all together, they jerked to a halt. There was silence. The dust began to thin on the light breeze. A door opened. Then several more. Black-clad men got out, armed with automatic weapons, all pointed at us. One of the men opened the rear door of the middle car, and another man got out. By the gold-plated gleam of his Bond-villain smile, I could tell he was the leader. He puffed a cigar, then flicked it to the ground and crushed it under his heel. He shouted an order, and his men snapped to attention, all the guns now pointing at us, the men shouting angrily.

The tension rose as they shouted at us. We didn't understand—it was all in Arabic, but they were getting anxious. I sensed that at any moment, they were going to open fire, rake our car with gunfire. Then one shouted in English:

"Get out now, or we kill!"

Ben and I exchanged a look that seemed to contemplate all our options but conclude we had none left. Breathing fast we fumbled with the handles, my hands shaking almost too much to operate the lever, but my door cracked open, and the hot desert air leaked in. I pushed the door open wide, and on legs that didn't feel like my own, I climbed out, for every second I expected to feel the bullets tearing into me. But they didn't. Instead a man came running up to me, gun aimed at my chest. He turned me around. I could feel pain in my lower back where he pushed the muzzle hard against me. Even though I knew I was asleep, I could feel that pain, and I wanted to cry out but didn't dare. The man with the gold teeth walked toward me. He inspected me for a long while, then sucked his teeth and spat on the ground.

"So, you have the money?" he said to me. Across his cheek was a long, ragged scar. When I nodded and pointed to the bag I'd pulled with me, he smiled. I fancied the cut was so deep it was actually a hole. I could see inside his mouth through his cheek.

"Do you have the product?" It was Ben's voice. Somehow he'd found a new wave of confidence and he sounded almost in control. The man snapped his attention away from me and onto Ben. Ben took a step forward to come to the other side of the van, and all the armed guards raised their guns at once. There was shouting. Ben stopped and the boss man raised his arm to his soldiers, commanding them to back off without needing to speak.

"First the money, my friend. First the money."

I kicked the bag forward with my foot, toward where the boss was standing, only it wasn't a bag. Now, it was a briefcase, leather, with twin catches on the front. One of the armed men picked it up and hefted it onto the bonnet of one of the Range Rovers. He snapped the catches off and lifted the lid. It was filled with stacks of American dollars. He picked one stack out and strummed his finger against the ends of the notes. He sniffed it suspiciously.

"It all there?" his boss asked him.

"One million dollars," the man said. How the hell he counted it so fast, I didn't know. It took me an hour to be sure our pile of euros was right.

The boss gave a slight inclination of his head, and another of his men understood the signal at once. He went to the back of the last Range Rover and lifted the boot. Inside, I could see packs of cellophane-wrapped white powder. Cocaine, heroin, I didn't know. But this wasn't going to plan.

"Here!" The boss man drew a knife from nowhere. At first, I thought he meant to slit my throat, but he spun it around and caught the blade, then held out the handle to me and beckoned me to follow him to the car. I took the knife and followed him. On his grunted instructions, I selected a package of drugs and cut through the packaging. The drugs were the purest white powder I'd ever seen; like the finest flour, it spilled out onto my hand and the desert sand. I put my finger to my mouth and tasted some. It tasted of strawberries. I had no idea if that was right. But I nodded to Ben, and the boss man gave me the biggest smile yet. This time every single one of his teeth was solid yellow gold.

His men moved into position to start transferring the load, and the tension that held us all released its grip. The men lowered their guns and began to laugh. I looked at Ben and smiled in amazement. But then all hell broke loose.

There was a shout, then a commotion from the guy who now had the money. I didn't understand what it was about, but then I saw him pull out a black plastic box from the briefcase with a red LED light blinking on the side—a tracking device. I knew what it was at once. I froze, not understanding, but out of the corner of my eye, I saw Ben react. Like an animal—or an action hero in a film—he threw himself at the nearest of the guards and stole his gun, using the butt to smash against the side of the man's head. Then they both went down, rolling in the dirt, but it looked like Ben had the upper hand. The gun went off, and everyone dived for cover—except the boss man. He pulled his gun from his waistband, a giant silver pistol, and he pointed it at the two men fighting on the floor. And then, before I could do anything to stop him, before I could even scream out, he fired, once, twice, three times. And then his gun turned into a machine gun, and he hammered the pair with a minute, then two minutes of non-stop deafening gunfire, flushing metal through their riddled bodies long after they were both dead. They jerked and danced, and the desert floor was red with their blood. He stopped, and there was silence. Silence except for the settling of their corpses. Then the man looked at me.

"So, you would cross me?" he said, and before I could say anything, he pistol-whipped me, and I felt my jaw snap out of place.

"You would dare to cross me?" He turned and fired a single shot into Ben, who had somehow now survived the previous assault and was gasping for mercy on the ground beside me.

"Me who controls this land? Then you will face retribution. Your family will die. Your girl, the one you call Julia—I will take her for myself. And you. You will die now. Knowing all this." He pointed his gun at my face, at point-blank range. He showed me his golden smile one final time, and then I heard the gun fire, and I saw the bullet in slow motion coming right towards my eyes. As it pierced the soft tissue of my lens I woke up.

Chapter Twenty-Three

"MATE IT'S TIME to get up. I want to get there early and check the place out."

Ben was in my room, wearing just his shorts, shaking me by the shoulder.

After my nightmare, I'd got up and gone to the kitchen to drink water. I'd run through everything in my mind. I'd nearly panicked and woken Ben up, but eventually, up on the roof terrace under a canopy of stars, I'd calmed down. At five in the morning, I'd gone back to my bed, still wet from sweat. Now, I glanced at my watch. It was seven.

"Mate, you look like shit," Ben told me.

I didn't answer. I just climbed out of bed and went to the shower.

When I got out, Ben was counting the money on the kitchen table. He'd made coffee, and I poured myself a cup.

"You all set?" Ben asked, but he didn't take his eyes off the money. Again, I didn't answer, but looked at the small piles of euros. Twenty-five thousand euros in cash takes up a surprisingly small amount of space. There were still small balls of polystyrene from where it had been packed inside one of the boards, before they were locked to the roof. If I'd convinced myself up to this point that this wasn't real, it was time to face reality. And if I wanted to tell Ben I wanted out, now was the time. I opened my mouth to speak.

"Yeah," I croaked. Bottling out again.

Ben didn't respond. He began to load the piles of cash into a sports bag, packing the money carefully as if it were a bagful of loose eggs. Only when he was finished and he'd zipped it up did he look my way again.

"You're good on the plan for today, right? There's nothing going to go wrong, but we've gotta be careful, just in case. You're going to be driving, and you stay in the van. You'll keep the engine running while I get out and make the exchange."

I felt sick at the base of my stomach. I could still feel the bullet from earlier when I'd dreamed about it piercing my eye. I put my hand over my face to try and shake the feeling.

"Jake mate, you need to relax. They're farmers. They're just a bunch of farmers selling their crop. It's gonna be fine. It's all gonna be fine."

The coffee still tasted like dirt in my mouth.

* * *

We took the same road we had the day before, slowing at the car wreck Ahmed had marked on his map and indicating before turning off into the desert, even though there were no other moving vehicles in sight. Close up the smashed car made my stomach turn, the whole front end was caved in, past the front seats, like a truck had ploughed into it and not even slowed down. Whoever had been sitting in it when it happened wouldn't have stood a chance.

We pressed on, there wasn't much of a road, just a track that wove through the bumps in the desert. Ahmed's map told us to go a couple of miles until we came to another abandoned vehicle, this time a pickup truck, picked bare of anything salvageable like an animal carcass stripped by vultures. We parked up nearby and sat there, not getting out. Not turning the engine off. In the distance we could still see the main road, a few trucks and cars trundling along the horizon. I looked at the pick up. I wondered how it got to be here, and hoped it didn't belong to the last people that had tried to buy drugs around here. I half expected to see a couple of skeletons sitting in the front, or scattered around in the dirt, but there was nothing. No sign of any life anywhere. Or death, for that matter.

We drove around a bit to see if there was anything else and eventually parked back up by the truck, the engine still on. The slight vibration it gave to the van was making me more nervous. I was about to turn it off when suddenly, Ben pointed.

"Shit," he said, and opened the glove box and pulled out his mini binoculars.

I looked where he pointed them. I saw something but I couldn't see what it was. It was black or brown—hard to see in the weird desert light where faraway things wobbled and danced in a silvery mirage. But even so, the way this was moving was weird. It wasn't the Range Rovers of my dream, at least. There wasn't any plume of sand thrown up behind it, but it looked kind of alien. Or like a giant crab slowly scuttling toward us.

"What is that?" I asked.

Ben was silent for a minute, watching through his glasses. Then he swore again.

"What is it?" I said again, getting irritated that he wasn't answering.

"Camel train," Ben replied. "Here." He passed me the glasses, and I quickly put them to my eyes.

I saw at once he was right. There were three camels ambling slowly toward us on long, ungainly limbs. Alongside them were three men walking. They were too far away for me to see their faces, but they were dressed in long brown robes, with turban-things wrapped around their heads.

"Shit, what do we do?" I said, watching them approach, then added: "Do you think that might be them? They're not on the road, and it looks like they're coming straight toward us."

Ben didn't reply. He just held out his hand for the glasses back, and watched as the three camels slowly came closer and closer.

It seemed to take an eternity for them to get to us, but eventually they were close enough to see them well without the binoculars. And from that point it was clear they were coming toward us. Either we'd accidentally stopped on their route, or more likely, they were our guys.

Eventually they reached us. The men stopped the camels maybe twenty metres away. No one moved for a minute. We watched them, and they watched us. The camels had bags strapped to their sides. Up close, we could see the men better. One was quite old. It was hard to guess how old; he could have been anywhere from fifty to a hundred, his face was chocolate brown and deeply lined. The other two were younger. They looked mean, untrusting. But there was one thing that gave me hope we were going to survive the next few minutes. I didn't see any guns.

"OK, let's do this," Ben said, more to himself than me, as he pushed open the door. I was about to tell him not to, but he was already out, and I watched him walk slowly toward the men. As he did so, the older man also walked forward until they met halfway between the van and the camels. I couldn't hear what they were saying, but I saw as the man took Ben's hand and shook it, using both his hands to encircle Ben's. And I saw he was smiling, and even from inside the van, it looked genuine, even if the teeth were the same colour as the desert floor.

Then the old man called the younger men forward, and Ben ended up shaking their hands as well, and then Ben turned around and pointed to me, and I knew what he was going to do before he did it. He beckoned me to come out and join them.

"What about the fucking plan, Ben?" I said, even though he couldn't hear me. "What about me staying in the van while you do the deal?" But I turned off the engine and pushed open the door.

Outside, I could smell the camels right away. A warm, milk-and-urine smell, like you get at the zoo. Or it might have been the old man; it was hard to tell. I walked over to him, getting that same floating, not-my-own-legs feeling that I'd had the night before, only this was happening for real. And then I was locked in the older man's bony-fingered handshake and the brown-toothed grin just as Ben had been, and he was saying "Welcome" to me over and over again, the odour from his mouth washing over me in the desert air. Then one of the young guys spoke.

"My name is Youssef. This is my father, Agafay, and there, my brother Omar."

There was a slight pause, but then Ben replied.

"I'm Ben, and this is Jake."

The old man turned to Ben and repeated his name as if it was a great honour to meet him, then did the same to me, grinning and nodding his head. Then he opened his arms wide, and I thought for a moment he was going to hug me. But instead, he said something in Arabic, then waited for Youssef to translate.

"My father invites you to drink tea with him," he said with a slight bow of the head. I looked at Ben, then glanced around, not just surprised at this turn of events but wondering how the hell we were going to drink any tea. We were a long way out of town, especially at the speed these camels walked. But Omar was already fetching things from one of the saddle bags, and he quickly set up a small stove and set a pan to boil. While he did that, the old man, Agafay, asked us questions, translated by Youssef.

"You have come a long way, yes?"

"Yes." Ben nodded.

"You are from England, yes?"

"Yes." Another nod.

"You are young men, yes?"

"Yes." A slight nod, this time accompanied by a raise of Ben's eyebrows.

"But you are brave men also. Yes?"

"I suppose so."

"Yes." Agafay nodded as if the question was now settled.

The four of us, Ben, me, Agafay, and Youssef, were all sitting down by now on tiny folding stools that Omar had unpacked from a camel. Now he came back, carrying a battered tin teapot, which he placed in the middle of us, and the old man did the honours, pouring a little glass of tea first for Ben, and then for me. Only when we'd both drunk and said how good the bitter, oily liquid was, did he pour more for himself and his sons. When we'd all drunk, in a kind of awkward silence, Agafay clapped his hands and gave another command to Omar, who disappeared back to his camel.

When he returned this time, I saw at once what he had. He was carrying a stack of brown slabs of hashish. I'd never seen that much before in my life, but I knew from all the calculations we'd done that it was a kilo. Omar handed it reverentially to his father, who inspected it quickly, then handed it to Ben with another bow of the head.

"Here, for you to inspect," Youssef said, and they both watched Ben's face as he examined the block. He handed one of the slabs to me too. It was wrapped in cling film, pulled tight against its oily surface. I didn't want to open it, so I just weighed it in my hand—it had a nice heft—and put it to my nose and sniffed in the deep, pungent smell. It looked OK to me. What am I saying, it looked amazing. I had a momentary out of body experience, just seeing myself there inspecting dope in the middle of the Moroccan desert. I felt so light headed I wondered if I might pass out.

Ben told me to go and get the money, and I did so, grateful to have a moment away. I carried the sports bag back to the little group and gave it to Ben, unsure what the etiquette was now. Ben unzipped it, pulled the sides of the bag open as much as he could, and handed it to Agafay. But it was Youssef who took it, and who began to count the money, placing small piles of notes on the ground in front of him, weighted down with rocks from the desert floor. We all watched as he worked. It was hypnotic. And when he'd finished, he nodded to his father, who turned to us with a satisfied smile. I had a moment's panic that we'd just spent the full twenty-five thousand euros on just one kilo of dope, but with another flurry of Arabic, Agafay ordered Omar to bring the rest of the dope, and Ben—clearly getting into the spirit of things—told me to help him, like he was the boss of our side the way Agafay was of theirs.

I'd calmed down enough by now to give him a dirty look for that, but

I did what he told me anyway. I opened the side door of the van and then went back to where Omar was standing, by the first camel. He pulled open the bag that was draped down the camel's side and showed me it contained stack after stack of slabs of hashish, each wrapped in the cling film and loosely tied together as four. He grinned at me then handed me two piles of slabs and he pointed to where the van was parked, still twenty metres away. Omar took another pile, but it was going to take all day if it was just the two of us. Instead of the others helping, something else happened.

Suddenly the old man leapt to his feet and shouted something. He looked angry. Then Ben was on his feet, and Youssef too. I'd known all along something was going to go wrong, and I just froze, expecting them all to whip guns out from under their robes. But that didn't happen. Instead, Omar bowed his head and went back to the camel. He grabbed the reins by its mouth and led it, and its companions, over to where the van was, meaning we could transfer the load of hashish much more easily. The old man laughed as he did it, and Youssef translated again.

"My father says young men are brave, but not always wise." I could see Youssef smiling as he said it.

It didn't take us very long now to remove the bricks of hashish from the panniers of the camels—which up close really stank, by the way—and count them into the van. There were four slabs to a kilo, so four hundred in total. I was shocked how much space it all took up; it pretty much filled the whole back of the van. I was wondering how I was going to fit this all inside the boards.

While we were doing that, Youssef packed away all the tea stuff, and the old man started up with another round of double-handed handshakes, and then a kind of manly hug, which I hoped for a moment might be for Ben only. I'd almost forgotten my fear at this point, but when I saw I was getting a hug as well, I had a fleeting thought that maybe this was the moment he was going to pull out a knife from under the robes and stab me. I didn't have long to fear, and instead of a blade, all I felt was a firm embrace. It was like I was the guy's favourite nephew.

"My father says to say thank you, and you are welcome any time," Youssef said. "He hopes very much to meet you again."

And then, with much nodding and waving, Ben and I retreated to the van. We watched them for a moment while they finished strapping everything away on their camels and then began to walk onward, continuing the path they'd taken as if stopping to sell us one hundred kilos of hashish had been nothing more than a tea break.

"Well, that wasn't too bad," Ben said when we were both back in the van, and he turned around to look at the load we had packed in the back. Then he laughed.

CHAPTER TWENTY-FOUR

BEN WAS HYPER that evening. Screaming with excitement, running up and down the stairs. In and out of the swimming pool, dripping all over the house, and in between everything, just stopping to look at our enormous pile of hashish. We'd backed the van right up to the front door to move the bricks inside. Now, they were stacked up against the wall of the courtyard, opposite the paddleboards they were supposed to fit inside. It looked impossible. Like there would never be enough room. Maybe that was why my mood didn't match Ben's. For him, this was a massive release of stress. I still had some work to do.

I got right on with it. I used chairs, placed back to back, and laid the first board on top; then I got the mini power saw, opened it up, and chiselled out about half of the foam. I took a couple of the slabs of dope and placed them inside, calculating how this was going to work. I chiselled out a bit more foam and tried again. This was going to happen. It was going to take me a good few days. But I was going to make this work.

Ben helped for a bit when he calmed down, but he wasn't much use —he always looked for shortcuts. And in the end, he got bored anyway and told me he was going to go and explore the area, and I was happy to let him go. He came back later with the contents of another tagine in a styrofoam box. Moroccan takeout. I was surprised how hungry I was, and when I'd eaten, I decided I was too tired to do anything more that night.

The next day, Ben went off exploring again after breakfast. I didn't mind being left with all the work. There was a radio in the house, and I found a station that played a mixture of old American hits and French pop that made a nice accompaniment to my work. The morning flew by and eventually hunger drove me to the kitchen where Ben had been back and left some more food, and that's how things progressed. By the time the sun went down I'd opened up all four of the boards. By midnight I'd scraped away enough foam from inside that I could pack all the bricks into the boards. I was dead tired by then so I did a length of the pool by starlight then found my bed.

The next morning I concentrated on just one board and prepared it to be sealed. First, I cut two sections of plastic sheeting to cover the bricks and tucked the first in around them as best I could, so that the epoxy wouldn't stick to the dope itself. Then I laid the second sheet over the entire hole. Then I had an idea and took everything out again. Into the empty shell of the hull, I spooned in a full jar of instant coffee. I didn't know if it would really help in putting sniffer dogs off the scent, but there seemed no harm in trying. Then I repeated what I'd done before, shouting to Ben to get lots more coffee.

I double-checked everything. I made sure I had all the materials and tools I'd need in the next stage ready. I didn't want to mess the next part up. I weighed precise amounts from the two bottles of clear, syrupy epoxy with my digital scales and mixed them together for a few minutes. Then I painted the mixture onto the plastic sheeting, and beyond where it overlapped onto the surrounding parts of the board, now sanded back so that my additional layers could be blended in. Then I laid on my first sheet of fibreglass, allowing the resin to soak through and wet out the fibres. And then I added a second sheet of fibreglass, touching it up with additional epoxy where there were dry spots. The air being so warm meant I had less time to work than back in Brighton, which nearly caught me out. The resin was already turning to jelly as I finished, but by the time I left it, I was satisfied. The first board was on the way.

Although it was dry to the touch a couple of hours later, I forced myself to leave it overnight, and then I trimmed off the excess fibreglass to begin the process of blending it in. The bottom of the board was now sealed, and the set fibreglass and epoxy gave it a surface that was hard and strong, but you could see the shadow of the brown bricks beneath, and the surface wasn't flat. I prepared my squeegee and filler and got to work fixing that. This was easier. I just had to get the consistency of the filler right so that I could draw the flexible blade of the squeegee along the bottom of the board, and it would fill the dents and pattern left by the fibreglass. Two coats, one to sort the larger holes, the second two hours later when it was dry, to sort the smaller ones. Then two hours of careful sanding, and it was looking good. Another two hours, and I couldn't detect a blemish on the surface, either by sight or touch. The repair was perfectly blended in, and even when you tapped the surface of the board, it was hard to detect what was original and what I'd put in. But it still *looked* a mess. Instead of a white, smooth surface, the bottom of the board was a mixture of browns and greens, from the filler and parts where the hidden contents still showed through the opaque resins and fibreglass.

While that first board was drying, I got started on the second. I was slightly concerned I was going to run out of materials, and I didn't want to skimp, so I drew up a shopping list for Ben, as well as giving him the task of disposing of the pile of hacked-out foam and the old surfaces of the board's undersides. We didn't want to fill up the bins at the house with all this, just in case someone got suspicious, and Ben said it would be easy enough to dump it in the desert.

I decided to paint at night when it was cooler. I hung up a sheet against the back wall and propped the board so that the paint wouldn't pool on the surface. There were a few bits of graphics, which wrapped around the board's edges and onto the bottom; I'd been careful not to damage this area when I'd cut into it, and I masked them off now. Then I shook the paint and put on the first coat. Instantly, it was transformed. It looked damn near perfect, except for a fingerprint where Ben wanted to see if the paint was dry. I told him to get the fuck out of my workspace and fixed that. Then I left it overnight again, getting up early to inspect it and adding a second coat, then a third. By lunchtime, I was confident it was dry, and I had my first chance to inspect the finished board.

It was beautiful. I thought of my dad and how he'd taught me all this stuff, I wondered what he'd think if he saw what I'd done. I decided he'd probably be rather proud. When Ben came in, I showed him my work and waited for the inevitable praise. He came over and stared at it closely. He gave me a quizzical look, like he wasn't sure if I was kidding with him, wasn't sure if this was perhaps a board I hadn't even started with, hadn't even opened up yet. Then he picked it up.

"Fucking hell, Jake, it weighs a ton."

My pride and sense of self-satisfaction disappeared in a heartbeat.

"Well, yeah, it's got twenty-five kilos of hashish in it. This board only weighed ten kilos before."

"Fucking hell. That's not great, is it?" He made a face.

"Oh, fuck you, Ben. You want me to work miracles? Look at it—it's fucking perfect," I began, the stress of nearly three days work suddenly coming out. "You can't see the join. You can't feel the join…" I stopped, realising he was kidding me.

"It's awesome Jake. It's a thing of beauty." Ben said.

"Yeah right," I replied, not quite convinced he meant it.

"Go and have a swim. I'll roll you a joint," Ben said.

I did what he said, doing lengths underwater until I calmed down. And Ben came out with the joint and a beer that he'd managed to find in a shop somewhere.

"It's perfect, mate," he said. "We're going to have no problems at all."

CHAPTER TWENTY-FIVE

I GOT BACK on with it, enjoying myself a little less now. Not because of Ben's lack of appreciation, but for another reason. I was getting to the end of the job, and that meant one thing. We had to start thinking about driving home.

You'll probably appreciate it wasn't the thought of three thousand miles sitting next to Ben that worried me. Nor his insistence on choosing the music on the iPod. My concern stemmed purely from the two international borders we had to cross before we got home.

We'd tried to get a good look at the customs area on the Spanish port as we came through, and Ben had even fired off some photos, holding his phone in a way that didn't make it too obvious what we were doing. Unlike the time we'd driven back the summer before, the customs section was empty, but that might just have been because all the incoming traffic from our ferry had already passed through. The photos didn't help much: slightly blurry images where you could see a row of sheds painted blue, tables inside just visible where, presumably, suitcases could be opened and examined. We couldn't see much else, but you could guess it. Inner rooms with tiny windows where the guilty would be led away to, the first step in a journey through the Spanish criminal justice system that would destroy our lives. Our plan didn't rely on evading the customs officers. We were banking that we had the gear well enough hidden that it didn't really matter if they stopped us. With no reason to suspect we were anything other than tourists, they might check the van, they might even rifle through our bags, but they'd never justify drilling into our boards. But as we got closer to testing this, I became less and less confident about that.

* * *

We left the day before our Airbnb dates ran out. The owner had told us to leave the keys where we found them, but we didn't want to run the risk of him or the cleaners turning up early and seeing what we looked like. All our dealings with him had been done through a fake email account that Ben set up, and we paid him through a fake PayPal account. Even so, we figured that if the owner had any reason to suspect something was odd about us, it wouldn't be that hard to track us down. That meant we had to spend a long time cleaning up. I made Ben do all the work while I put the finishing touches to all four of the boards. The last thing we did was load them onto the roof rack and strap them down, then thread the cable lock around the whole lot. It would be pretty annoying to get them nicked after all the work we'd put in.

The drive back up to the port at Tangier started off uneventfully, but we got held up in Rabat, and that made us late for the ferry. It was a single-lane road, more or less a straight line that stretched to the horizon with a steady stream of cars and trucks on it. You could sit back and follow behind a truck at forty, but if you wanted to go any faster, it meant overtaking all the time. And even Ben's van could do sixty. Because the road was so straight, you could always see traffic coming toward you. It was just a case of judging the gap, gunning the engine, and going for it.

It's addictive once you get started doing that, and I was hammering along, watching the kilometres tick down to the ferry port in Tangier, eating my way up toward each new truck and then sailing past them in a blast of yellow dust, with the flashing lights and horns of oncoming traffic warning me when I got too close. A couple of times, Ben told me to cool it, but I ignored him. Driving dangerously was keeping me from thinking about what was coming up.

There was no customs on the Moroccan side, just a passport check by a guy in Spanish uniform. He didn't look very interested in a couple of British tourists especially since we were almost the last to arrive. We got sent to the back of the queue for the boat, but then, because we had the roof piled so high, when they started boarding the little ferry we got pulled to the front again. When we clanked over the metal plates into the hull of the boat, we were the first on and got told to park with the nose of the van nearly touching the raised off-ramp, where you drive off. It was open to the sky above, and when we left the van and climbed up to the seating area, we could look down through the boat's front windows at a hundred kilos of the finest Moroccan dope hidden in our four boards. When we looked up, we could see the Rock of Gibraltar over the narrow stretch of shocking-blue sea, flecked with whitecaps where the wind was hammering through the straits. We drank coffee and sat in silence, as the ferry cast off and carried us away from Africa and back toward Europe.

The port in Algeciras crept into view as we neared the Spanish coast. We left the looming Gibraltar behind and edged closer. Ferries take so long to dock, especially when you're nervous. There was a queue of people waiting to go down the stairs and get back into their vehicles. We watched the deck hands hurl thin ropes to men standing on the dock, and then those men hauled these ropes until they dragged much thicker ropes up from the filthy water and secured the boat to the land. Then there was a tone and an announcement, first in Spanish, then in bad English: "All passengers should now returning to their vehicles." Oh God, I thought. Here we go.

It was Ben's turn to drive, and he climbed into the driver's seat. A mixed blessing for me. It meant I wouldn't have to worry about stalling, but I had nothing to distract myself from what was coming up. I checked I had the passports ready about fifty times as the sound of metal rang out in the enclosed hull behind us. I fiddled with my phone. I guessed that was what most people would be doing, getting onto a new network, but my hands were shaking as I held it, and I felt so sick I wanted to throw up. There were a couple of motorbikes beside us. I prayed the customs guys would stop them, not us. Anyone but us.

The off ramp, raised vertical in front of us, began to lower, and the port opened out in front of us, behind it the city of Algeciras. It's not much to look at, but the stretch of apartment buildings in the distance looked beautiful to me. If we could just get there, we'd be safe. At least, for now, and right now I would take that. Ben started the engine. He didn't look at me; his eyes were on the guy whose job it was to wave the cars off. Ben was humming. He does that when he's nervous.

The motorbikes were let off first, then us. Ben revved too hard to take the slight rise up the ramp; I felt my heart rate climb. I wasn't sure if I could handle this. I forced myself to breathe. Slow, easy breaths. Calming breaths. That passed a few seconds, and we followed the bikers through the maze out of the port.

Up ahead, we could see the customs area. "ADUANA" in big letters on a gantry that hung over the road, behind it those blue sheds. Two men stood side by side, waiting for the flow of traffic to reach them. As the first bike neared, one of them held out his hand, pointing into the first bay.

"Fuck," Ben said. "They're fucking stopping people." I felt him accelerating a little.

"Take it easy, just keep going," I heard myself say. We were nearly level with the two men now. I didn't want to look at them, but I thought that might look wrong, so I fixed my eyes on them and prayed. They glanced at the van. Then the first man waved his hand in a slowing motion, his expression irritated. My pulse doubled. They *were* stopping us. This was like a bad dream.

Ben slowed the van further, but the guy's expression got more irritated. He changed his hand signal now. It wasn't "slow down" anymore but "speed up, keep moving." Keep going. Get out of here. Proceed to go. Collect two hundred pounds. You look like nice boys, back from your travels. Back from your silly little surfing holiday. Welcome back to Europe. We're not interested in you. Get the fuck out of here. I didn't breathe. Ben aimed for the gap between the blue sheds, the exit for the port in sight, and Ben must have had to fight so hard to keep the speed down now. And then we were out. Passing through the chain-link fence that marked the boundary of the port, and then onto the road, straight onto a roundabout. Spanish cars suddenly all around, smarter, cleaner than the traffic in Morocco. We got sucked into the flow of cars and carried into the town, along the beautiful waterfront. I realised I was out of breath. I really hadn't been breathing, and then Ben saw a gap by the side of the road and pulled into it, forgetting to indicate. An angry horn sounded behind us.

"What's wrong?" I managed to ask.

"Nothing. I've just got to stop for a bit."

I understood. Ben got the van more or less parallel to the pavement and killed the engine. Then he put his head in his hands, and leaned forward on the steering wheel. He stayed like that for a long while, and when he finally rocked back upright and dropped his hands, his face was streaked with tears. His whole body was shaking. And he was white. Even with the tan he'd picked up, his face was just white, and he wasn't smiling this time.

"Fucking hell, mate. That scared the shit out of me." He burst into tears again.

It was good to know it wasn't just me feeling that.

Chapter Twenty-Six

FRANCE IS BIG. I said that before, right?

On the way back, it was the last bit that got me. Northern France. It's so empty and flat, and Ben's van felt ponderous, lolling around on its springs as we bumped our way northward, the engine somehow hanging in there. We'd been driving for so long by then, drunk so much coffee and Red Bull, that we weren't speaking much, just odd words here and there. The rest of the time, we'd just stare out the windscreen in a trance as the tarmac rolled toward us, the faster cars zipping by on the left-hand side, their indicators going all the time in that strange way the French drive. But by then, even that seemed familiar. We felt nearly home. All we had left to do was the customs border between France and England. And for some reason we'd never thought of that as too much of a problem.

Ben had booked the Dieppe-to-Newhaven ferry for the return trip. They're both smaller ports, a little bit away from the main crossing points of Dover and Calais. They're a lot less busy, and we figured this meant there would be fewer customs officers stationed there. We actually researched it. Newhaven is just twenty minutes down the road from Brighton, and we'd driven down there to check it out. We went ready to pretend we were meeting someone off the boat if anyone challenged us, but no one did. No one even looked twice. We parked at the back of the terminal car park, where we could see the cars streaming off the boat, and we watched them drive past the customs gates through Ben's binoculars. We watched four ferries come in, sat in the van having a sneaky spliff. Every time, all the cars just drove straight off. I didn't see a single customs officer the whole time.

So yeah, we weren't too worried. We were just tired. A bit sick of each other's company. Watching the road feed itself toward us. And I was passing the hours by daydreaming. As each mile brought us closer to the flat, I was thinking about Julia, whether she would be in when we got there, and how she'd react when I told her that we'd done it.

We got to the port at Dieppe early enough that we had time to stock up on duty-free beer before we checked in. There's no customs on the French side of the Channel. You just show your ticket and drive straight on. Park in the bowels of a ship, and then walk up the softly carpeted stairs into a weird world of plastic café tables and the subtle smell of sick.

The nerves kicked in a bit at that point, but not as bad as the other ferry. Even so, the Newhaven boat takes four hours, and once it casts off, there's no backing out. Once it docked we'd have to make the short drive through another customs channel and hope like hell nothing went wrong. If it did, if for some reason they stopped us and found it... Well, that would be that. Game over. The beginnings of a long stay in an unpleasant correctional institution, criminal records. Buggered by men who hadn't seen women in twenty years. So the nerves were jangling a little bit.

It was altogether nicer to just keep going back to the Julia daydream. I wondered how I'd tell her. Maybe she'd come into the room, by accident, while I was working on the boards. She'd see everything, just as I had the skin peeled back and the slabs of resin exposed. She'd smile at our secret. Maybe we'd smoke a little to test it out. After that, well, I still had that packet of condoms in my room. Hell, in my mind, we ended up with the whole load of dope piled on the bed and us fucking like rabbits on top of it. Like I said, I was daydreaming a little bit.

* * *

The dull green coast of southern England hardened on the horizon:

the low hills of the downs, the smudges of towns along the shoreline. Ben was fiddling with his phone. I stared out the window at the choppy sea sliding past the salt-smeared window.

And then the harbour arms came into view, and we slowed, and then we passed through the rocky opening, turning around in the calm of the inner harbour. The announcement on the tannoy came, always later than you imagine, when the ship already seemed to be docked, and we joined the queue of drivers waiting to get back to their cars.

Chapter Twenty-Seven

FOR THE FIRST thirty seconds after we drove off the ferry, everything looked fine. Then the cars in front of us slowed then stopped. One of the few good things about Ben's van was the driving position was higher than in most cars, so you could see more clearly what was ahead of you. I didn't much like what I could see.

"Ben," I said. I was driving. It just happened that way because Ben had done a long shift getting us to the ferry port. "I can see guys in the customs area. Look, in yellow jackets."

"Don't worry about it. It'll be fine," he said, but he craned his neck to get a better look.

"Look, there at the front. They've pulled over the first two cars off the boat. What's going on?"

I didn't need to tell him this—we could both see just fine. And now, the car that was third off the boat was called forward into another bay. We watched as a small team of yellow-jacketed customs officers worked with each car, searching them.

"What the fuck's going on?" I said.

There was nothing to do but watch, and from our raised vantage point, we could see they were doing a pretty thorough job of searching each car. They were removing the luggage from the back. They even had a sniffer dog running around, on a long leash.

"What the fuck?" I asked again. I didn't hear how tight my voice was, but Ben must have done.

"Calm down, Jake. We've planned for this. It's just a routine check. We know they do it from time to time."

"How can I fucking calm down? They're doing a routine search of every car, and we've got a hundred kilos of dope on the roof. We didn't plan for this."

"Calm down. Jesus, Jake. We don't want to draw attention to ourselves."

He had a point with this, and I took a few deep breaths. I watched as the border guards finally finished with the first car, and it drove away. To freedom. The line pulled forward one as they took the next into a bay and repeated the process.

"Look, they're doing every car. They're going to do us." It was the sheer surprise of it that got me more than the fear. I just hadn't been worried about this crossing. I'd had my head in the clouds. Up my arse, maybe. And now, suddenly, we were facing disaster. The maximum sentence for smuggling dope is fourteen years in prison. So even though I could hear the panic rising in my voice, I wasn't doing anything to stop it.

"Mate, calm down. Tell me a joke or something," Ben said.

I turned to look at him.

"I don't know any fucking jokes. When I learn some in prison, I'll write you," I replied.

"I'm just trying to distract you. OK. I've got something. I think Anna fancies you."

"What?" That threw me. Maybe that was his intention. "Where the hell did that come from?"

"Someone told me."

"Who? What? *Anna*? What the hell are you on about?"

The border guards finished with the second car, and it too drove away. They signalled for the next car to pull into the spot, wandered over to the driver, and asked him to open it up. They really were doing every bloody car.

"I'm just trying to get you to think about something else," he paused. "OK. I've got some news. Something interesting." Ben grinned at me. "Did you know Julia split up with Andy this morning?"

And of course that was interesting. Shocking. Just to hear Ben mention Julia's name was strange, given how I'd been thinking about her so much over the last few hours. Then some implications dawned. Julia didn't have a boyfriend anymore. The smallest of smiles crept onto my face. Then it changed to a frown.

"How do you know that?"

"She texted me. On the ferry."

She texted him on the ferry. We were about to be arrested for smuggling drugs, but Julia had texted Ben to say she didn't have a boyfriend anymore. Julia had texted Ben. Not me, Ben.

"Why did she text you?" I said, my voice strangling out the words.

Ben didn't answer, but he glanced over at me with that grin again. A naughty grin.

"I couldn't tell you, not while she was going out with Andy."

"Tell me what?"

Again the grin. "We've sort of been seeing each other, on the quiet."

It was like I didn't hear him. Or I did, but there was still, somehow, room in what he was saying for my fantasy relationship with Julia to not come crumbling down. But the foundations moved. Like in an earthquake. I wanted to undo the last few seconds, to un-hear what Ben had just told me.

"I don't believe you." These words sounded angry and I realised they were inappropriate as I said them. They seemed to confuse Ben too. This wasn't the reaction he'd expected. So he kept on, still sounding friendly, trying to convince me.

"Honestly. She's been sneaking into my room last thing at night, and then out again before anyone woke up. And then sometimes, when we were all watching TV in the evening, we'd have to wait until everyone went to bed. I'm amazed you didn't notice." He grinned at me, and I had to fight to keep the feeling of sickness and horror off my face. I reached for whatever other objection sprang to mind.

"But she's seeing Andy. She's with someone. Who does something like that? That's totally out of order."

There was confusion written all over Ben's face now.

"She was seeing Andy. He's a prick. You said so yourself."

"Yeah, but fucking hell, Ben. Two-timing someone? That's just well out of order." Christ, I sounded like a schoolkid.

We both sat there in silence for a while. The sudden tension made the air taste different. I don't know why I kept on about it. Maybe I didn't believe him. Maybe I needed proof.

"What do you mean you're..." I could hardly say the word, "seeing her anyway? What does seeing mean?"

A half-smile reappeared on Ben's lips. Like he wondered if his revelation could turn out the way he'd intended after all.

"What do you think it means? You want details?"

"No, I mean..." I didn't know what I meant. The words were just falling out of me. "I mean, how did it happen?"

Ben gave me another smile, which I blanked.

"It was the day you had that interview. Do you remember? When you came back pissed and knocked on my door, wanting a joint? Well, that evening, it was just me and Julia in the flat, and we were just downstairs, watching TV, when she said she wanted to ask me something. Something personal." Ben bit his lip and glanced over at me; he seemed reassured by my face. His eyes told me: You're gonna like this.

"What did she ask?" I said, but I had a feeling I probably knew.

"She asked me if I liked her tits! She came out and asked me, and she just took her top off—she didn't have a bra on or nothing, and she asked me to feel them and tell her what I thought." Ben stopped and glanced across at me again, gauging my reaction. "Pretty crazy, hey?"

"So what did you do?"

"I did exactly what you'd do. I felt her tits for a bit, and then I took her upstairs and fucked her."

And that was what really floored me. I realised at that moment that I had blown it. I'd had exactly the same opportunity, only I didn't do it. Heaped right on top of my fantasy being shattered, right on top of being arrested any minute, I also felt like a loser.

Somehow, buried under my misery and shock and fear, I realised I had to fake surprise at this story. Fake being impressed.

"No way!" I forced a look of surprise. "She really did that?"

"Yeah. You see, she's been thinking about getting them done. You know, plastic surgery, making them bigger. So she wanted me to have a good feel, tell her if I thought it was a good idea."

"And what did you say?" How did you do it, Ben? Where did I go wrong?

"I said yeah, it was a good idea. I mean, she's got nice tits, but they can always be bigger, right?"

I pictured the two of them down there on the sofa, Ben's hands all over her breasts. I could see it perfectly because I'd been there. I could still remember how soft her skin felt. Ben's voice interrupted me.

"Hey, mate..."

I looked over. Said nothing.

"You need to pull forward."

Blankly, I looked out the windscreen. The border guards had finished searching another car, and the line in front had moved on one. Spots of rain started to dot the windscreen. Automatically, I put the van in gear and closed the gap to the car in front.

"Yeah, and... you'll like this," Ben went on, somehow missing my shocked, hurt face.

"What?" I asked.

"Well, she hasn't got the money for the operation. On her tits. I mean, she really wants it, but she can't afford it. And it's a good idea, you know, if she wants it."

I frowned.

"So I said to her that when we get back, you know, with the dope, I'll buy it for her as a present. The operation. I'll buy it with my cut!"

I was quiet for a moment.

"You told her about the trip?"

For the first time, Ben looked a bit sheepish.

"Yeah, I had to. I told you she was coming to my room, and you were in there during the days, making such a mess with the boards. She asked what it was all about. I had to tell her."

She'd known. That time when I hinted what we were doing. She already knew. Because she was shagging Ben every night. I didn't know what to say or think, so I just said:

"Yeah."

Ben grinned at me again. I guessed that in his mind, this had ended up the way he wanted it.

"She won't mind me telling you. That we're seeing each other. She knows you're my best mate."

I nodded and fixed a sickly smile to my face, suddenly hating Ben with every ounce of my being.

"Don't tell her you know about the tits, though. That's kind of private, you know what I mean?"

Chapter Twenty-Eight

THREE CARS IN front the men wait for us, dressed in their uniforms and high-visibility jackets. They look suspicious. I've got the engine running—all the cars in the queue have—but the engine doesn't idle smoothly in Ben's van, remember? So I have to keep revving it. I can see one of the uniforms keeps glancing at us, like that's annoying him.

"Don't rev it so hard," Ben says, getting a bit nervous now. "Don't draw attention to us."

I can't bring myself to look over at him. My best friend in the world, who's just knifed me in the back.

* * *

The brake lights on the car in front go off, as the queue crawls one place forward. I have no choice but to follow. What else am I going to do, reverse back onto the ferry? Even if I wanted to, there's a solid line of traffic blocking us off, and concrete barriers tight up against us on either side. We could make a run for it, just open the doors and leg it, but what good would that do? They'd probably catch us before we got out of the port, and even if not, how long can you last on the run? So our van tinkles as I move forward, from the bottles of wine and beer in the back. If only that was the problem.

Just to spite Ben, I give the engine a big rev.

"Easy," he says, anxiety spreading into his voice now.

I almost can't bring myself to answer him. But I can't tell him how I feel about her, not after what he's just told me. So I go with the other problem. Even though I barely care about it now.

"We're gonna get caught and go to prison. And you know what Ben?"

He looks across at me.

"What?"

"It's all your fault."

I stare at him, and I see the confusion and hurt in his eyes, and it's what I was hoping for. It makes me feel just a little bit better. But then he blinks it away and I see his confidence come back, but it's an effort.

"Jesus, Jake, what's got into you? Have a little faith. They're not going to find it. You did a good job."

For some reason this snaps me right back into the present. They really are searching every car, which really does mean we're in big trouble. A sudden hope flares up in my brain like a match striking: Can I blame all this on Ben? Just blurt it all out to the customs guy when he leans down to tell me to get out of the van? It was Ben's idea, so surely that makes him more guilty than me? But no. That's never going to wash. Ben might have come up with it, but I'm sitting right here in the van with him. I'm in this just as much as he is. And like when the phosphorous on a match is all gone and the flame hasn't caught the wood, it died straight out.

The car in front moves forward another place. Just one more car in front of them. We're close enough now to watch how this works. The customs officer, the same one who looked pissed off at me for revving the engine, beckons the car at the front of the queue into one of the bays where they do the searches. He goes round to the driver and taps on the window. I guess he tells the driver to get out because the door opens, and a man steps out. They walk together to the boot, and the driver opens it. It's a big car, a Volvo, and I can see little heads in the back, kids. Then the customs guy starts poking around. The driver leans in like he's trying to help, and he gets told off. He puts his hands up like they're gonna shoot him or something. Then they both calm down, and the customs guy points to the wall, and the man goes and stands and watches from there.

Then they get the dog, a spaniel or something. Another officer has it on a lead, and its little tail is doing circles, it's so excited. It jumps into the boot of the car and sticks its nose down. Tasting the smells coming out of the bags. Tasting the air in the car. Tasting with its nose, thousands of times more powerful than any human nose. I get a horrible feeling in my gut, like I've been punched. We sort of planned for a dog, but we didn't really. We were messing about then. Ben might have been serious, but I was just showing off how well I could fix up the boards. I still wanted Ben to like me back then.

Tasting the air in the car.

That phrase suddenly strikes me. We might have the dope well hidden now, but a week ago we didn't. Back then we just piled it up in the back of the van. Surely there's going to be some smell left that the dogs are going to pick up. We didn't think of that, did we?

And now I know we're going to get caught. There's just no way around it. And forget what I said earlier, I do care. I care about what's going to happen to me, I care about what my dad is gonna think. I feel my heart rate soar as I watch. I feel dizzy, like I'm about to pass out. My stomach feels like someone keeps punching me there, over and over again. I can't believe I've put myself in this position. What the hell are they doing with a dog?

"Jake mate, calm down," Ben's voice cuts through my panic. "We planned for this. We didn't expect it, but we planned for it."

The words sound faraway, but they pull me back. Back into the van, back to the horrible reality.

"They're doing proper checks. We counted on them not doing proper checks." Suddenly I'm back to trusting Ben will sort it all out. I can hear it in my voice.

"Mate, you did a good job hiding it. They're not going to find it. Relax."

I look across at Ben. Right now, I don't know if I despise him or if he's my only hope. But the thought of all that dope loosely piled in the back of the van crashes back in. My head starts to shake, it doesn't feel like it's me controlling it, it's this simple, unfortunate fact. My head shakes even more.

"You're wrong Ben. We fucked up. We had the dope loose in the van remember? There's no way that dog's not going to sniff that."

And Ben suddenly gets it too. I see his face drop, his mouth fall open, as if to speak, but no words come out. We had all the dope just piled in here. Rubbing against the seats. No way the dog's gonna miss it.

Oops.

* * *

Just then, the customs guy walks two steps toward us, calling us forward again. It's our turn. I don't move. I can't move. He comes closer, looking pissed off that I'm holding him up. There's nothing else I can do. I slip the clutch, and the van crawls forward.

Chapter Twenty-Nine

I FOLLOWED THE guy's directions and stopped in the search bay, then turned the engine off. For a couple of beats, the silence was reassuring. Then the officer's face appeared at the window, indicating me to wind it open. I paused to try and get my heart to slow down, but then I did what he said.

"Hello, sir, would you mind waiting over by the wall with my colleague while we check the van?"

Yes, as it happens, I would mind.

I nodded and tried to smile, as if this was exactly how I was hoping my holiday was going to end, and I got out and followed Ben to the wall. A second officer was there. The rain had stopped at least.

"What's all this about?" Ben asked him. I was amazed by how calm his voice sounded.

"It's just routine, sir. We're checking all the vehicles coming in today. Nothing to be concerned about."

Unless of course you're smuggling large quantities of drugs, his glassy smile seemed to imply. My mouth felt dry.

Then the first officer called me back and asked me to open the van for him. I don't get why these guys aren't able to operate a simple door handle.

"Are these surfboards?" he said, indicating the roof.

"Paddleboards," I corrected him, my mouth dry. The look on his face said he wanted a clarification. "Like surfboards but a bit bigger."

Please don't ask me to take them off.

"I'm going to need you to take them off the roof, please. We need to check them over."

"Sure." Shit.

Ben came back to help. My hands were shaking as I reached up to unstrap the boards, I could feel the customs officer watching me. He must have seen I was nervous.

I could see the drugs dog running around another car in the bay opposite us, being worked by another team of customs officers. There were about ten customs officers in total, working in groups to get through the queue of cars quickly, but I could only see the one dog. A final, desperate hope hit me. Maybe they didn't use the dog on every car? Maybe we'd still slip through the net?

We got the boards unstrapped and unlocked the cable, and with Ben at the front and me at the back, we lifted the first one off the van and onto the concrete floor. Without needing to look at each other, we both made an effort to make it look lighter than it was. Then we took the second board and put that on the floor too, trying to put both close to the wall, away from the car.

"And the other ones, please, sir?" the customs guy asked, pointing the stubby aerial of his radio at the two final boards still resting on the roof. Ben and I walked back round the van to unstrap these as well. Then, as we lifted the third board off the car, something went wrong.

It was Ben's fault. There was a curb separating the pavement from the bay where the van was stopped, and he didn't step up to get over it. He stumbled and dropped the board onto the concrete. Because of the weight, it fell pretty hard, and I could see what happened at once. A crack opened up where it hit the floor. Maybe there was a cavity underneath that I didn't fill properly, and the epoxy coating caved in, or maybe Ben just dropped it bloody hard. Either way, our final line of defence, the physical barrier stopping any smell from reaching that dog, had just failed. Ben stared at the crack, then at me, and I could see how shocked he was, like he couldn't believe what had just happened. But there was nothing we could do, we had to go back and get the fourth and final board, and as I did that, I could see the dog and its handler had finished the car they were doing, and were standing there waiting for where to go next.

We lifted the last board off the van, and like before, Ben and I somehow communicated the need to use this board to cover the crack in the other one. We put it on top, and the officer used his radio again to indicate we needed to step back away from them.

For a moment, we were all watching the dog handler. It seemed he could either come and check us out, in which case we were finished, or he could go to another car. It did seem like the dog was only being used to check one car in three. I held my breath. Come on, give us a fucking break.

But then our guy called out to the dog handler, beckoning him over to us, and the sliver of hope slipped away. I wanted to close my eyes. I didn't want to watch.

Even though I wanted to kick it to death, I had to admit it was a cute-looking dog. Brown and white, and that silly little tail whipping around. I watched as the handler spoke with our officer, the dog twirling round his legs as they spoke. They were too far away to make out what they were saying, but there seemed to be some sort of issue. They weren't using the dog to search the van like I'd seen them do with the cars.

Around us the other officers were still working in the other bays too, and right then it just happened that every bay was ready for the dog to come and check the cars over, but there was only one dog. I dared to watch our officer's face and it looked like this was what they were talking about. I saw him shrug his shoulders, still holding onto his radio, like they were complaining about how they were supposed to do their job if they weren't given the resources. Still they stood there, a few metres away from the open door of the van, not searching. Then our officer pointed to the paddleboards and I half heard him tell the dog handler to just do them. The van sat there, I could almost see the drug fumes escaping through the open door, but it seemed they'd decided they didn't have time to search everything, and they'd let it pass. I couldn't believe it. On such a random decision they were letting an easy bust slip through their fingers.

Or were they? The little dog pulled at the lead as the handler pointed at the pile of paddleboards. This wasn't over.

The handler walked the dog up and down the length of the boards, and I watched in the way you watch a car accident. You don't want to, but you can't take your eyes off it. The dog put its little paws lightly on top of the pile, then jumped up and padded around, sniffing and wagging its tail. And then it came to the crack. Ben's crack. My heart stopped. But the dog didn't pick anything up. Its nose just kept on roaming past the crack, and by then the handler seemed to have lost all interest too. He gave a jerk of the lead, and the dog jumped off the pile of boards, and looked around for something else to sniff. The handler said something to our customs guy, who shrugged again, and we watched as the handler led the dog off to check another car.

"Thank you very much, sir," our customs guy said to me. "If you could load your surfboards back up now."

We didn't need telling a second time. I nearly ran back to the van to shut the doors. I didn't want any more of the smell to leak out. Then we loaded the boards back up. It was like we were moving through treacle, and the whole process of balancing all the boards back on the rack, and strapping them all down properly took forever. All the while, the customs officer was waiting next to us, but now he was just impatient to get rid of us, and we were both so desperate to get away our fingers were fumbling with the strap buckles. But finally, we were ready.

"Can we go?" Ben asked the customs officer.

He didn't say anything for a moment, and I thought he'd changed his mind. But it was just that he was already waving the next car into his bay.

He barely registered Ben's question, just glanced at him. He didn't smile.

"Yes, sir. Have a nice onward journey, sir."

Chapter Thirty

YOU KNEW RIGHT? About Ben and Julia getting together? It was obvious wasn't it? I mean, everyone seemed to know already. Anna, our mates, even those we didn't know that well. It was like I was the last to know. Apart from Andy I suppose, but who gives a shit about him?

Everyone seemed to know about me and Julia too, or at least how I felt about her. Maybe that's why no one let me into Ben's little secret. That's what made me feel such a fool, made my face burn with shame. Everyone knew but no one said anything.

* * *

"Motherfucker!!!"

Ben was screaming—literally screaming out loud—for most of the short journey back to the flat. I could hardly drive in a straight line for all the punching the air, all the high fives, all the yelling and swearing he was doing.

Plus, I was in shock. Glassy-eyed and empty. Exhausted by the whole thing.

"You did it, Jake. You're a fucking genius. They had a fucking dog right on us, and it didn't suspect a fucking thing. You're a legend." He leaned over and tried to hug me, right around the steering wheel.

"Fuck off, I'm trying to drive."

* * *

We got back to the flat. I don't know how, but we got there. There wasn't anywhere to park, but I put the van up on the pavement outside the front door with the hazard lights on, while we took the boards off the roof and carried them up the stairs. I just wanted to get them inside, where no one could see them. Where we could just forget about what was inside them for a few hours.

And when I came back after moving the van, Julia was there, and Ben was telling her what had happened with the sniffer dog, and by the way she was draping herself over him, I knew at once he'd told her I knew about them. She looked... different somehow; maybe it was because she couldn't quite meet my eye. Maybe she just didn't want to. Maybe she was just too full of whatever she was feeling for Ben. I don't know. It hurt too much to think about it.

They both went out and got a takeout for the three of us, to celebrate getting the dope back home, but I didn't feel like eating so I disappeared off to bed. I wanted a different homecoming and the only place I could have that was alone in my bed.

I didn't feel any better the next morning. I didn't want to see Ben, I *really* didn't want to see Julia, and I didn't want to think about what they'd been doing all night. But I swallowed it. All the hurt and the pain and the feeling of betrayal, I swallowed it up and did everything I could to not let it show. What else could I do?

But I drew the line at seeing those bloody boards. Ben wanted me to start opening them up right away, but he saw the look on my face and didn't push it. Instead, I took a long walk alone along the seafront, I just wanted to let everything that had happened over the last couple of weeks wash over me.

* * *

I didn't notice at first but it was a beautiful day, bright and warm and not a breath of wind so that the sea hung still as glass reflecting the pale blue sky. I walked for miles, the sun shone and the seafront was busy. Old ladies hobbled past me, walking their little dogs. Mothers pushed prams, dudes swerved past on their skateboards. A pair of council seafront officers walked past in their silly blue uniforms, looking a little bit like customs officers. It was strange, I could walk past all these people even after what we'd done and none of them seemed interested. None of them knew my secret. I felt invisible.

And slowly, gradually, I stopped thinking only about how much I hurt over Julia, and began to realise how much I'd just changed my life. For the better. All these people around me, they all had their own money worries, their own debts, but now suddenly, as a stroke, I'd wiped mine away. I found myself walking a little taller, holding my head up just a tiny bit. I wouldn't say I was smiling exactly, the thought of Julia, or just a half-pretty girl walking by would still have me wincing and feeling the flush of red at my cheeks, but as compensation goes, going from drowning in debt to suddenly free has a certain power. I was miles from the flat, and now suddenly I wanted to get back there, to open up the boards and finish the job.

That afternoon, I knocked on Ben's door and saw what a mess he was making, trying to pull the dope from a jagged hole in one of the boards. Julia was in there too. She'd never looked lovelier, it was like she was doing it on purpose. She was lying back on his bed, watching him work and wearing a tiny pair of dark blue shorts that showed off her smooth tanned legs like they were on display in some exhibition. Seeing her like that almost broke my newfound determination, but I tore my eyes off her and told Ben I'd take over. He yielded at once, and went and sat next to Julia, putting his arm around her, but she shrugged him off.

"If you're just going to watch Jake work, the least you can do is get him a beer," she told him.

"He hasn't done anything all day, he's been on the beach." Ben protested, like I'd been slacking off and he tried again to slip his arm round her waist.

"Come on. And get one for me while you're about it." She pushed him away again and this time he did what she said, pretending it was a big effort. So for a few moments it was just her and me in the room.

I hadn't been expecting that, and the sudden silence between us was awkward. I started poking around in the mess Ben had made and hoped we could last until Ben came back. Then she called out to me.

"Jake,"

"Yeah?" I stopped and glanced at her before looking away again. She had a smile on her lips, a small, sad smile.

"I wanted to say I'm sorry I couldn't tell you. About me and Ben, I mean."

I wasn't ready to have this talk. I couldn't find any words. I didn't even let myself look at her.

"You understand don't you? Until I broke up with Andy I couldn't let anyone know."

Dumbly I nodded.

"We can still be friends though can't we? I mean you're Ben's best friend, he really likes you. I hope we can be friends as well."

"Yeah," I croaked. "So do I." We lapsed into silence.

"And," she paused, and then took a big breath. "And maybe it's best if we don't tell him what kind of happened between us?"

At this I did look at her. In surprise. She was embarrassed by it as well. I don't know why but somehow that helped. It really helped. I looked at her, at the way her body was curled up on the bed, those legs now folded underneath her. I felt a spasm of pain, a mixture of desire and regret that I couldn't have her. I nodded again.

"Sure."

Ben came crashing back into the room, three open bottles of beer in his hands.

"Jake," he said. "I found out why the dog didn't smell anything through the board that cracked," I hardly heard what he was saying, I was still watching her, smiling now as she took a beer from Ben's hand.

"There was still a really thin layer of whatever stuff you put in there blocking it off. So it was still sealed. Lucky huh?"

Julia raised the bottle to her lips and tipped her head back, exposing her long neck. I watched the muscles move as she drank. Ben said something else and I didn't hear. Julia pressed the cold bottle to her face and caught my eye. Ben said something else.

"*Jake*!"

I dragged my eyes off Julia for the last time and listened to what Ben was saying.

"What?" I said.

"The way you fixed up the boards. Even though it cracked it didn't go the whole way through," he said.

I blinked a couple of times to flush Julia's image off my retinas.

"Give me that beer will you," I said, and got to work.

PART TWO

Chapter Thirty-One

I THINK BEN would have happily spent the next week hanging out with Julia and the big pile of dope in his room, but he'd already set in train the plan for what happened next. So a couple of days later we packed the dope up again, this time in some sports bags that were on special offer from Sports Direct, and we carried it back down to the van.

I didn't know too much about it before Morocco, and since Ben had been inseparable from Julia since we got back, there hadn't been much opportunity to ask, but I knew the basics. Danny, Ben's dealer, had a contact named Paul, who was going to come with us in the van and introduce us to his contact, a man called Jimmy, who was going to buy all the dope in one big deal. Only then would we finally be finished.

This Jimmy character, Ben assured me, was totally expecting us. He had the money ready, and he was going to sell the dope to his network of dealers, who were mostly people like Danny, as in they dealt predominantly with the student scene—this was what Ben had told me before we left, back when I hadn't been listening because all I could focus on was buying the stuff and getting it through customs. And now I didn't really care about what happened to it all. I just wanted it over with. The dope gone, and my debt with it. But anyway, that was the plan, just it didn't last long after we actually met Paul.

* * *

"The fuck is this?" were his first words to me, on the street outside

Danny's flat. He was tall and slim, maybe ten years older than us, and he was pretty sure of himself. At first, I didn't think he wanted an answer, but from the way he kept staring at me, I realised he did.

"It's a van. A camper van," I said, and then when I worried it might sound like I was taking the piss, telling him something more obvious, so I tried to soften what I'd said. "It's alright. It goes. It's better than it looks."

"I don't give a fuck what it is. I'm not driving to Scotland in a fucking caravan. We'll take my car."

Scotland? I looked over at Ben, but he looked away.

In fairness to Ben he had told me the idea was to sell the dope a long way away from Brighton, the idea was to minimise the chance we'd ever hear about it again, which worked for me, but Scotland? That was miles away.

"What's your car?" Ben asked.

"Over there," Paul answered. He pointed to a dark metallic-blue BMW with blacked-out windows. Just imagine what car a flash drug dealer might drive, and you've pretty much got it. Ben looked kind of impressed, though.

"Alright," he said.

"Hang on, mate," I interrupted, then lowered my voice so only Ben could hear me. "What are you doing? I thought we agreed to take the van?"

Ben shrugged. "The van's pretty slow. We'll get up there quicker," he sounded shifty and I stared at him.

"Well how are we going to get back?"

Ben hesitated at this, but clearly Paul had been able to hear after all because he lowered himself down and leaned on the van's window so he was level with Ben and me. "With a hundred grand, you can afford a train ticket. And like I say, I ain't driving to Scotland in a caravan."

"Alright," Ben said again, and he opened the door.

"Alright. Let's go," Paul said. "You tell me this heap of shit moves? Well shift it and we'll load up." They went off together and I thought about refusing, but after a minute I fired up the van's engine, and moved it as close to the BMW as I could, and then jumped out to move the sports bags across. But while I was doing that, Paul stopped me.

"Wait up, boys. I need to check it." From somewhere he'd pulled out what looked like a handheld radio, like a walkie-talkie, and he waved it over each bag. He unzipped one of the bags and thrust this thing inside, then did the same with the next bag.

I watched him for a while before asking. "What's that?"

Paul didn't seem to hear me, so I asked again, louder.

"What's that thing?"

I'd been getting more and more nervous the whole day about meeting this guy. It had made me irritable.

"GPS sniffer," Paul answered. "Looks for devices emitting radio signals. Tracking devices, listening devices, that kind of shit. You don't get anywhere near Jimmy without this."

I didn't want to look impressed, but I was. I mean, he might have been bullshitting us, but it looked real enough, and he did it pretty diligently. I also got the idea that whatever vehicle we'd turned up in wouldn't have been good enough. It wasn't about our van, it was about going in a car he knew was clean. For all his brashness, I got a very strong sense Paul knew his shit. And the dope seemed to pass his test. His machine didn't go beep once.

"I'm going to need your phones too," Paul said when he was done. He pulled out a padded envelope from inside his jacket. It looked like it was lined with tinfoil. "Come on boys. Turn 'em off. Take out your SIMs and stick it all in here. You'll get them back when we're done."

I looked at Ben, hoping he'd protest, but he just shrugged and took out his phone and held the button down till it shut down. Paul turned to me and smiled sarcastically. "Now you, pal." He smiled at me.

I'd come to know that smile very well, but that first time I saw it I just got a very bad feeling. It was the way he looked like he loved himself way too much. Gelled hair, leather jacket, stubble on his face. Teeth artificially whitened. I didn't smile back, but I did what he asked and handed it over. Then we all got in the car, me in the back and Ben in the passenger seat. The first thing Paul did was fiddle with all the buttons, the heated seats and the stereo and the traction control or something, I don't know what. Then, when we finally set off, he was driving too fast.

"Can you slow down, please," I said from the back. "We shouldn't draw attention to ourselves." I was being an arse I know, but I was in my post-Julia angry phase by then.

"Can you shut the fuck up, please?" Paul answered at once. "Do you know how far it is to Scotland from here?"

"Well, however far it is, it's going be considerably further if we get stopped for speeding and the police notice the car's full of hashish." We glared at each other via the rear view mirror. I knew I was being an idiot but I couldn't help it.

"Where the fuck did you find him?" Paul asked Ben, ignoring me and turning up the music so I couldn't hear Ben's reply. But he did slow down a little, and I sat back, trying to force myself to relax into the leather upholstery. I had to admit one thing: it was a nice change to get out of Ben's stinking van.

* * *

For the first few hours of the journey, we travelled in silence—well, we didn't talk much. We were listening to some R&B crap. Paul's arrogance extended to his driving, he stayed in the fast lane, burning up behind people, then sitting too close and flashing his headlights if they didn't move over. When the traffic thinned out though he suddenly switched the music off and began to talk.

"So, this is your first time doing this?"

Because I was in the back seat, it could only have been Ben he was talking to.

"Yeah, sort of. We've done some before. Just a slightly bigger scale this time," Ben replied. We'd agreed to be as vague as possible. It seemed safer that way.

"Uh-huh," Paul said, not sounding particularly interested, then he went on.

"So... Danny didn't tell me how you got it in. Through customs?" He glanced across again.

"Danny doesn't know," Ben said. "I'm sure you'll understand, we think it's best if we keep that information to ourselves." Ben looked across at Paul and smiled, but Paul just kept his eyes on the road and said nothing. I thought he'd dropped it but then he spoke again.

"Not sure that's gonna work," he said. "Jimmy's going to want to know, you see. And you don't want to be 'keeping it' from Jimmy. Do you know what I mean?"

He glanced again at Ben, and then I saw his eyes check me out in the rear view mirror, interested to see how we both took that.

It sounds crazy, thinking back about it. I'd given hardly any thought to who this Jimmy guy was or what he might be like. I'd just taken Ben's word for it that it was all sorted. That this was just a delivery drive, even if I didn't really understand why we had to make it.

But when Paul started talking like that, I really began to see that this still wasn't over. We had no idea what we were getting ourselves into here. And no defence if something went wrong.

"OK," Ben said suddenly, making a decision. "There's nothing too much to know. We hid it in surfboards and drove it back."

I watched Paul's reaction to this. His pretence of being uninterested had slipped. He turned to Ben.

"Surfboards?"

"Well, paddleboards, to be exact. You know, like all the celebrities are into."

Paul said nothing, and Ben went on explaining.

"They're bigger, you see. You get more space and..."

"Yeah, I get it."

Ben shut up.

"So you hid it in paddleboards? Then what? You just drove it home?

In that shitty van?"

"Yeah."

Paul put his head on one side, like he was working his way through the practicalities.

"How'd you get it in there? Inside the boards?"

Ben jerked a thumb toward me in the back. "Jake. He's a genius at fixing stuff up. He opened them up, packed it all in, and put them back together so no one could tell the difference."

"The guy in the back's a genius?" Paul said, sounding doubtful, but this time, it was Ben who smiled.

"Yeah. And you know what?"

"What?"

"They stopped us. At the customs. We just got unlucky, and they were stopping everyone, and we thought we were fucked—they even had a dog sniffing over the boards. And they didn't suspect a thing!"

I saw Paul's eyes appraising me again in the rear-view mirror.

"Yeah, Jake's a genius." Ben warmed to the theme. "You should have seen the boards, they looked like new."

"No shit." Paul said.

I couldn't decide how to take this. On the one hand, I felt a small surge of pride at Ben talking about me like this. On the other hand, if I allowed myself to think about him sleeping with Julia it still left me hollow and out of breath. And then, it was his plan that meant we were sitting in a car, driving to Scotland with someone who was probably going to rip us off and steal all our money. It was a complicated feeling.

For a moment, no one spoke, and the only sound was the low growl of the car's big engine, and the hum of air and flying bugs smashing against the windscreen.

"And where did you say you bought all this from?"

"He didn't," I interrupted. "And I don't think this Jimmy needs to know everything, does he? Maybe the less we all know about each other's business, the better?" Ben might have decided to tell all, I still wanted to stick to the plan.

Again Paul went silent for a little while, just gunning the big car forwards. Then he turned around to speak to me, totally taking his eyes from the road.

"How much do you know about *this Jimmy*?" Paul asked, and watched me while hundreds of metres of unseen road flew towards us.

Chapter Thirty-Two

"I JUST KNOW he's got the money, and he wants to buy the dope," I said in the end. "Can you please look where you're going?"

To my relief Paul turned around, but he still watched me in the rear view mirror.

"Then you don't know shit. He's got plenty of money. That's for sure, and he's interested in buying your little stockpile, but he's going to want some questions answered, questions that I'm here to ask. And if I don't get those answers, then *he* doesn't get those answers. And he's not going to like that."

Paul paused.

"You do know his nickname is Crazy Jimmy, don't you?"

Obviously, I didn't, and from the way Ben wouldn't meet my alarmed look, he didn't either. The fucking idiot.

"Do you want to know why his nickname is Crazy Jimmy?"

I didn't really, but I had a feeling he was going to tell us.

"When you meet Jimmy you'll see he's kind of a scary guy anyway, but if he gets angry he's liable to get real angry. I mean the sort of angry with serious consequences. I mean people get hurt. Or worse." Paul shook his head as if he'd seen it happen too many times.

"I guess these days you'd say he's got *anger management issues*. I'm sure he could get help if he wanted to, you know, counselling or something. Hypnotherapy. They make them stroke rabbits don't they?

The fur calms them down. But he doesn't do any of that. I think he likes it to tell the truth. He likes how his reputation precedes him. You know what I mean?"

Neither Ben nor I replied.

"Well the point is it's not a good idea to do things that Crazy Jimmy doesn't like. That's what tends to make him go a little crazy. Do you understand?

"Do you understand?" Paul asked again, when neither of us responded.

"Yeah," I said.

"Good. And since we're on the subject, I should tell you that if Jimmy doesn't like those answers..." Paul winced. "Then this isn't going to end well for you. Do you understand that?"

I was cursing Ben for setting this up at that point, and especially for abandoning our van. I hated the fact we were trapped.

"I understand," I heard Ben say from the front. "It's alright. I get that he'll want to know the provenance. That the dope is legit—isn't stolen—whatever. That it's not going to cause him any trouble. We can do that." Ben turned around to me in the back.

"Can't we, Jake?"

I was scared, but somehow, I was more angry than scared.

"Yeah. We can do that."

"Good," Paul said. His tone had lost its menacing edge and was back to all business. "So, where does it come from?"

I listened as Ben told him our story. At first, he tried to keep some details out of it, obscure the facts a little, but Paul was good at probing and good at insisting everything was explained properly. And if there was any comfort to be taken, it was in the fact that Paul didn't seem to mind that we were total amateurs. In fact, he seemed to like it. My problem was, I was increasingly thinking how this made us a whole lot easier to rip off. Or, if Jimmy really was as crazy as Paul made out, to murder.

We drove straight through the night. Paul didn't seem to need to take rests, but we had to stop for fuel around three in the morning, somewhere near the border. I said I had to go for a piss, and Paul told me to go in a bush where he could see me. I guess he thought I might try and make a run for it. I might have too, even with all our dope in the boot. Then we got back in the car, and the constant drone of it and the warm comfortable seats meant I must have slept for a bit, because the next thing I knew, Paul had opened all the windows and was shouting at us.

"Yo, compadres. Wake up."

Cold air was rushing into the car. I sat up in a hurry, blinking. It was still dark, six in the morning now. When Paul saw that we'd both woken up, he shut the windows. They hummed up, and then the road noise was cut out again.

"We're nearly there. I need you to put these on." Paul reached across in front of Ben and opened up the glove box, where he pulled out a couple of black material bags, with little drawstrings on the bottom.

"Put these on your heads. Pull the cords tight, go back to sleep. I'll wake you when we get there."

Paul tossed one of the hoods into the back, and I picked it up.

"What's this for?" I asked.

"So you can't see where the fuck we're going. It's a good thing. It means I don't have to kill you if this all gets fucked up. Put it on."

I watched as Ben put his on, and wishing I could think of an alternative, I did the same. As the fabric hid the sight of the car and the back of Paul's head I wondered if that would be the last thing I ever saw. A part of me marvelled at how willingly I was giving myself up. I almost welcomed the hood and the chance of oblivion it promised. But then the cheap nylon smell of the fabric and the touch of it against my face and the way it covered my mouth and trapped my breath all made me realise just how fucking scared I was. I had to fight to keep my breathing shallow so that I didn't suck the material into my mouth. Some time later I realised I should have been trying to work out where we were. The last sign I'd seen was for Glasgow, but it was impossible. I'd missed miles fighting against my panic and now I had no idea where we were, what sort of road, or how fast we were going. Paul had put his music back on too, so I gave up. I let myself fall into a kind of limbo where I waited for whatever was going to happen next.

CHAPTER THIRTY-THREE

"WAKE UP. WE'RE here."

I felt the car had stopped moving.

"Take your hoods off."

I did so, and the brightness of daylight hurt my eyes. I'd already sensed it was daytime, but the hood had still cut out most of the light. Squinting, I saw Paul getting out of the driver's seat. He stretched outside the car and then unbuttoned his fly and took a piss against the wall which stretched out in front of us. Right in front a tall iron gate blocked our path. On either side was a high stone wall, and two CCTV cameras were mounted on the posts holding up the gates, like a pair of birds of prey. All around us, as far as I could see, were mountains, rising up steeply, their tops lost in the mist.

"Ah, that's better," Paul said, shaking himself dry.

"Where are we?" I heard Ben say.

Paul went up to a metal grille and pressed the button for the intercom. He leaned in and spoke for a minute, then straightened up. He stretched again. Then he walked back to the car and got in.

"Good sleep ladies?" he said, as the gate slowly swung open.

The drive curled around the side of a lake—a loch, I guess, since we were in Scotland—and led up to a house, a modern building like a white square box. There was more CCTV here.

"Welcome to Jimmy's," Paul said.

I didn't look across at Ben, but I could sense he was nervous. Me? I was fully shitting myself. As I got out of the car, I looked around, hoping I'd see something to reassure me. To our left was a stand of trees that extended behind the house, cutting off the chance that anyone could see us from there. In front of the house was the loch; I could see the far bank, and even a couple of buildings, but it was a long way away, much too far for anyone to see what might happen here. To our right was the long drive we'd just come down, and the end of that was the sort of place you could take a piss without worrying about being seen. It all meant one thing: No one knew where we were. If anything went wrong, we were in big trouble.

Paul led us to the back door and rapped on it hard with his knuckles, and we all waited.

The door cracked open, and I heard a man's voice; I could hear at once he was on the phone. He opened the door enough to see who we were and glanced around outside as well, like he wanted to check there was no one else around. Then he swung the door fully open and just stared at us, continuing his phone call into a little earpiece.

That's when I got my first sight of Crazy Jimmy. He was middle-aged, dressed in jeans and a black shirt, with short hair and a neat beard. His whole look was groomed, like he'd worked on it, but like he had a way of looking cool naturally as well. He had the mobile phone in one hand but no wires to the earpiece. It must have been Bluetoothed.

"Hold on," he said, presumably to whoever he was speaking to on the phone. Then he stared at us, his face empty of expression.

"Paul," he said eventually by way of a greeting, but he gave nothing away as to whether our arrival was welcome or even expected. Jimmy ran his eyes over Ben and me.

"Just do it like I told you to and get on with it," he said suddenly into his phone, and then he cut the call and pulled the earpiece from his head.

"Which one of you is Ben?" Jimmy asked, and Ben raised his hand like a kid in a classroom when the headmaster unexpectedly comes in.

"You're younger than I thought."

Jimmy continued to stare at us.

"Fucking hell. Like policemen. You know you're getting old when they look like they're not even shaving yet."

Jimmy exchanged a look with Paul. A look that said something, but it was too cryptic, too fast for me to read anything from it.

"So, you want to come in? You've come a long way to see me."

Paul moved forward, but Jimmy held up his hand to stop him.

"You checked them over, right? Phones?"

"Yeah. It's all good."

"The product?"

"I told you. It's good."

"No issues on the way up?"

"Jimmy, I did it just like you told me."

Jimmy sniffed and pushed the phone and his earpiece into his jeans pocket.

"You better come in, then."

We followed Jimmy in, Ben going after Paul and me last. We walked through a narrow corridor over worn flagstones; the house seemed to be a modern shell built over something older. We went up a glass and steel staircase, and the space opened up, and I drew my breath in. We emerged into a big modern room. One end was a kitchen, and the other had low-lying sofas arranged around a giant TV. But the most striking thing was the front wall: it was just glass, outside a big balcony that stretched the full length of the room, and beyond that the loch, where wisps of mist hung over the still water.

"Have a seat," Jimmy said, pointing to the kitchen table. It was empty apart from a laptop resting on it, and he pressed the lid shut as Ben and I sat down. Paul didn't sit; he walked to the window and stood against the glass, looking out at the loch.

Jimmy hadn't sat down either. He stood in the middle of the room, still staring at us, his head cocked to one side as if he wasn't sure whether he should just kill us now. Then he spoke to Ben.

"So, you're the one who set this all up? This is your thing, right?"

I think Ben wished he hadn't been so quick to sit down. Now, Jimmy and Paul had the height advantage, along with every other advantage going.

"Yeah."

"And how you feeling about it now? You feeling good?"

"I'm feeling OK."

"You're OK. You're feeling OK. That's nice." Jimmy repeated back to him. "You know, I was very surprised when I got the message through Paulie here, that a couple of guys wanted to see me with a shipment of product. Very surprised." Jimmy stroked his beard.

"And normally, I'm not a big fan of surprises. You should know that about me. If you're sitting in my kitchen, which you are, looking at my beautiful fucking view, that's the first thing you should know about me. Don't fucking surprise me, got it?"

Ben didn't say anything to this. There wasn't much he could say. I just kept my head down. I wasn't enjoying his view. I wasn't enjoying anything.

"So, what do you know about me?" Jimmy asked Ben.

And when Ben hesitated, Jimmy went on.

"Come on, you must have done your research. What do you know?"

"We don't know anything. We just heard you were the man to see. That you could, you know, handle a big shipment."

"And who the *fuck* told you that?" As Jimmy spoke, he slammed his hand down on the table next to Ben. There was a shocked silence in the room. Then Paul broke it.

"Calm down, Jimmy. You know the story. They talked to Danny. Danny called me. I checked 'em out. You know all this. No need to put them in the lake."

Jimmy ignored this and turned back to Ben.

"That it? You didn't want to know anything else. You agreed to come here just on what that fucking gobshite told you?" He didn't point or say Paul's name, but it was obvious who he meant. Paul didn't flinch at all.

Ben still didn't answer.

"Jesus fucking Christ," Jimmy said and turned away. He walked a couple of paces until he was at the kitchen worktop, then turned around and walked back, rubbing his hand across his face as if he were deep in thought. Then Paul piped up again.

"How about offering them a cup of coffee?"

Jimmy swung toward him.

"Come on, Jimmy. I've driven all fucking night to bring these boys to see you. Can we at least have a cup of coffee while you decide if you're gonna shoot them or not?"

Jimmy stared at Paul for a moment. Then he relented and jerked a hand at a coffee percolator. It was already full.

"Go on. Go fucking wild."

Paul pushed himself away from the window and put four cups on the worktop. He filled each with black coffee, then slid one in front of each of us. Neither me, Ben nor Jimmy touched them, but Paul took his to the window and blew on it, then took a sip.

"Where's the product?" Jimmy asked.

Ben and I hesitated so Paul ended up answering. "It's in the boot. Packed in bags."

"How many bags?"

"Six."

Jimmy seemed to consider this for a moment.

"Paulie. You—" He pointed at me like he'd forgotten my name, although I'm not sure he knew it at that point. "Go and get em. A bag each. Bring 'em up here."

I didn't move. I didn't know if he meant right now.

"The fuck you waiting for? You think I'm not busy?"

I got up at once, pushing the chair back across the floor so that it squealed in protest. Paul gave me an ironic smile, and then with mock politeness, he gestured for me to go first.

I walked back down the stairs and out to the car. Paul zapped the remote to open the boot and we each shouldered one of the sports bags; then Paul shut and locked the car again. Paul didn't say a word the whole time, instead he whistled. He was clearly feeling pretty relaxed about the situation still.

Paul led the way back upstairs, and I did what he did: put the bag down on the table, then stepped away.

"Sit down," Jimmy said, so I did that instead.

As I did so, Ben cleared his throat and started talking. Maybe he'd managed to break the ice a bit with Jimmy while I was gone.

"So, what we've got here is one hundred kilos of pure Moroccan dope, of the highest quality—" But Jimmy cut him off instantly.

"Shut up."

Ben's mouth hung open for a second, but he did what he was told too.

"Did you weigh it?" Jimmy asked, but none of us answered.

"Did you weigh it? You just said a hundred kilos. Did you check that?" When still none of us answered, he swore under his breath.

"You again." He pointed to me. "That cupboard, there's some fucking kitchen scales in there. Pull 'em out. You might have to get on your hands and knees to find them cos it's a right fucking mess. I'll make sure no one fucks you up the arse."

I did what he said, and rummaged around in a cupboard full of cake tins and old baking trays, thinking how weird this was, that I was getting to see the inside of a major drug dealer's kitchen cupboard. But I found the scales in the end. Digital scales, slim smoked black glass, stained with something. It looked harmless, cake mix, not blood.

I put them down on the table next to the bag, and Jimmy took over. He pressed the "on" button, then unzipped the bag all the way and plumped open the sides to have a good look at the contents. He pulled down the sides of the bag so we could all see.

"Very nice. We've got ourselves a big pile of nine bars. Let's just refresh all our memories on some weights and measures. Four nine-ounce bars make one kilo, which means each of these is going to weigh in at two-fifty grams. Four times two-fifty is one thousand grams, or one kilo. We all clear on that?"

No one said anything, but I was thinking through the numbers in my head. It made sense. What didn't make sense was the horrible realisation that it hadn't ever occurred to us to weigh the stuff. We just took it on trust. Jimmy reached into the bag and ran his fingers down the first stack, pulling a few of the bars out at random.

"Ready, boys?" He dropped the first bar onto the scales. The display rolled up nearly instantly. Two hundred and twenty eight grams.

He glared quickly at all of us and swiped it off. When the display was back to zero, he dropped the second slab on.

Two hundred and thirty one grams. Oh, fuck.

The third was one gram more at two hundred and thirty two, and Jimmy was shaking his head.

"Still think you've got a hundred kilos of finest Moroccan?" Jimmy said to Ben.

Ben didn't reply, nor did anyone else.

"First thing you do. *First fucking thing you do* is check the bastards aren't ripping you off on the measures."

Jimmy was still shaking his head.

"I'm assuming you haven't tested it either?"

Ben looked too shocked to answer, but to my surprise, I found myself speaking into the silence.

"We had a few joints to check it. It's good stuff. It's pretty strong."

Jimmy let this sentence hang in the air for a long time. Ben seemed to have taken a big interest in what his coffee looked like. Finally, Jimmy went on.

"Good stuff, eh? Good stuff." Jimmy turned to look at me like he'd only just noticed I was capable of speech.

"That's interesting, because it doesn't look that different to fucking dog shite to me. But while we're in the business of ruining your day, let's find out." He pulled a bag out from under the table, a leather briefcase thing, and out of it he pulled a small cardboard box. Inside was a selection of little plastic bottles and cards. I couldn't make out what it said on the side, but it looked like something medical.

"Pick a bar for me," Jimmy told me. "You choose. Which one of these looks the most like 'good stuff' to you?"

Not knowing which to choose, I pointed at the closest bar of dope.

"OK," Jimmy said, and he sat down. With a finger, he slid the bar of dope over in front of him, and unpicked the cellophane on the corner until the bare hashish was exposed. Then he turned his attention to the box. He poured an equal amount of two clear liquids into a single glass vial and shook it for a moment. Then he produced a lighter and held it under the corner of the nine bar I'd chosen, until he was able to crumble away a little of the dope. It expanded into a floury powder, and he carefully dropped this into the vial so it fell into the liquid. Then he plugged the top and shook it again, for longer this time, a full half minute before holding it up to the light coming in from the huge window.

"You know how this works?"

No one answered but I shook my head.

"Course you fucking don't." Jimmy sighed.

"There's over eighty different strains of cannabinoids found in marijuana. Most of them, we don't have a clue what they do, but there's one we know about. Tetrahydrocannabinol—let's call that THC because it's a fucking long word for people that can't even handle kitchen scales. Now, it might be that you've brought me a big pile of camel shit wrapped in cling film. Or, it might be you're really, really lucky, and you've managed to buy some hashish. This little test will tell us." He stopped and gave me a black stare.

There was a silence that dragged out until Ben broke it, his voice reedy and uncertain.

"Well? What does it say?"

"You have to wait ten minutes before it says anything," Jimmy answered.

The silence came right back, and I stared at the pile of dope on the table. It was dope, I knew that much, and the quality had seemed good. But what was this test going to say? I didn't know. Then Jimmy said something totally unexpected.

"So, what else has my gobshite of a brother told you about me, then?"

Ben rode the surprise better than me, but his mouth still dropped open. Jimmy read it at once.

"OK, so that's something. He didn't tell you we were brothers? Jesus wept. Why else do you think I would let an arsehole like that into my house? Why else do you think you're here? We'd normally be doing this in an abandoned warehouse somewhere. Don't you go to the fucking movies?"

I stole a look at the two of them now. Jimmy was older, at a guess I'd have said by about ten years, but now, I knew I could see the family resemblance. It was there in the way they stood, in the shapes of their bodies—thick, powerful upper arms that filled the fabric of their shirt sleeves. You could see it too in the shapes of their faces, although Jimmy was dark and Paul almost blond. Now I knew it, I was suddenly stunned I hadn't noticed before.

"Did he give you the Crazy Jimmy story? Well?"

Ben nodded, and Jimmy almost broke into a smile.

"Fucking Paulie." Jimmy turned to us. "He likes a joke does my brother. It's all bullshit. We fought a lot as kids. That's all."

"It's not all bullshit," Paul interrupted. "One time he shot my rabbit with an air gun."

"It was a fucking accident. And it didn't die did it?"

"You still fucking shot it."

Jimmy rolled his eyes like this showed how Paul liked to kid around.

Ben and I exchanged glances for the first time. He looked as confused as I felt.

Then there was another surprise.

Chapter Thirty-Four

A SMALL WHITE West Highland terrier suddenly burst into the room and bounded up to Jimmy, its claws making it skate across the floor, nearly crashing into the furniture. Then it saw the rest of us there and seemed to want to visit us all at the same time, its stumpy little tail wagging away.

"OK. Let's put this away," Jimmy said, moving at once to do it himself. He scooped up the slabs of hash, slipped them back into the bag, and zipped it up; then he pulled it from the table and slid it underneath, not exactly hidden, just out of the way. The testing kit was bundled back into its box and put into the cupboard. And just as he finished, a small girl in a bright green coat and red-and-white spotted boots appeared in the doorway.

"Hi, Paul," she said, but she looked at me and Ben too and didn't come any further. "I didn't know you were coming."

"Hello, Alice!" Paul said, a big smile overtaking his face. "My favourite little niece. I came up just to see you. Come over here." He bent down with his arms open. "Give us a hug, then?"

The girl—she was maybe three years old—looked a little uncertain for a moment longer, but then began to take her boots off.

"OK, but I'm not allowed to keep my boots on." She sat down on the floor and kicked them off, leaving them piled up in the doorway. Then she ran lightly over to Paul, who swept her up and started teasing her by blowing the hair out of her eyes.

"We walked all the way to the shop," Alice said to Paul, and he made impressed noises while Jimmy watched them. I couldn't read his expression. Then a dark-haired woman came into the room. Presumably, the kid's mum. She was dressed in black leggings and a long, tight, knitted grey jumper pulled tight over three bumps, her breasts and stomach. She was tall, startling pretty, and very obviously pregnant.

"Hello, Paul," she said. She was smiling, but she too seemed cautious to come in with us there. "Jimmy said you might be coming. How are you?" She had a light Scottish accent; her voice purred with it.

Now, she did walk over to Paul, and he balanced the girl on one arm while he gave the woman a kiss on both cheeks.

"Hi, Sarah. You're looking as gorgeous as ever."

She smiled a thank-you but didn't say anything.

"I see you've come with friends. I hope you're all being good." Sarah's eyebrows rose. She had the kind of face you just wanted to stare at.

"You know me Sarah," Paul said. "I'm always good."

The woman gave him an indulgent look and turned to Ben and me.

"I'm Sarah. I'm Jim's wife."

I wondered if I was expected to kiss her too but she took the lead and held out a hand. She had long, slim fingers, and up close, I could smell her perfume. I mumbled my name, unable to properly meet her gaze. Her grip was cool and soft.

"And how do you know Paulie?" She asked me.

She was just making conversation, I realised at once, but it caused a tangible shift in the atmosphere in the room. I had to answer, but I could sense from Jimmy and Paul I absolutely couldn't answer her honestly. Problem was I didn't know a thing about Paul other than he was a drug dealer.

"We're um…" I started then stopped. Then I had a flash of inspiration. "We're mates from work." I turned to Ben, hoping this would be enough and she'd move on but instead she continued to face me. I felt a red glow creeping up my face. I noticed how green her eyes were.

"Really? You look very young for that," she answered, and that left me flummoxed. I was beginning to shrug my shoulders when Paul rescued me.

"He's the youngest pilot on the books," he said, then seemed to notice Ben also sitting there. "They both are." Paul smiled at Jimmy as he said this, like it was pretty funny, but Jimmy's face was set in an angry stare.

Sarah seemed to read it all then she looked at Jimmy. "Well you all look busy here so I'm going to take Alice into the other room." Sarah sent a look to Jimmy and went to scoop the girl up, but she said she wanted to stay with Paul.

"No Alice, I think they're discussing daddy's work."

The dog stayed in the room, though, curling up on a mat next to the window and keeping its eyes on Jimmy.

* * *

"OK. Let's get this done. Then maybe we can all get on with our day," Jimmy said when they were gone. Just a hint of Sarah's perfume stayed in the room. He opened the cupboard and pulled out the testing kit again. He pulled the little glass vial out of the box and held it up to the window again. It had turned an orangey-red colour.

"So what does that mean?" Ben asked.

Jimmy turned to him slowly. "It means your suppliers must have run out of camel shit."

I felt the beginnings of some relief. I'd known it was dope, but if Jimmy was admitting that, it had to be a good sign. But the relief didn't last.

"Instead, they've put in the lowest-grade crap they could find. This is fucking shite. The dregs scraped off the presses."

I knew it. In a way I'd always known it. We'd come all this way, we'd risked so much, but in the end, we didn't know what the fuck we were doing. It gave me courage I hadn't expected.

"So you don't want it?" I asked. It didn't feel like I had anything to lose.

Everyone in the room turned to stare at me. I had to go on.

"If you don't want it, just say so, and we'll take it elsewhere." I didn't know how we were going to do that, but I was sick of this.

"Don't be so hasty," Jimmy said. He surprised me by not sounding angry. He sounded amused. "I didn't say I didn't want it. We're just establishing what it is you have for sale." He gestured at me to calm down.

"Now, most of the hash on the streets is fucking shite, so the relative poor quality of this shipment isn't necessarily a deal-breaker." He took a long, slow breath before going on.

"What are you looking for? How much per kilo?"

Although this was Ben's side of things, I knew the figures just as well as he did by then.

"A thousand," I said.

Jimmy whistled.

"A thousand?" His eyebrows flicked up his forehead. "That's high. Even for a starting bid. You'd be lucky to sell it for that to the end user. No, no. I think we're looking at half that."

"Five hundred a kilo?" I asked.

"And don't forget you don't have the full one hundred kilos."

I was silent, miserably doing the maths in my head, the whole point of our plan falling apart around us. I nearly didn't hear Ben when he joined in.

"No way. We might not have a fancy testing kit but we tried it out and it's good stuff. Way better than what you can normally buy. So if you don't want it we can find loads of other places to shift it."

Jimmy turned to him. "Oh really? And how exactly are you going to find these other places?"

"Well, we found you, didn't we?"

For a long time Jimmy just stared at Ben, his face unreadable. But then he answered.

"Yeah. You did. You did find me."

Jimmy turned away from both of us and looked out suddenly over the loch. He walked to the window, as if suddenly the view was the only thing that interested him. He tapped the vial of liquid against the glass. Then he turned back, and when he spoke again he changed the conversation.

"Listen, you boys have all had a very long journey. When you arrived I was just about to have some breakfast. How about I fix us all some scrambled eggs?"

There was a momentary pause in the room, as we all took in this shift, but then Ben said:

"Sure."

Chapter Thirty-Five

JIMMY TOLD HIS brother to make four rounds of toast and then broke a whole box of six eggs into a bowl. He cut the corner off a pat of butter and dropped it in. Then he pulled open a drawer and pulled out a cheese grater and a spice bottle. From the bottle, he shook out a little round nut and began to rub it against the grater so that a powder fell into the mixture.

"Freshly ground nutmeg. That's the key to decent scrambled eggs. Did you know that?"

When no one answered, Jimmy continued.

"For hundreds of years, this stuff grew on just a few islands in Indonesia, the Banda Islands. Nowhere else. They became known as the Spice Islands. Now, back in Europe at that time, everyone thought this little nut would stop you getting the plague. You know, boils all over your face, dying. All that. So you know what happened? A few very enterprising people worked out that if you could sail a ship and find those islands, and if you could fill your hold with this stuff and sail it back to Europe, you could make yourself very, very rich indeed."

He finished grating from the nut, and he tapped the grater and placed it down on the empty work surface.

"Nowadays, of course, it grows all over. You can buy it anywhere. This comes from the shop down in..." He stopped. "Well. I bought it for just a couple of quid. My point is, you can't get rich from this anymore.

You need to find something else." He stopped; it seemed the history lecture was over.

"But it's still the secret to fucking good scrambled eggs." He pulled a pan out of the drawer and set it going on the hob, with another knob of butter melting against the heavy iron base.

Paul had sat down with us at the table now. We were all waiting to see what was going to happen next. And that turned out to be watching Jimmy cooking the eggs and ignoring us completely. He poured the egg mixture into the pan and stirred it slowly. It was like he'd forgotten we were in the room. But then, suddenly, he turned to us.

"Let's indulge in a little fantasy. Let's imagine that over breakfast here, we come to an arrangement. It's not going to be eighty-five a kilo, but let's imagine we reach a deal, maybe fifty, fifty-five, somewhere in that region. What happens then? Are you going to invest that money into arranging another deal? Are we contemplating a *regular* arrangement here?"

Ben started to say something, but Jimmy cut him off.

"And that question is aimed at Jake," Jimmy said sharply, still with his back to me.

I froze, unsure how to answer. In the end, I went for the truth.

"We're not really drug smugglers. We just did this to help pay off our student debt. Maybe have a bit of money to set ourselves up, but this was just a one-off."

Jimmy still had his attention on the stove and the eggs. And moments later, he was satisfied they were done. He brought the pan over to the table and carefully spooned some onto all our plates, where Paul had already placed some toast.

"Let's eat."

Jimmy sat down, and we all ate in silence. I'd never much rated scrambled eggs before, but I had to hand it to Jimmy: these were pretty good. Must have been the nutmeg. When Jimmy had finished, he placed his knife and fork together on his plate and sat back.

"Was. You used the past tense, Jake. This 'was' just a one-off?"

"Is," I corrected myself. "This is just a one-off."

"OK. And this question is to either of you. What do you think is the single biggest issue I have to deal with in this business?"

Neither of us answered.

"Come on. You're newcomers into the industry. I'm interested to hear what you think. Ensuring a regular supply? Minimising my risks? Maintaining a secure distribution network? What's the most challenging of all?"

I looked at Ben. He looked at me.

"Security?" I said.

Jimmy frowned, gestured for me to elaborate.

"Getting caught by the police?" I said.

This time, he smiled.

"Some of my best friends are police officers. No."

Again, Jimmy shook his head. Then he leaned forward and made his hands into a steeple, leaning on the table.

"It's manpower. Whatever you do, you need people. To shift bags, to drive cars. Just to come up with ideas. It's difficult to find people, good people, I mean."

Something made me glance at Paul at that point. And his face surprised me. He was beginning to smile. I couldn't work out why.

"I've been in this business for a long time, nearly fifteen years. How many times do you think I've had kids, like you, come to me with a deal the way you two have?"

"I dunno," Ben managed when Jimmy rested his eyes on him, waiting for an answer. "A few?"

Jimmy shook his head.

"Not once. Not one single time."

Chapter Thirty-Six

JIMMY SAT A long time, completely still, watching us. Then he spoke.

"I'm going to make you boys an offer. Actually, I'm going to make two offers. I'd like you to consider both very carefully."

I looked across at Ben and listened.

"Now, you've asked for a thousand a kilo. I tried a little trick on you back there. I tried to make you believe your product isn't worth that, and Ben here saw through that. And I like that. So my first offer is simple. Exactly what you asked. A thousand a kilo. For however much product you've brought. In cash. Right now. And afterwards, Paul will drive you to a train station—I'm afraid we'll need to use the hoods again—but he'll put you on a train home, back to your lives. And you'll never see me, or my brother, ever again." Jimmy stopped.

For a moment, I waited for him to go on, but he was watching us again, so I turned to Ben, holding my breath.

"Why don't you boys step out onto the balcony and have a little chat about that?" Jimmy said. "Just say the word. We'll shake hands, and we'll be done."

But then, Ben spoke for both of us.

"What's the second offer?"

I thought I saw Jimmy smile, but maybe I imagined it.

"I've just offered you exactly what you came here for. Why would you want to hear the second offer?"

He was ignoring me now. Totally focussed on Ben. I realised we all were, but I was probably the only one who didn't understand why.

"What's the second offer?" Ben said again.

This time, Jimmy definitely smiled. Paul too. I still couldn't work out what the hell was going on.

"Look around you, kid," Jimmy said. "Go on. Have a good look." He leaned back, and both Ben and I did so, tentatively at first, glancing around at the glossy white kitchen cabinets, the wide open windows and steel balcony, the view out over the loch.

"All this comes at a cost, kid. And I'm not talking money. Are you sure you want to hear the second offer?"

Ben hesitated for a moment, but not for long. "I want to hear it."

The two of them stared at each other, until Jimmy was the one to look away.

"I told you I've been in this business for fifteen years. Fifteen good years. Very good years. But things change. I've got a daughter. And a second on the way. And a dog." He bent down and stroked the ears of the little terrier.

"Which all means I have to make some changes to the way the business operates. I can't be going away as much as I used to. I need to rely on other people. Creative people. People who can handle themselves in difficult and unusual circumstances. And people like that are hard to find."

No one said anything for a moment, and he went on.

"And then Paul gets to hear about a couple of guys—not dealers, not junkies, but *university graduates,* who want to come and bring me a shipment of product. So we got to thinking. Perhaps we should meet these boys? See what they're made of. Do you know what I'm saying?"

Ben nodded.

"I think you do. I think you did from the moment you walked in here."

I looked at Ben, expecting him to look as confused as me, but he didn't. He was smiling.

"The details," Jimmy went on. "We'll have to work out the details."

"Of what?" I blurted out. It seemed like everyone else in the room was able to communicate through some sort of telepathy, but I still didn't understand.

"A job, Jake. I'm offering the two of you a job. To come and work with us. To make some real money."

PART THREE

Chapter Thirty-Seven

IF YOU EVER find yourself flying into the island of Tenerife, off the west coast of Africa, make sure to get yourself a window seat on the left-hand side of the aircraft, because the view you'll get is spectacular.

Almost the entire island is formed from a huge mountain which rears steep-sided out of the Atlantic Ocean. On the day I flew in, the volcanic top of the mountain poked out of a duvet of clouds like an alien world floating in the sky, and as we descended, the clouds dissolved to reveal a landscape of deep greens on the upper slopes, ringed below by the activity of humans—peculiar and insignificant from the air. Roads buzzed with little toy cars, wind turbines spun, tiny resorts glimmered, their blue-water pools like jewels inlaid in the ochre rock. For most of the five-hour flight, I was stuck next to a kid playing video games on his tablets, all bleeps and stupid tunes when he collected gold coins, and then turning around to argue with his brother about who was best, so his sharp elbows dug into my ribs. Then the view got good, and he started whingeing to his mummy he couldn't see anything because that man was in the way. I took my revenge silently and kept blocking the window, my nose pressed up against it. Drinking in that view.

I still felt the fear, that raising of my heart rate, the anticipation of doing something dangerous. But it was a familiar feeling now. It no longer felt like it might overwhelm me. I controlled it.

The glide seemed to take forever over a landscape too rocky and craggy to place a basketball court, let alone land a plane this big, but eventually, the whines and clunks below my feet told me the landing gear was deployed, and I had to trust, as we slipped ever lower, now toward the red roofs of villas and the dirty white of apartment blocks, that an airport would come into view in the final seconds. And just when it seemed it might not, and we really were descending towards a sudden, fiery death, then it was there, reassuringly flat tarmac and wide run-offs to the side, lined with planes waiting to take off. We hit the ground, and the engines roared into reverse. A few people on the plane tried to get everyone to cheer, but it failed to catch on. I wouldn't have minded if it had. Now I'd learnt to fly myself in tiny light aircraft that bucked and lurched around the sky I had a new appreciation of the smooth effortless comfort of commercial airliners. Just five hours earlier, I was in the Manchester rain. Here, it was sunny, and the baggage handlers, already unloading the plane, were working in shirt sleeves.

When I walked through the plane door and into the sunshine, I spent a few moments breathing in the warm, fresh air, looking around at the slab-side of the mountain on one side of the airport, and the ocean stretching away on the other. I glanced at the bus at the bottom of the steps, standing-room only already with tourists and their cameras and their tablets and their moaning kids, and their worries about whether they could get reception on their phones, or if they'd be able to find a bar that showed the football. I smiled at that. Thinking how far I'd come. How much I'd changed. And as I watched the tourists, squabbling and pushing for space on the bus, I smiled again at the fear. For how it had made me different.

I spent a few minutes walking up and down the line of hire car desks, listening and watching, before choosing the one I wanted.

Buenas tardes, necesito alquilar un coche para una semana, *por favor…*

My language skills were coming on by then, Mum would have been so proud.

The woman behind the desk had teeth as white as her blouse, which was unbuttoned to show a shaft of nicely tanned cleavage. I walked away with the keys to a little red Fiat, and the certainty that a pair of deep brown eyes were watching me depart. Maybe in other circumstances I'd have practiced a bit more of my Spanish, but I had work to do. Instead I found the car and drove the sixty kilometres north to the island's capital, Santa Cruz, away from the tourist resorts in the south and along a highway hugging the edge of the land before it plunged into the ocean.

I stopped for the night in the *Atlantic Marina Hotel*. On a whim, I upgraded to a front-facing room, paying the bill in cash. I always tried to do that by then. There was no one chasing me, I was sure about that, but it made me harder to track, just in case.

When I got to my room, I threw my bag on the bed and took a shower to wash off the grime of travelling. Then I poured a drink from the minibar and pulled open the door to the balcony. Outside I could hear the hum of the city and the lights were coming on as darkness descended. It was warm, comfortable. That's when I got my first glimpse of her, looking beautiful and elegant in the evening light. I raised my glass and said a silent toast.

CHAPTER THIRTY-EIGHT

I'VE TOLD YOU about the first time. Now I have to tell you about the last. Well this was the last. There were others of course, but if I told you about each of those this story would go on for ever, and I'm not in here long enough for that.

Our secret, the way we operated by then, was as simple as it was clever. We simply never did the same thing twice. We built up no patterns, left nothing that anyone could track us by. It kept things interesting too. Once we'd brought in a shipment by lorry from Tunisia via Italy and Poland hidden in washing machines. We'd done light aircraft trips—never with the same origin or destination, never the same plane. We'd carried suitcases through customs. But this last one was the biggest we'd ever tried. If this worked we wouldn't need to work again for a very long time.

* * *

I had a lot to get done, but I allowed myself the luxury of a leisurely breakfast. My meeting with Carlos wasn't until eleven. I took a swim in the hotel's outdoor pool, twenty lengths, the sun already hot on my back. Then I worked my way through a plate piled high with fruit, and then sat back with coffee and looked around me. The hotel's other clients were mostly business people, a few older couples. Despite my casual look, I didn't appear out of place. No one would remember me.

Carlos the Broker—that wasn't his official name; it was just what we'd taken to calling him—had an office in a small block near the main highway into town. it was all cool marble, a wide view out over the ocean, and a showy receptionist, the whole office was designed to impress people who needed all that to feel comfortable. I accepted the red-lipstick smile from the receptionist as she showed me into Carlos's office, where photographs of boats filled the walls. He rose at once from his chair and shook my hand with an enthusiasm that betrayed how, even if he felt aspects of this deal were unusual, it was profitable enough for him to overlook them.

"Mr. Smith! How lovely to meet you in person. How was your trip?"

We'd agreed how to handle this. Businesslike and polite, but offering nothing.

"Very pleasant, thank you." I accepted the invitation to sit, not at his broad wooden desk but in a more informal area, where we were equals.

"Coffee?"

I nodded.

"Maria!" I was flashed another smile as the receptionist walked past to a coffee machine on a low table by the window. From the way she had to bend down to fetch our drinks, a move which pulled her skirt tight against her arse, I guessed the table was low on purpose. Carlos flashed me a look to check I was watching, and I saw no reason not to.

There were pastries laid out in front of us, and Carlos waved his hand over them, but neither of us touched them.

"There is a very fine little restaurant on the quayside," Carlos went on. "Once we are done with the paperwork here, I would like to invite you for lunch. A little celebration." He smiled broadly.

"That's kind, but I have a prior engagement." I accepted my coffee from Maria, not allowing my eyes to be drawn down to her chest as she leaned in to hand it to me.

"Of course." He assimilated the brush-off and adjusted his strategy. He was probably happy not to go through all that schmoozing bullshit anyway.

"Another time, perhaps? Shall we?" Carlos opened a leather-bound folder on the table in front of him. "There are just a few papers to sign, and I can check that the money has gone through online. Then she'll be all yours." He smiled again, a reassuring smile, which belied how keen he was to complete this sale.

He'd marked where I had to sign the documents and I scribbled the same signature six times. The last one was a bit loose, but good enough that Carlos didn't notice anything. He pressed the button to bring an iPad to life and I saw it was already logged into a banking app. I had no worries about the money side of things.

"Are you sure you won't have a pastry?" He asked, as we waited. *Why the hell not?* I thought. It's not every day you buy your first boat.

* * *

Apart from the week's intensive course, taken to prepare me for this trip and where we never left the choppy, enclosed waters of the Solent on the south coast of England, I'd never so much as set foot on a yacht before. You don't tend to, growing up like I did in south London. And the boats we went on for the course were small, knocked-about vessels that rolled under your weight as soon as you stepped aboard. The *Prima Donna* was different. She was twice the size for a start, at fifty-four foot long, and with a mast that stretched up into a sky a thousand times bluer than the one I had sailed under in the Solent. When I put my foot on the scrubbed teak side deck and climbed aboard, she barely moved at all.

She was too large to fit into the standard berths at the marina, so had to be moored at the end of the pontoon. I had to walk out the whole length of the floating wooden footpath between line after line of smaller craft until I reached the giant T shape where the bigger boats were moored. Directly in front of *Prima Donna* were two even larger yachts, shinier and more impressive. But I wasn't disappointed by this. What we needed was the biggest boat we could get away with while still being just a little upstaged wherever we put in. No point drawing more attention to ourselves than necessary.

I held onto the guard rail and walked toward the back—the stern, I knew it was called, now I'd done my course. I jumped down into the cockpit, looked around for a moment, and searched in my pocket for the key which Carlos had presented to me once the money had gone through. Maybe he thought it odd I didn't want to look the boat over before buying it, but I didn't want to make it obvious that a guy who knew nothing about boats was buying one of the most expensive on his books.

I looked around me one last time before I unlocked the door. All around me, the air was filled with the noises of the ocean. There were birds wheeling around and the knocks and clangs of ropes slapping against masts. Outside a giant rock breakwater, and visible through the harbour entrance, the wind was blowing the sea into steep walls of chop. Further out, these were streaking the water with smears of white. I pulled open the hatch and hoisted myself down the steps, glad my job didn't involve taking the *Prima Donna* anywhere on my own.

Downstairs—down below—she was beautiful, all polished wood with touches here and there of brass. There was a table with wings folded down where I stood now, pleasantly surprised at how much headroom there was, and in front of me, a corridor led forward where I could see the doors of lockers, the toilet, and the cabin at the bow. Behind me was the galley and opposite that, the chart table, a bank of computers and screens mounted on the wall. She had everything; she could practically sail herself, Carlos had said that morning. That was lucky since I didn't know how to sail it, and my confidence in my new *skipper* was pretty limited too.

I chose the rear cabin for myself. Not that I'd ever thought much about it, but I'd always assumed the captain of a boat would sleep right at the front. Apparently, this isn't the case. The cabin that's tucked away at the back is usually more spacious and more comfortable, and since I was going to be here on my own for a while, I decided it might as well be mine.

Then I got to work. I spent the rest of the day and all of the next running my errands. To the supermarket to buy supplies; to the various hardware stores I'd identified earlier, where I could buy all of the other equipment and materials I needed. There was a trolley that yacht owners could use to wheel their gear from the marina's car park out along the floating walkway to where their boats were moored, but even with this, it was still a pain to get everything out to the yacht, and then onboard.

As beautiful a boat as the *Prima Donna* was, at that point I just didn't get the point of the whole sailing thing.

Chapter Thirty-Nine

I SHOULDN'T EVEN have been out there alone at that point. The *Prima Donna's* new skipper—who insisted I call him that, partly due to the genuine benefit of staying in character as much as possible, but mostly because he just liked it—had pored over the surveyors' reports and floor plans with me and discussed how this would work. The original plan was for the two of us to come out together, both to buy the boat and fix it up.

But the original plan changed at short notice when he got the news that Aussie Mick, who handled the distribution end of things, was unhappy with some aspects of the operation. Most likely he wanted more money. I understood why that meant the skipper had to delay his arrival, but on the other hand, I really could have done with someone who knew *a bit* more about boats than I did.

I'll give you an example. The lockers and cupboards in the front of the boat were full of gear, and there wasn't going to be room for all of it once I'd finished. But since I knew just about nothing about sailing, I didn't know which bits of kit I could safely get rid of, and which we needed to keep. Some bits were obvious. The anchor, I guessed, was a keeper, but the lockers at the front seemed to be filled with sails. Far more than it looked like we needed. I checked up on deck, and the boat was already fitted with the big sail at the front and the main one at the back—so why did it need the ones down below? Spares? I didn't know.

I made the best of it and cracked on. For the first few days I was doing nothing but working and sleeping. Until something happened that changed that.

* * *

At first, I'd assumed the boat moored in front of the *Prima Donna* was empty. It was another sailing yacht, even bigger than mine and called *Miss Adventure*. But it turned out to not be empty after all. One morning, when I was taking a break from all the chaos downstairs, something caught my eye on *Miss Adventure*. A figure was moving on deck. I frowned initially. The fewer people around, the fewer people who might wonder at the noise and mess I was making—but then I got a better look at who was moving around, and my frown turned to a look of interest.

At first, I just saw her from the back, walking along the side deck of the yacht. Long, tanned legs in little navy blue shorts and—because there was a bit of a chill from the wind, I suppose—a white cashmere jumper that struck me as not looking very nautical, but what the hell, she looked good in it. Then she turned around and walked back toward me, and I got to see her face. She was concentrating on where she was stepping, so I felt able to have a good look. About my age, pretty but not in the way that you might imagine a woman on a superyacht would look, not in-your-face looks. Hell, what am I saying? She was gorgeous. Hair touched blond from the sun; tall, slim. She stopped concentrating, and I should have looked away, but I found I couldn't tear my eyes off her. Then she was stepping over the guardrail and walking down the pontoon toward me.

"Hi," she said brightly in an unmistakable English voice, "I'm Jenny. We noticed you turning up the other day. I thought I'd come and say *hola*." The way she said it, it was clear she already knew I was English, I wondered how she knew.

"Hi," I replied.

It turns out it's very much the done thing for people on yachts to chat to their neighbours when they're tied up in port. Lucky old me, eh?

Maybe it's something to do with how they don't have anyone much to talk to when they're all sailing around out at sea. Who knows? Who cares?

"She's beautiful. Is she yours?" Jenny touched her hand to the teak deck, at waist height to where she stood on the pontoon. She had graceful fingers, long and slim. I looked from them to her face: blue eyes set deep, framed by eyelashes that were surprisingly dark. Her teeth white, her lips just open. I could have stared at her all afternoon.

"Sort of," I said. "Me and a friend have bought her. He's coming out in a few days."

"Really?" she said to this, her eyebrows arched and her eyes wide. "I was joking. You look far too young."

I shrugged. "Yeah, maybe." I didn't really want to dwell on this so I went on: "How about your one?"

"*Miss Adventure*? Is she mine? God, no." Jenny laughed, a lovely sight.

"I'd love it if she was though," Jenny talked quickly. "That's my dream one day. One day I'm going to find a million dollars and buy her and sail her all around the world." She smiled a friendly smile.

"But for now, I just work aboard." She screwed up her nose at this. It looked so pretty I was unable to reply.

"I'm sorry I talk too much." Jenny went on. "She's owned by a couple of businessman. They're hardly ever on board though, mostly they just get us to sail her around from place to place."

"Us?" I asked, for a couple of reasons.

"Me and a couple of others." She smiled.

"That's an actual job?"

Jenny wrinkled her nose again and laughed so that her breasts moved beneath the softness of her jumper.

"Yeah, course it is." She gave me a look like she couldn't decide if I was being funny or not.

"Is this boat *really* yours?" she asked.

It was something I hadn't really considered properly up to that point.

"Yeah," I said, a bit thoughtfully. "Yeah, it is."

"Are you not going to invite me onboard to show her off?"

That surprised me, and I wasn't really ready for visitors, but I agreed anyway. I held out my arm to help her climb on, even though there were plenty of other handholds. We held onto each other's hands for a little longer than we needed to.

"She's beautiful," Jenny said again when I'd followed her below, watching how her hair fell to her shoulders. We stopped in the saloon; I didn't take her any further forward since I was still working up in the front. "What are you doing, though? What's all the wood for?"

I felt my pulse creep upwards. There was nothing on display that would raise real suspicions, but her being on board was an unnecessary risk. I didn't like that, but I liked her being there all the same.

"I'm just fixing a few things up. We're sailing her back to England in a week or so."

"Cool. We're off to the Caribbean next." She put her head to one side. "Hey, we're all off to a party tonight. Why don't you come along?"

I thought for a moment, and as I did, she reached out and touched my shoulder.

"Come on, it'll be fun." She smiled at me, with even, white teeth.

"OK."

"Great. There's a restaurant on the quayside. We'll grab something to eat first. I'll pick you up."

We looked at each other.

"I'd better go. I'm supposed to be fetching bread."

"OK."

I watched her step off the boat. She must have known I was still looking as she walked away because she turned back to me and smiled again.

"I'll come by at about eight?"

* * *

When she did so, she'd changed into a tight black dress that stopped halfway down her thighs. Her hair was tied up to reveal her slim, shapely neck. She introduced me to the skipper of her boat, a Scandinavian guy with hair so blond it was almost white, and a couple of other people they were with. They were a fun, easy-going bunch, and they seemed to see where this was going, so they left Jenny and me to talk together most of the time. We sat opposite one another in the restaurant, and she told me how she'd gotten into sailing and the job, and about all the places they'd been. She was some sort of deckhand-cum-hostess-cum-model, there to make sure the boat's owners and their guests would have their every need attended to. I didn't ask but I guessed she was employed as much for her looks as her culinary skills.

We ate fish and drank wine; her skipper kept ordering more as soon as the bottles on the table ran low so that I was worried who was going to pay at the end. When I tried to offer my share he stopped me and wouldn't take no for an answer.

Then we went on to the party, in a loft-style apartment a few streets back from the harbour. Jenny held onto my arm as we walked there, drawn in by the heavy bass tones of the music. The door was open, and a trail of people were sitting on the stairs in the hallway, drinking and laughing. In a way, it reminded me of our old flat, back in Brighton.

We wandered around—it was too loud to talk—and we smiled and pushed through the throng of young, beautiful people, and we danced, and we smoked outside on the balcony, and then we found a quiet corner, and Jenny kissed me, her tongue pressing into my mouth and her hands resting in my lap. She kissed me with an urgency that told me this was something she'd been thinking about the whole day. She shook out her hair, and I stroked it and curled it around my fingers. And as the party died down, she asked if she could come back to the *Prima Donna* with me.

That was when I really got it, this sailing thing. I left the hatch open so that that the bright stars threw a little light onto Jenny as I unzipped her dress. It fell to the floor, and she smoothly ensured her bra and pants followed. Then she lay herself back on the saloon table and pulled up her knees to open her legs. She squirmed to find a comfortable position as I took off my shirt and pulled down my underwear. Then I leaned into her, the moonlight cool on my back.

Yeah, I kind of got the attraction of sailing that night.

Chapter Forty

BETWEEN THE SKIPPER not being there to help me out, and Jenny popping in as often as she did, I didn't get as much work done on the boat as I'd planned, but rather than leave anything undone, I just limited the areas I was working on. What that meant in practice was I finished the extra compartments up in the bow, but I didn't get to do the ones I'd planned in the stern. I couldn't see that it mattered; we weren't adding that much extra weight, and the *Prima Donna* was a big boat. It'd be fine, I told myself.

And a couple of days before we were due to leave, the skipper finally turned up. I drove back down to the airport to pick him up, back down the oceanside road. It seemed forever since I'd arrived there myself and the flood of tourists with their sticky children and their angry sunburn was a shock after the time I'd spent isolated on the yacht, with only my tools and Jenny for company.

I saw him before he saw me. Doing his best to blend in, but looking nothing like the holidaymakers all around him. He was dressed in a Hawaiian shirt and shorts, eyes hidden by mirrored shades. All his gear in a discreet holdall carried by his side.

"Hey Skipper!" I called out, and he veered left in the arrivals hall to intercept me.

"Hello Jake," he said pushing his shades up into his hair. For a moment we stood there unsure how to react. Then I couldn't help myself,

I grabbed him in a hug.

"Good to see you Ben," I said.

"Get off mate. And call me Skipper. It's important to keep in character."

"Whatever mate. Skip." I replied. I was happy to indulge him and before long we were both smiling at each other. We'd come a long way since that first trip in his shitty old camper van.

"So, how'd it go with Mick?" I asked, as we turned to walk outside to where I'd parked. "All sorted?"

"Mate don't ask. He's a pain in the arse. I think we got it sorted."

"What was the problem?" I asked. I was only making conversation. This had never been my area of the business.

"Just the usual."

"He want more money?"

Ben didn't answer but I saw the muscles around his mouth tense before he looked away.

"It's sorted Jake. Honestly you don't want to worry about it."

I accepted that. He did his part, I did mine. We'd got on just fine that way this long, I didn't think it was about to change.

He smiled now, then clapped me around the shoulders.

"Don't worry about it. It's fucking *boring*. Let's get out of here. Show me my fucking *boat*."

* * *

Ben had pushed hard for this idea. He loved boats. He'd had some uncle with a yacht when he was growing up, and him and his brother used to do trips across the English Channel, cruising around Jersey and out to the Scilly Isles. I'd been cautious if that was enough experience for what we had planned but Ben had convinced me.

Now we walked around the deck together, Ben tracing the routes of the ropes, checking the tightness of the hatch covers. Then we went down below, and I showed him all the work that I'd been doing. I pointed out I'd only been able to set up the front lockers as we'd planned, and I asked him if he thought that mattered, but he was relaxed about it, and we moved on. After we'd checked everything, he climbed back into the cockpit and stood behind the wheel, as if this was the part that really interested him.

"Maybe we should take her out for a test sail tomorrow," he called down to me. I was grabbing a couple of beers from the fridge down below.

Then he must have seen Jenny, climbing off her boat and walking over to ours, because his back straightened, and he ran a hand through his hair, then pushed his sunglasses up to hold it in place. His tongue ran lightly around his lips in a smile of anticipation. Then I heard her speak from the pontoon.

"Hi, I'm Jenny. Is Jake around?"

I watched from below as Ben's eyes sharpened, and his mouth fell open. I poked my head up to see. Jenny was leaning on the guardrail, the tops of her gorgeous breasts pushed up against it, her legs on display too, her sun-kissed hair blowing in the light breeze.

"Hey you. You want a beer?"

"Sure."

I collected another bottle and climbed back up, then introduced her properly to Ben. We drank in the afternoon sunshine and chatted easily together. I savoured the taste of that beer, that feeling of relaxing in the warm sunshine, everything just perfect with the world. Most of all I enjoyed the jealous look in Ben's eyes every time he glanced at Jenny, and she glanced at me.

* * *

We left two days later. Our first time taking the *Prima Donna* out from the marina. There was a bittersweetness to it. Jenny watched and waved from the deck of *Miss Adventure*, where earlier, we'd been lying together in her little cabin, almost unable to stop holding onto one another, but promising that we'd meet up again, somewhere, and soon. I didn't have much time to think about that now, I was so busy following Ben's instructions: pull all the ropes in and coil them up; take in the fenders, the great plastic bumpers that hung down the side of the boat. For all his previous assurances I could see Ben was nervous, being in charge of the *Prima Donna* for the first time. We left under the power of the engine, a reassuring, purring throb that made her thrum as she cut through the calm water. It was strange, watching the view of the marina change as we moved at last. It was like I'd forgotten the boat could move.

I waved to Jenny until I could no longer see her, only the tall mast of *Miss Adventure,* and then I made my way back to the cockpit and stood by Ben, watching the rocks of the harbour wall slide past just a few metres away. Outside its protective arm, I could see the water was lively with whitecaps.

"You jammy bastard, Jake."

I knew exactly what he was talking about.

"You're shagging a… hostess or whatever she is. While I'm stuck dealing with Aussie fucking Mick." He was pretending to look annoyed, but I knew he wasn't really.

"You realise I have to get my own back now?" He said. "I'll have to show you what a boat like this can do."

The yacht shook gently as it drove through a set of small wavelets. We cleared the shelter of the marina, the *Prima Donna* beginning to find its rhythm as it rode into the swells. Ben pointed at more ropes and told me to pull them, not moving from his position on the wheel, in charge. I did what he told me, and with a lot of effort, I winched up the mainsail, and then pulled out the genoa at the front and winched that tight too. Once I'd finished winching, sweat had broken out on my brow and I felt like I'd just done fifty press ups. Then I looked up. The sails were enormous, a huge expanse of white filling the sky, and buckling and cracking since we were still motoring into the wind. Then Ben kicked the engine into neutral and laid us off, and the sails filled with wind. At once, the yacht yawed over to one side, and I swore and grabbed hold of what I could to keep from slipping over. Ben steered more and more off the wind so that the whole of the sails filled with wind. The boat was leaning right over on one side now, and surging forward, waves already crashing over the front and sending rivers of water down the side decks.

"Fucking hell," I said, not meaning to speak out loud. The boats I'd practiced sailing on back in the Solent hadn't been *anything* like this, but then, they were tubby little cabin cruisers, and there hadn't been much wind.

"You know she's been all the way around the world?" Ben told me. "She's an ocean racer; that's why I chose her. Shouldn't have any problem taking us where we need to go."

And that first experience was nothing, just a light breeze to get me started. As the island lurched and gurgled away in our wake, the wind picked up, and the boat threw herself forward, faster and faster, crashing now through some of the ocean swells, surfing down the valleys between others. She lay down harder too on her side; the deck I'd come to feel familiar on was now a steep slope that bucked and crashed as we ploughed through the walls of ocean. I clung on, my feet not on the floor but on the angled sides. The detail of the port behind us quickly faded, and with it the mast of *Miss Adventure* acting as my marker for where Jenny was. Then even the tall, mountain top of Tenerife faded as well, and then we were alone in the ocean, a charging thoroughbred racehorse of a yacht at full speed, heading for the Moroccan coast.

Chapter Forty-One

"HERE, TAKE OVER for a minute." Ben had seemed settled in his position behind the wheel, bare feet braced wide apart, a yachting jacket zipped up to keep off the worst of the spray. We'd been sailing for about two hours. We were passing the southern tip of the island of Fuerteventura.

"Steer one thirty-five."

"Where are you going?" I guess I sounded worried, because he grinned at me.

"I'm going to take a nap. I'll be on watch tonight."

I felt my eyes widen.

"You can sail a boat. You'll be alright."

I made my way cautiously and awkwardly over to the wheel. It was hard to move anywhere with the angle of heel, but when I got there, he moved to one side, to let me stand beside him. I copied his position, widening my stance. Then I joined him with my hands on the wheel.

"If the wind picks up any more, we'll have to shorten sail. For now, just keep an eye out for the bigger waves. Let her head up into them. Let 'em roll underneath us." Ben gave me a grin. He was doing what he loved.

"You got her?"

I nodded, and Ben let go. Immediately, the wheel began to slip through my fingers, spinning round one, then two full turns. At once, the yacht began turning into the wind, the sails losing their shape and flapping angrily. Ben grabbed the wheel again and fought it back around. Slowly, the boat fell back onto its original course. It was like it was alive, like you had to tame it.

"You sure you got her?"

Annoyed with myself, I gripped the wheel much harder and nodded.

"Yeah, sorry about that."

"Don't worry about it." He let go.

"Well, wake me up if there's an emergency." He thought for a moment. "Or if you see dolphins."

I watched as Ben made his way forward to the hatch. I don't know how, but he seemed already to be in tune with the movement of the boat, not clinging on but moving lightly and easily. He dropped down below, and I concentrated instead on steering the boat. My eyes swept between the compass, mounted on a pedestal right in front of the wheel, and watching the waves sweep down on us from upwind. The wind was from the north; Ben said it almost always is in this part of the Atlantic, so that it builds up great rolling ocean swells, like creases in a rug, that are shaken out down the entire western coastline of Africa. We were crossing them now. One by one, they picked us up, carrying us higher in the sea where the wind was stronger, then allowing us to slide part-sideways in to the deep valleys between them. And as the hours passed, I found that if I let the yacht bear away, she would ride down the face of these ocean valleys, picking up speed, and the whole boat would thrum with vibrations. The rigging would whistle and hum as the wind screamed past ropes iron-tight with the tension from the sails. I was awestruck. Somewhere between euphoric and terrified. On one level it reminded me of a game, like something on the Xbox that Ben and I used to play, only it was nothing like that. It was so much bigger, it encompassed me. I was part of this awesome machine, its power like nothing I'd ever experienced, power I had no idea even existed. I found myself wanting more and more. Looking out for a bigger wave so that I could set up another sleigh ride down its face, with the fresh spray whipping past on either side.

The colours were amazing. I'd never seen anything as white as those sails against the sky. And the ocean was such a deep blue, it was close to black. I don't know how deep it runs there, but it's inky, the streaks of white where the wave's tops are blown apart by the wind like snowdrifts against coal. It was hypnotic.

"Hey, Jake." I snapped back to the present, seeing the hatch slide back and Ben's head appear. "You taking it easy up there?"

I'd been watching a big roller approach us from the side, and at that moment, I spun the wheel hard to turn her bow off the wind. The wave picked up the entire yacht and sent her careering downhill, sheaths of water flying through the air on either side. For a full thirty seconds, we rode the swell down, the boat's steering light and responsive to my touches on the wheel; then we reached the bottom and crashed hard into the swell in front. Rivers of water came sweeping down the side decks, Ben reached above him and closed the hatch cover so that the water from the coach-house roof ran straight into the cockpit and drained away behind me.

"I'm having fun!" I shouted, matching Ben's grin from before. "Why didn't you tell me how much fun this is?"

"I did. You didn't listen." Ben yelled back. "But you can have too much fun. Pull her into wind. We need to reef."

I steered as Ben pulled the ropes and did whatever he had to do to make the mainsail smaller; then he took the genoa—the sail at the front—in as well, rolling it back up around itself. When we returned to our course, the noise and the speed of the yacht were both less, and Ben pointed to a low smudge on the horizon.

"That's Africa," he said. "We don't want to crash into it."

* * *

He needn't have worried. As we came closer, the wind dropped. It went from force six—like sticking your head out the window of a fast-moving car—to a light breeze, and then twenty minutes after that, it had dropped to nothing. Our speed dropped with it. From fifteen, nearly twenty knots surfing down the swells, to just cutting sharply through the water, and then, with the coast of Africa now looming large across the horizon, to almost nothing. The sea became almost glassy-still. We put the engine back on and took down the sails and motored slowly closer for a while, Ben flicking through the GPS and the radar as we waited for word. Then we saw them.

Chapter Forty-Two

THERE WERE THREE boats, small, open wooden vessels, painted blue and already close enough that we could see the figures in them. Ben had a pair of binoculars pressed to his eyes, and he focussed on the boats now.

"That them?" I asked, a little nervous now. This was always the worst part, where you feared something might go wrong.

"Yep. That's them," Ben replied, and using his foot he pulled back the throttle lever so that our speed dropped to just a ghostly glide through the water.

"Get a couple of fenders out there." Ben pointed to our port side. I swung open the locker under the cockpit seat, and dug around for where I'd stored them. Then I stepped carefully to the middle of the boat and tied them to the guardrail. Then I waited. The only sound was the higher-pitched whine from the outboards on the closing boats, and a little lapping noise as the near-still sea fussed at the *Prima Donna*'s waterline. It was late in the day now, and the sun was low behind us, shining on the three boats as they closed in. Now, I could see a familiar figure standing in the front of the first boat, his hand up, shielding his eyes from the glare.

Ten metres away, the first of the fishing boats throttled back off the plane, coming to match our speed. Even from that distance there was no mistaking the driver was a local, the guy at the front too, standing ready with a rope. But the figure in the middle wasn't. He dropped his hands now and formed them into a funnel around his mouth.

"Nice fucking boat boys!" he called out, it was weird to hear Paul's voice this way after not seeing him for over a month. "Any chance of joining you or is this a romantic cruise?"

"Sure," I shouted back. "Come aboard."

Moments later, the first boat was alongside, the driver shouting instructions that I couldn't catch. I offered to hold a rope but the bowman pushed my hands away, instead threading it through a cleat and holding it secure, pulling the two boats close.

"Good to see you, mate." Paul said, once we were secure. He looked good, a white t-shirt highlighting the tan on his face and arms. As always he looked larger than life. We gripped hands for a long moment.

"Let's get the stuff onboard, and we can get out of here, huh?"

Around Paul's feet, filling the bottom of the boat, were a dozen cheap shopping bags, the kind you can get in markets all around the world. Although they were zipped up, I knew each was filled with cling-film-wrapped cubes of product, ten in each bag, arranged that way because it was the biggest size we could lift onto the yacht easily from the much lower fishing boat. Paul handed them to me one by one, and in turn, I passed them back to Ben, who dumped them down below in the saloon. It took three, maybe four minutes to empty the first fishing boat, no more than that. Then Paul pumped fists with the boat driver, whose white teeth flashed in the evening sunlight, and then he took my arm and I pulled him aboard the *Prima Donna*. We didn't waste time. He waved the second fishing boat to come alongside from its position a few score metres behind. When it too was alongside he dropped back down into it, and we did the same as before, him lifting the bags of product from the fishing boat, me taking them and passing them to Ben who placed them out of sight inside the *Prima Donna*. Then the third boat came alongside.

"Hey, honey," Julia said to me when she was close enough. I'd nearly forgotten how pretty she was. "Missed you."

"Missed you too," I replied.

"Come on guys, let's get this done fast." Paul heard the exchange and cut it short. It wasn't because he was unsentimental. He just wanted to minimise the time the product was exposed. That was how they worked, they did everything practical to reduce risk. With the four boats there at that point, if an aircraft happened to fly over and saw us it might create suspicion. It probably wouldn't but it might. Better to get it done and get the fuck out of there. That was what Jimmy had told us time and time again. Julia handed me the first of the bags.

"Don't drop it," she said. "That's a lot of money there."

I closed my grip around the bag's handle and took the weight.

* * *

Now, I'm going to stop you for a second here. How much do you think that bag was worth? I've already told you it weighed ten kilos, and you know a kilo of Moroccan hashish is worth about a thousand pounds? So each bag was worth about ten grand, right? Wrong. Dead wrong. You see it wasn't Moroccan hashish in those bags. It was extremely pure cocaine, on the final leg of a long journey from the rainforest refineries of South America, where Paul had negotiated its purchase, via container ship from the Columbian port of Buenaventura, through the Panama Canal and across the Atlantic to Agadir on the coast of Africa where Julia had intercepted it and diverted it into these fishing boats. And now here I was, ordinary little me from my ordinary life, pulling it aboard for the final voyage back to the UK. So, how much do you think that bag was worth? Go on have a guess. Ten thousand? Try *eight hundred thousand* and you're getting closer. You really don't want to drop that.

But then again, there was a float in every bag, so if we did drop them, we'd just pick them up again. We weren't idiots. We knew what we were doing by then.

* * *

We emptied the third boat, and this time, both Paul and Julia said hurried goodbyes to the local driver, Julia giving him a hug and kissing his cheeks. He was beaming and I wasn't a bit surprised. Not because of Julia, because of how much cash he'd just made. Then Paul pulled her roughly aboard the yacht and it was my turn for a hug. Then when she was done with me she made her way back to the cockpit where Ben was still standing at the wheel. I couldn't hear what they said but I watched them embrace and then kiss each other deeply, and I smiled. It made me feel good.

"The fuck you smiling about? Let's get this hidden away." Paul told me.

* * *

We worked fast to load the product into the compartments I'd created, and I got to work right away finishing them off so that they'd pass a cursory inspection. We had way too much on board to save us if they ripped us apart—but what reason would anyone have to rip apart the *Prima Donna*? None at all. She was totally clean.

And then the four of us sat together in the cockpit, while Paul motored us north along the African coast. We drank cold beer and watched the sky to our left descend from oranges and reds and golds until it reached purple and then became punctuated with pinpoints of silver blue sparkling stars. Eventually it matched the shimmering black darkness that hung over the Sahara.

Chapter Forty-Three

BEN DIVIDED US up into two watches. Neither Julia nor Paul had any sailing experience so it made sense for each of us to lead a watch. I thought he'd put himself with Julia but he didn't. He said it wasn't a good idea for a couple to be on watch together. He and Paul took the first watch, they sent Julia and me below to cook some food.

It was warmer down there and Julia stood so close to me our bodies were touching in the tiny galley as she chopped vegetables and I fried them on the stove. After a little while we heard the sounds of the sails going back up, and then the throb of the engine changed tone, and then went silent altogether, replaced by the gurgling sound of water flowing past the hull. Then the yacht took on a little heel, not as much as before, just enough that she pressed herself forward through the water.

* * *

It took me a while to come to terms with the whole Julia thing, in case you're wondering. When Andy was off the scene she and Ben became an item officially, and that meant she became a part of our thing with Jimmy and Paul. At first I had to work hard to hide how I felt, to smother my resentment at Ben for having her, and my resentment at her for taking him away from me. But over the weeks and months that followed, my eyes were opened to a world I hadn't known existed, and certainly never imagined I'd be a part of. I came to see how well she and Ben fitted together. In a strange way I developed a sense of pride at how well they worked together, and especially of how they both still valued me as a friend.

And their closeness meant I became closer to Paul and Jimmy than would otherwise have happened. I think Paul suspected how I felt for her, and I know Jimmy knew because his wife Sarah talked to me about it a few times, telling me gently to accept what Ben and Julia had together, and assuring me that I would have the same one day. I came to see that Julia was never right for me, and I never right for her. That it hadn't been *love* I felt for her but the shock and novelty of sudden and unexpected proximity with a girl more beautiful than any I had encountered up to then.

Speaking with Sarah helped me most of all. She was equally beautiful in her own way, dark where Julia was light. Deep, where Julia was—for me at least—just a little bit shallower than I needed. Their second child had been born by then and Sarah would calmly and naturally expose one of her own breasts in the middle of our conversations to attach the baby for its feed. Perhaps the contrast helped me grow up a little.

Ben did buy Julia her fake tits, though, in case *that's* what you're wondering. Right after we agreed to Jimmy's deal. We went back to Brighton with a nice pot of cash, and that was one of the things he got sorted out early on. She showed me them too, once they were done, so I got my before and after viewing. I think I preferred the before, but she was happy about them. And I know Ben was.

We ate all together, the autopilot steering us north, and we popped the cork on a bottle of champagne that I'd bought in the Tenerife supermarket for just this occasion.

My first night onboard—my first night sail—was beautiful. Ben had told me it would be, and Jenny had too. The wind stayed light, and we tacked north against it, changing sides every couple of hours just for the variety of it, and to pump a little blood by changing the sails across. The boat was much more mannered than it had been on the crossing the day before. It cut crisply through the water, close hauled, those huge sails knifing through the air. Above them, the sky was ablaze with the universe of a billion stars. Julia and I put the deck stereo on loud and argued good-naturedly over what music to play. Everything I liked she hated and vice versa. Yeah. Julia and I were never meant to be. Once I accepted that we were able to become just about as close as friends could be. We drank coffee to stay awake and talked. It was good to see Julia again.

Chapter Forty-Four

OUR VOYAGE WAS sixteen hundred nautical miles—about two weeks, Ben thought, on a yacht as fast as the *Prima Donna*, although that depended upon the weather. For the first week or so, the wind stayed light from the north, meaning we had to keep beating against it, covering twice as much distance as we'd have done had it been behind us. It didn't matter; we had enough food and water onboard for three weeks, and if we did run short or needed spares, we could break the voyage by stopping on the Portuguese coast, in the north of Spain or France. But since that would have technically left us liable to a customs inspection, it was a lot better if we didn't have to.

One good point about that week of light winds was that everyone got the chance to learn how life aboard worked. We grew from a bunch of novice sailors, at best, into two teams who at least understood the basics of setting the sails, steering a course, and keeping ourselves fed and warm. It was easy enough in the daytime, when we all tended to be awake anyway. The nights were harder. Julia and I had the hardest watch of all, from midnight until four in the morning, an entire shift of darkness where we had to fight to stay awake, and where the passage of time seemed to slow right down, and we yearned to see the lightening on the horizon to prove the world was still turning and daylight would return.

We saw whales blowing a few times. Once, we even saw a pod of humpbacks breeching, maybe a half mile from the yacht. And we often had dolphins around us. They'd follow for hours at a time, just playing in the wake. It was beautiful out there. I had no idea the oceans had so much life.

If only it had stayed like that.

* * *

Julia and I were halfway through our morning watch when I first realised there was a problem. It was chilly, and we were dressed in the jackets and warm trousers we normally only had to wear during the night. Ben was there too with Julia curled up against him for warmth. Then Paul came up on deck and looked around. I noticed he didn't have his usual cocky smile. He looked anxious.

"What's up, mate?" Ben asked, he'd clearly noticed as well.

Paul didn't answer; he was scanning the horizon ahead of us.

"You looking for something?" Ben nudged Julia off him and joined Paul.

"Latest weather forecast doesn't look so hot," Paul told him quietly.

Julia looked at me and then to the pair of them.

"Let's have a look." Ben went downstairs and for a while it was just Julia and me on deck, now scanning the sky. However much we'd come on as sailors in the voyage so far, we all knew we'd been lucky with the weather, calm and dry so far.

A little while later Paul came back.

"Is everything OK?" Julia asked at once.

"Yeah," Paul said, looking around. The wind was still light, still from the north. We were heeling over maybe fifteen degrees, by then we hardly noticed it. But it was colder. We'd all noticed that.

"Might get a bit bumpy later is all."

We all stayed quiet for a while, listening to the wake bubble out behind.

"How bumpy?" Julia asked in the end.

Paul scanned the sky and puffed out his cheeks.

"Depends if you believe the weather forecast."

"Well what does that say?"

"It says it's gonna get a bit bumpy."

Again, we all looked around at the horizon. It didn't look any different, a little darker maybe in the west.

"It's alright, this old tub should be able to take it." He patted the top of the coach house roof. We'll be OK."

But if Ben believed that too, he still made us prepare. We altered course by thirty degrees—a big deviation from the course we had been on where our bow was pointing directly on the western tip of Ireland, a thousand miles away around the curve of the globe. We were trying to cross around in front of the worst of the weather that Ben was monitoring on his computer screens. We strapped down everything that could move. He told me to cook three meals, one for us all to eat now, and the others that could be kept in the fridge, so we wouldn't need to cook if things got rough. And while I was down below doing that, the first of the rain began to beat down on the cabin roof.

Chapter Forty-Five

THE WIND WAS stronger now, and Ben used it, driving the boat fast to get us out of the track of the storm. She lay down hard on her side, rivers of water washing down her lower deck, she thrummed and vibrated as she speared through the waves. On deck everything was drenched. We were lucky she'd come with a locker full of ocean-rated waterproofs branded with a *Prima Donna* motif. These probably saved our lives. Even wearing them cold shafts of rain and salt spray flushed down our necks and up our sleeves. It was cold and wet even down below. Helming was the hardest, alone on deck and facing into a driving rain that made your eyeballs sting. Whoever else was on watch was usually huddled up on the stairs that led below, sheltering under the sliding hatch, alert if needed but a little bit drier and warmer.

We'd all seen how the swirl of isobars on the weather charts grew deeper and stronger with each run issued, and we'd heard the sombre voice of the shipping forecast warning of storm force twelve. But I don't think any of us knew what that meant. Not really. But even on our new course, it wasn't clear if there was anything we could do to actually avoid it, the developing storm was just too big to sail around. It was moving too fast.

For a while Ben seemed to be enjoying it. He seemed able to tap into the energy that flowed around us. He told us often how the *Prima Donna* had raced around the globe, and must have come through storms before.

And while that might be true, we also knew that none of us had, not even Ben. And even for us sailing amateurs, we could all see that storm force twelve is as high as the chart goes.

* * *

We passed through the belt of rain and the visibility improved. The boat slowed and became more mannered as the wind eased a notch or two as well. For a while I wondered if maybe we were through the worst of it. But the sea retained a weird lumpiness to its movement, waves coming from almost any direction and sometimes crashing together. And then behind us the sky took on an ominous appearance. A great wall of black clouds appeared and then spread out behind us, filling the horizon in both directions and seeming to stretch as high as the atmosphere. It was like the approaching of the night only it wasn't dark, it flashed and crackled with white flashes of lightening, and the rumble of thunder was almost constant.

The weather seemed to change minute by minute and soon the wind came back. Our speed picked up but it made little difference, still the approaching black clouds built above and around us, catching us around sunset. No spectacular sunset tonight, instead our deck lighting illuminated a wild sea sliding past either side of us, the chaos of the front edge of the storm.

The wind picked up quickly again as we were overhauled but this time it kept building. Our speed increased too, but the storm was moving way faster than we could. Now travelling downwind, we were getting picked up and surfing down waves that were getting bigger and bigger. In some ways, it was similar to that first day, but now it was dark, which made it far more frightening. Dark, that is, apart from the lightning—strobe light flashes of near- daylight brightness that seared onto our retinas a glimpse of the raging sea chasing us. And as the storm closed in on us, the wind just got stronger and stronger.

By then, we were all on deck, wearing safety harnesses and clipped onto anchor points in the cockpit. The movement of the boat was too violent to stay below, too erratic. And the boat wasn't pitched over on a constant heel this time; it was rolling wildly from side to side. The masthead lights lurched around as the mast swung through its crazy arc. First Julia then Paul were lost to seasickness, they clung on moving only occasionally to puke down the side of the boat. It didn't affect me, my own stomach only felt tight with the tension. I had myself braced, just holding on as the boat flung itself down the swells.

By now, Ben was at the helm. He'd been there since the weather really turned bad. Maybe he felt responsible for getting us here, or felt that he was the least likely to make a mistake. Certainly he wasn't enjoying himself anymore.

"Jake!" Ben shouted to me. He was only a few metres away, but I could hardly hear him through the roar of the wind and waves.

"Jake!" he said again.

"Yeah?" I raised my head and looked at him.

"We're not going to outrun this. We need to come around and push our way through it."

I knew what he was saying. He'd told us before the storm really hit that we might get to a point where we had to turn around again, this time pointing the bow of the yacht into the oncoming weather. It meant we were officially giving up escaping the storm, instead accepting we were stuck with it, and trusting the *Prima Donna* could fight her way through. The problem was, this meant we had to make a turn which would put us side on to the waves, even if just for a short moment. And that was flat-out dangerous. If one of the bigger swells came through and hit the side of the boat, it would just pick us up and roll us sideways. There would be nothing to stop us being knocked flat, the mast slamming into or under the water. We could lose the mast, or we could fill with water, or both. We might just be pushed under and never come up, the air in the cabin pressed out and the yacht's hull directed toward the ocean floor, a kilometre below us.

I was the only one fit to do anything—the other two raised their heads, but it was clear they would be of no help.

"We do this now, or we don't do it at all," Ben yelled at me.

"We're going to need power all the way through. I need you to keep the sails sheeted."

I climbed stiffly to my feet, still holding on with both hands, and looked at the ropes he was asking me to pull. We rolled heavily, and I nearly fell, just managing to catch hold of a rope and falling with my back against the cabin roof.

I heard Ben's voice behind me. He was shouting, but the wind was whipping his words away.

"Now!! We're coming round now."

Looking back, I could see him under the deck lights, fighting to turn the wheel as fast as he could. As he did so, I winched in the sheet on the genoa, trying to work quickly enough that it didn't have a chance to flog itself to death. There wasn't much of it there by then anyway; it was mostly furled up, but we had some out because it made the boat more balanced. I left it as tight as I could get it so I could do the main sail, which was also heavily reefed by then.

With a great yawing final roll, the yacht's hull turned off its downwind course, and for a helpless moment, we were sideways to the swells. A small wave broke just upwind of us, and a frothing surge of water hit us from the side, like a nightclub bouncer punching a drunken man in the stomach as he lurched around a darkened street. I thought for a moment that was it—our mast lay nearly parallel to the water, and a half-ton of water flowed down the stairs into the cabin—but somehow, we recovered.

"The main. Sheet the main harder," Ben yelled, fighting the wheel to get us to turn more. I grabbed the winch handle and rammed it into the top of the winch, then cranked it around. Slowly, we turned, and as the sails bit again, the movement changed: no more rolling but jarring and thudding down as we began to hit the waves head on. We took a heel as well, more than we'd had on that first day, and Ben screamed at me again, this time to release the main again. It already had three reefs but I let it flog to reduce the power we were taking.

But we'd made it around. We were settled into our new pattern, heading back upwind, up and over the mountains of waves as they rolled toward us.

It was better, but not by much. We must have been right in the middle of the storm by then, and it seemed right on the limit of what the yacht could take. Even though it was night time by then it wasn't that dark, and what we could see of the ocean was terrifying, it was more white than black, the waves were being blasted by so much wind that their tops were mostly foam that streaked the sea for miles at a time. For maybe half an hour we rode the swells back upwind, just about managing to maintain forward momentum sailing uphill then plunging down the backs. Every so often a bigger wave would come along, and we'd slow to a complete stop and the whole boat would jar and shudder and slip backwards until the wave rolled underneath us. We'd hold on tighter than ever and Ben would fight the wheel to hold us straight.

And then a really big one hit us.

CHAPTER FORTY-SIX

WE HAD NO chance. One second, we were at the top of a wave and then what we could make out of the ocean in front just went black, the next wave was as high as our mast, and steep too, coming straight at us like a cliff. We plunged down straight into it, just as the wind pushed the top of it into an avalanche of white water. I felt the boat thud down and stop right at the base of the giant wave, way too low for us to get over it. Then I sensed rather than saw the water crash over the front of us. There was nothing to be done. Water smashed past up to my waist, cold, angry, surging water, shoving me over and down into the cockpit with a mess of ropes.

I thought I was gone, then I felt the jerk of my safety line stopping me being swept away. But there was so much water I didn't know if I was on the boat or not, I remember thinking that probably made no difference now. I hadn't had time to take a breath, and my lungs were already burning. I sucked in water but stopped myself. Instead I tried to pull myself towards whatever my harness was still attached to.

I floundered around, desperate to breathe, fighting in the blackness. Something hit me on the side of the head, I felt it but I hardly cared, I needed air. Inside my head I was screaming, I didn't want to die like this. Then finally my head broke through the surface and I sucked in a lungful of air. It was wet air, heavy with salt and spray but it was the sweetest breath I ever took.

I was still on board. Just. My safety line was wrapped around a cleat, its thick webbing enough to hold me on board against the worst the ocean could throw at us. And the *Prima Donna* was still there too. Her deck lights still burning through the storm. Somehow Ben was still fighting us forward at the wheel.

"What happened?" I asked, touching my head to see if there was blood. I could feel wetness, but then, I was soaked through.

"The genoa went," Ben replied. "It was washed into the water with that wave; it filled up. I thought it was going to drag us down. Then... I don't know, maybe the shackle sheared off or something? Anyway, it's gone."

I didn't answer that. I had nothing to say, and instead, I let myself slump over the rail and threw up a mixture of vomit and seawater, coughing it up in lumps while the yacht rolled underneath me. But Ben wasn't finished with me.

"Mate, I think we're struggling because we've got too much weight at the front. So when you're done with that, I need you to move all the coke away from the front. We get hit with another wave like that, with all that weight up front, we might not come up again."

I stared at him, mouth open, panting from the effort of what I'd just done.

"You want me to throw it overboard?"

In a weird moment in the storm, Paul interrupted.

"Throw forty million pounds overboard? You fucking do Jake, you're going straight after it."

Ben laughed. "No mate. Just get it in the aft cabin. We should have done it before we hit the storm. Paul if you can, help as well…?"

In the end the three of us stumbled downstairs, Paul, Julia and me. We were greeted by chaos. There was food from the galley all over the floor, and sloshing from one side to another with all the water we'd taken on. The pump was doing its best to get it out again, but it was barely keeping pace with how fast we were shipping it. We fought our way forward, and I prised open my first compartment and looked at the contents, packed tight enough that the storm hadn't moved them. Each package weighed twenty kilos, and we made a human chain to move them back, since there was no way to carry them down the length of the yacht as it pitched and smashed through the waves. We were thrown around, smashed into the cabin walls and even the roof sometimes, but we did it. We emptied the bow hiding places and filled my cabin in the back with the cargo. And Ben was happy about it. He shouted from the wheel that the steering was much lighter, the boat responding better to his attempt to steer through the waves, and we could feel it too. The *Prima Donna* felt happier too; she felt in control again.

I wouldn't say it was comfortable after that. It was still like being on a rollercoaster with your eyes closed, and every now and then, being hit by a heavyweight boxer. When a really big wave hit, or even just a smaller one from an unexpected angle, the whole boat would jar down with an impact so hard, I feared the hull might just crack in half. But we were right in the storm by then, and at least, it didn't seem to be getting any worse. In fact it seemed to be getting better.

We all felt it in the boat's movement. The sea around us was more black and less white, the bigger waves were coming less often and when they came we rode them better. Paul and Julia both improved as well. They were sitting up, able to talk and even to smile a little.

Later Ben was still steering, a grim look on his face, his eyes tired. I hardly noticed when Paul got up and walked unsteadily to the hatch.

"Next run of forecast should be in," he said, and disappeared below.

I looked at my watch, confused for a second, then I saw we'd been beating through the storm for five hours since the big wave hit us, I had no idea so much time had passed.

Suddenly I jumped. There was a new noise I didn't recognise; couldn't place. I suddenly realised it was music. Paul must have put the stereo on. Then he turned it up. Somehow he'd found the soundtrack to Rocky, the sound was fighting with the noise from the wind and the waves. Then Paul's head reappeared in the hatch. He was clasping a bottle of whisky.

"Wind's easing. We're through the worst of it. That calls for a drink, right?"

He unscrewed the top of the bottle and drank deeply. Then he handed it to Ben who hesitated for a moment before doing the same. Ben passed the bottle to Julia. She took a swig and looked like she was going to throw it straight back up, but smiled gratefully. She passed it to me and I let the liquid burn heat back into my stomach while Paul turned to the storm and roared at it, a defiant noise that seemed to carry out into the night. I drank again, and passed the bottle back to Ben.

CHAPTER FORTY-SEVEN

WE MADE IT through that night, the longest I ever knew. When the dawn did come, the sky was clear, and it revealed a sea like nothing I'd seen before. It was scarred with white, the little whitecaps I'd grown used to grotesquely enlarged into smears of foam hundreds of metres long. Under the sun, it had an awesome beauty. A world alive, soaked with energy. The wind was still blowing forty knots, but that was much less than we'd faced earlier, well within what a yacht like the *Prima Donna* could cope with.

As soon as there was enough light to see properly, Ben inspected the boat for damage. There was a short length of rope and a snapped metal shackle where the genoa had washed overboard, but nothing worse than that, and we could fix it, using one of those spare sails from below. The pumps had got rid of most of the water, and we tidied up too, dumping the ruined food over the sides. Julia made some hot food, and we all managed to keep it down. The wind eased more, and on the next run of the weather charts, the situation looked a lot better.

We discussed the options of diverting to somewhere in Spain or France. It was possible there was damage to the underside of the hull that we couldn't see, perhaps even the keel or the rudder. On any normal voyage, you'd head for the nearest port to get things checked over properly, but that was difficult with what we were carrying. So we did the only thing we could do. We hoped for the best. And as best we could, we planned for the worst. We checked over the life raft, making sure it was ready to deploy just in case we needed it, and then we got on with it.

* * *

The sea is different near land. The birds you see are different; the waves move through the water differently. Even the colours change. We felt land before we saw it but then, three days after we sailed through the storm, the low green hills finally appeared over the horizon. But we didn't stop. We plotted the final leg between Ireland and the west coast of Wales, still heading north.

Those final forty-eight hours, going up the Irish Sea, will stay with me for the rest of my life. We all knew how to sail the *Prima Donna* by then, and with the wind behind us at last, we kept close to the east coast of Ireland where the water was flat, and we powered north. Past Dublin, and then Belfast, where we could see the mountains of Scotland as smudges in the distance, and then suddenly they were all around us, towering purple and green and brown, dramatic and lit up under the sunshine. They say Scotland's Firth of Clyde is one of the most dramatic places to sail anywhere in the world and I can well believe it. And we felt like conquering heroes, like champions of the world as we sailed that boat home. Towards the safety of land after the ocean had thrown all it had at us.

And then Paul phoned his brother, to make sure everything was ready to unload.

Chapter Forty-Eight

THE VILLAGE OF Inverkip was our destination, just a few dozen miles around the coast from Glasgow and boasting Scotland's premier yacht marina. We nearly got there too.

Inverkip is too small to feature much of a customs force, but Jimmy and Paul traded on being careful, so the coke was going to disembark in a similar way to how it had come aboard. Jimmy had worked out an arrangement with the skipper of a local fishing boat to transfer the product down into its hold. It could then steam into port as normal, where the packages would be hoisted up onto the hard, hidden inside fish crates and covered in ice. From there, it would be loaded into a refrigerated van and driven to our distribution centre where Aussie Mick would take over. Jimmy had this one sorted. It was going to work. It was safe.

"We're all good," Paul said when he put the phone down. "Rendezvous will be tonight. Shouldn't take more than an hour. Jimmy's putting together a little celebration meal, says we might all appreciate a good steak."

We all liked the sound of that. We'd lost all our fresh food in the storm, we weren't starving but there's only so much tinned meat and vegetables you can eat. We were all keen to get off, to have a proper wash and stretch our legs. Spend a bit of time alone. I had an idea I might take a little trip out to the Caribbean.

We adjusted our course to take us to the place Jimmy's guy had chosen, a little bay on the Isle of Bute. The spot was perfect, tucked up inside the fingers of lochs that led toward the port of Glasgow, well sheltered from the Atlantic swells so that we could transfer the product even if the wind was up, but nowhere that could easily be overlooked by the land. The coordinates fixed a point a couple of miles offshore, under cover of darkness there was no chance of anyone seeing what was going on. And then, as the sun set, we got lucky anyway. A mist rose up over the surface of the water. The wind dropped to nothing, and we had to motor the last few miles through an eerie, beautiful, white silence.

In position, we hove to, sending a signal to the fishing boat that we were ready for them, and then we tracked her in on our radar. And while that was happening, we moved the cargo a final time, stacking it ready in the cockpit and saloon so that it would be easier to unload. There was a weird atmosphere while we worked. It was as if we were all already ashore in our minds. I guess that was understandable. We were at the end of a long and testing voyage, and our work was nearly done. Just one final push.

We were under motor, making the barest speed through the water, really just to hold ground against the tide, when I saw the fishing boat coming out of the gloom: no lights, not even the red-and-green running lights that we had on.

"There they are," I shouted, and everyone seemed to snap themselves more alert. The rusty-red hull of the fishing boat could just be made out in the grey gloom, perhaps fifty metres off our port side.

I was in my favourite place, standing on the steps that led down to the cabin, where I'd waited out the storm, and now my legs were being warmed pleasantly by the engine. But I could still see everything that was going on. And from here, I watched the fishing boat come slowly closer. Its decks were higher than ours, but it was much shorter. A squat ugly-looking boat. Paul had told me the owner would make five times as much in this two-hour trip as he normally made in a two-week fishing trip.

I watched a figure in yellow oilskins climb down from the wheelhouse on the other boat and flash out our pre-arranged signal with a torch. It wasn't necessary; there was no one else it could have been, and there were no other vessels within three miles showing on the radar, but that was the way we'd arranged it. On Paul's instructions, I flashed back our reply.

Since it was so calm now, we'd already put our fenders out. We'd be able to raft up together. Loading the fishing boat would be as easy as handing the bags over the rail, one after the other. No need to faff around with the inflatable boat, or using a hoist. Half an hour, and we'd be on our way. I could almost taste that steak.

The fishing boat closed a little more, now within hailing distance. There was a voice shouting through the gloom, muted by the damp heaviness of the night air.

"Hold your course. We'll come to you."

"We have fenders on our port side," Paul shouted back. We weren't using the radio now, nothing that could be picked up by other boats.

The fishing boat began to make a long, slow turn, so it could come alongside us. And I want to try and give an accurate account of exactly what happened next. But it's hard now because I've had to tell this part so many times, all the details. Where everyone was at this point, who said what, and in what order.

Ben was standing forward, in front of the mast, standing with his feet planted apart, a rope ready in his hands to throw. Julia was sitting on the aft seat, readying another rope. Her head was turned downward as she secured her rope around the cleat, and I remember how her knees were pressed together, in a weirdly ladylike posture. Paul was all man, though, all alpha male. He was leaning over the wheel, steering with his body as he liked to do, his hands cupped to his mouth, shouting at the skipper of the fishing boat to come in closer. For some reason, the turn they'd made still left them too far away from us to easily throw a rope. They were either being unnecessarily cautious, or something else was happening.

"Fuck's he doing?" Paul muttered. "He's going to have to come around again."

I noticed another man had appeared on deck now, also dressed in yellow oilskins, so that now there were two figures on deck. There must have been a third in the wheelhouse because someone was driving the boat.

That was when it started.

The first thing I saw were a couple of flashes of light. I thought the two fishermen were lighting cigarettes. I even had time to think it a strange coincidence that they both lit up at the same time. And there was a noise too, audible over the low growl of the two engines, but not a noise I recognised, a kind of popping sound.

And I looked at Ben. I don't know why. Maybe the way he was moving caught my eye. It was like he was suddenly dancing, his limbs and head jerking to an unheard beat. Then he crumpled and fell down on his back, hard against the grab rail on the roof, and my brain started to catch up. I pulled my head down into the cabin, turning as I did so to where Paul and Julia were, out in the open, exposed. And I was just in time to see Paul begin the same weird dance as Ben.

With Julia, it was all a whole lot clearer. I heard her scream, and I saw her hands come up to her face before she too jerked, and then it was as if some unseen force took her and threw her backward into the cockpit. And then I saw a line of round holes appear on the seat back, one after the other, as bullets slammed into the yacht.

Then the *Prima Donna*'s engine suddenly roared. I felt it vibrate under me, and I was almost thrown backward into the cockpit. Behind us, a sudden surge of foamy white water was already spreading out behind us. I thought Paul must be thinking to escape, but when I looked, there was no one at the wheel. And then I saw Paul, slumped in the floor of the cockpit, half-draped over the throttle lever. His face was staring up at mine, eyes open. I don't know if he put us into gear intentionally, or if that was just the way his body fell.

In seconds, we were already powering away from the fishing boat, and even over the roar of our engine, I could hear shouts. I half fell down the companionway steps and down below all hell was breaking loose.

We didn't have any lights on, but the cabin interior glowed green from the screen of the radar, and in this light, I watched the weird sight of familiar things zapping into life on both sides of the room. The cabin windows burst in, bottles exploded, something hit the metal body of the gimballed oven, and the front glass shattered. Then the radar screen snapped off, and all I could see were little bursts of yellow where metal hit metal and sparked in the darkness. I fell again onto the floor and covered my head as wood and metal exploded all around. Then the engine began to whine, like a kettle coming to a screaming boil. We were still accelerating at this point, the bow raised in the air, and then the motor suddenly gave up, and the stern levelled again as we slowed. And the firing stopped too. And all I could hear was the sound of water flowing past the hull and what was left of the engine ticking uselessly.

I was too shocked to move at first. I lay on the floor, still covering my head, trying to make sense of what just happened. I knew Ben was dead —at least, on some level I did. None of it seemed real, and had he walked carelessly down the steps behind me, I wouldn't have been surprised, as if this were just a crazy incident that only took place in my head. But I knew that wasn't it.

I wasn't sure about Julia or Paul. I thought maybe they were only injured, but there was little I could think to do. We were totally unprepared for this. We had no weapons. I found myself staring at the radio, but I couldn't think who to call. Instead, I forced myself to climb the ladder out into the cockpit, just enough so that I could see what was happening now.

The first thing I saw was Paul: he was alive, but he didn't look in a good way. I know now that the second burst of gunfire from the fishing boat was aimed at the engine, to stop us from getting away, but some of it had obviously hit Paul. It was too dark to make out details, but the shape of him was all wrong. He was crumpled up in the front of the cockpit, in a shape that humans don't make, and as he opened and closed his mouth, a steady trickle of blood fell like a solid line to the deck. Just looking at what was left of him almost made me sick. Sick at what was left of my friend.

And somehow, it was then that I realised that I was going to die too. I could see the fishing boat now, very close behind us. I could hear shouts from the deck: they were arguing about whether they should have fired or not, and one man was taking charge, telling the others to get ready to jump down. To make sure we were finished off. Maybe I had a moment then when I could have made a run for it, dashed to the rail, and dived in. But it was only a split second, and I didn't take it. Instead, I cowered back down in the cabin as the fishing boat came right up to us, fast. They were metres away now, and I could hear the men on board clearly. Then the bow cracked into the side of us, giving a glancing blow and sending the *Prima Donna* slewing sideways in the water. Then more shouts, and then the unmistakeable sound of a pair of boots landing on the deck.

"Hurry up. Now you've made all that fucking noise, we need to do this fast." I knew that voice, I recognised the Aussie rasp to it.

Bang. A second pair of boots crashed down. The yacht rolled lazily under the weight of them, and I heard them, one set moving forward, the other back, toward the cockpit near where I was lurking, on the steps down into the cabin. Then I saw the feet.

"Hello, Paul!" the man said, and I watched Paul's eyes swivel up to look at him.

"Nice trip? I heard you had a bit of bad weather?"

I'd thought Paul was already too far gone to reply, but he forced himself to make an effort.

"You're dead," he whispered. It was only because everything had gone so quiet that I was able to hear him. And above him, the man laughed.

"You're fucking dead Mick. Jimmy'll gut you alive," Paul said, and this stopped the laughter.

"Your big brother? I don't think so mate. I've got a bit of bad news there. It seems Jimmy's had a little accident. Somehow he managed to get himself shot. Silly boy."

Paul's face was already screwed up in pain, but it grew worse at this.

"So sorry to be the one to tell you that Paul. So sorry." He started laughing again.

And then the man raised his gun, a black shadow in the night and as I watched it spat a yellow burst of fire. Paul's head thudded against the cockpit floor, and I ducked my head down, too terrified and sickened to watch any more. Then from the front, the automatic gunfire opened up again, and I could imagine what that was: Ben lying there, being finished off if he wasn't already dead.

Then the man at the back turned his attention to Julia, and I knew that was my only chance. If I didn't move, I'd be dead in seconds, and there was only one way I could go, forwards, inside the cabin toward the front of the yacht.

The saloon was still full of the coke, ready to unload. I thought for a moment about hiding underneath it, then felt a spasm of sickness at how that idea would end, and then I had a revelation. There's nowhere to hide on a yacht, even a good-sized one like the *Prima Donna*. There's no way to escape. But of course, on this yacht, there *was* a hiding place. One that I'd built myself: the secret compartments in the bow that I'd crafted to hide the coke should anyone come aboard.

I moved just in time, getting to the front of the saloon and into the forward cabin just as a voice shouted down the ladder.

"Anyone down there? If you want to live, you better come out now."

As quietly as I could, I eased off the cover of the compartment I'd put in the bunks in the bow cabin. I'd raised the bunks up to increase the space underneath them, and put a false floor in. I'd never envisaged having to get in there myself, but I found I could just fit in, holding the floor in place above me. It was wet and cold, and I was shaking with fear. It was pitch black in there, and I had no idea if I'd be visible from above.

"Last chance. If anyone's down there, come out now, or I'm gonna put a bullet in your head."

I didn't move. I heard a whistle. An impressed whistle. I guessed Mick was downstairs now, seeing the pile of coke.

"Anyone down there?" This was another voice, the man on the foredeck who'd shot Ben.

"No, it's clear. Just the biggest pile of coke you've ever seen."

"Let's have a look," the second man said, his voice excited. I could hear the sound of his footsteps descending the companionway steps and then another whistle.

"Fucking hell. Fancy a line?"

"No, I fucking don't, and nor do you." Mick said, his voice a serious growl. "Get up the front and check properly. We don't want any surprises while we're unloading."

"Alright. Maybe later huh?"

"Just fucking do it."

I heard the boots coming closer, my heart, already beating fast, hammered so hard I thought he must hear it through the wood. Then the door that separated the saloon from the front cabin banged open. Then the toilet, the little shower. Then the locker that sat opposite it. I had a secret compartment in there too, where we'd stored a few of the bags. I had a horrible thought that he'd see it, and realise the yacht had other hiding places to check, but all I heard was the scrape of coat hangers on the rail; then the door banged shut. Then he was in the cabin with me, just a couple of feet from where I lay. I could see the light from his torch through the cracks at the edges of the lid of my compartment. Then it got brighter as he pulled up the mattress and peered underneath.

"Anyone there?"

Breathing sounds. The light playing around the edges. Like the guy was considering what he was looking at. The hiding places were only supposed to work with a casual inspection. We were playing the odds again. No one was expecting this yacht to be carrying cocaine, so no one would ever have any reason to look too hard. Only now, someone was looking. Looking for me. He was inches away with a gun in his hand.

Something hit the wood by my head. Somehow I knew it was the tip of the gun, he was using the muzzle to test the wood. I trembled, doing everything I could to hold it still.

"I said is there anyone there?" Aussie Mick called out from the saloon.

"No. It's clear."

"Then let's get this shit onboard and get out of here."

I heard the footsteps go back to the saloon. I lay drenched in sweat, shaking with fear. For the next ten minutes, I listened to the sounds of the coke being carried out onto the deck and, presumably, passed across and onto the fishing boat. They moved quickly. I guess they must have tied alongside us. And they didn't talk much. I couldn't think, lying there in the darkness. My brain was replaying the image of Paul's head burst open, and I imagined what had happened to Ben and to Julia, what they'd been thinking as the bullets hit them. And every few moments, my mind came back to me. I tried to think if there was anything on display that would show them there was still someone hiding on the boat.

A voice interrupted the sounds of footsteps and grunts: "Last one's onboard."

"You sure?"

"Yeah. What now?"

"We're gonna sink her. She's going already from the bullet holes. We'll get the bodies in here, and we'll shut the hatch so they don't float out. Water's deep here, no one'll find her for years, maybe never."

I remembered looking at the rendezvous point on the chart plotter. I'd noticed the depth then, although thought nothing of it. There was nothing else said, but a moment later, just aft of me, I could hear the footsteps again, and the sound of dragging, which must have been them pulling Ben's body back to dump it in the saloon. It was obvious that it wasn't easy. They were moving slowly.

It wasn't a big chance, but I figured it was the only one I had left. If I could get out into the cockpit before they got there, and perhaps when their attention was on Ben's body, then maybe I could get into the water before they saw me. It was two miles to the shore from here, and in the mist, I wouldn't be able to see which way to swim, but the idea of drowning, trapped in the cabin with the bodies of my friends horrified me.

I pushed the false floor off me and sat up in the darkness, cracking my head hard on the side of the yacht. With tears flowing from my eyes, I pulled myself out of the forward cabin, through the now empty saloon and cautiously back up the steps that led up to the cockpit. Paul was still there, or what was left of him, but I couldn't see the men who'd done this, and I risked looking out, to see where they were. There was a noise I couldn't identify, but I didn't have long to try. That was when they saw me.

Aussie Mick dropped Ben's body to reach for his gun.

"Fucking hell, there's another one! I thought you fucking checked?" I ducked back down. There really was nowhere to go now, but I ran anyway into my stern cabin, where less than three weeks before, I'd spent those perfect nights with Jenny. Maybe something told me that if I had to die, it might as well be here?

I slammed the door shut and grabbed the mattress from the bunk to try and jam against it. I don't know what I hoped to achieve. There were all sorts of noises above me now as both men scrambled to get back and kill me. But one noise above all the others had grown stronger. It had been muffled by the fog but now it was clear, almost drowning out everything else. The roaring *thud-thud-thud-thud* of blades chopping through the air. Then the sound of a voice over a loudspeaker, and through my cabin window, I could see the world outside had been lit up.

"Drop your weapons and put your hands on your heads. This is the police."

I don't know what those fuckers thought about that, but with a helicopter hovering just over their heads, I guess they didn't have much choice.

Chapter Forty-Nine

WELL HOW DID you think all this was going to end? Ben and Julia were going to disappear into the sunset? Paul and Jimmy were going to shift ever-bigger loads until they retired and tended roses in their garden? We weren't just bringing in a little bit of dope by then. We had over two hundred kilos of cocaine, worth over twenty million pounds. How do these things always end?

* * *

Mick was getting a fortune for his part, we all were, but the thing about money is you can always have more. It was like Jimmy said when he offered us our jobs. The hardest part is getting the staff.

I guess there's an irony that Mick found this out for himself so early on. It was his hit on Jimmy where it all went wrong for him and his guys. He wanted Jimmy and Paul taken out at the same time so neither could warn the other, or figure out what was going on, but that meant having to delegate the hit on Jimmy. He gave the job to two young guys, I met them once. I could have told Mick they weren't up to it.

I learnt about it later. Apparently they followed Jimmy's car, pulling alongside at some traffic lights and shooting him three times through the window. So far so good, but the silly fuckers didn't manage to kill him right off, and what's worse, in their excitement one of them blurted out that Paul was going to get it too, when he tried to unload the coke. I don't know, it was like the guy wanted Jimmy to die knowing how clever their plan was. I guess he'd watched too many films or something.

But as they drove away Jimmy was able to get straight on his mobile and call his contacts in the police. He told them exactly where and when the rendezvous was and what was going to happen. He phoned them before he even phoned for an ambulance.

That act of selflessness cost Jimmy his life, but it saved mine.

Really, how else was this going to end? You thought I'd end up starting my adult life with my debts wiped clean? Maybe a little nest egg? That I'd join a management training programme and be just like everyone else? Come on. You've seen the movies. It was always going to end this way. It always does.

* * *

I didn't get bail. The judge agreed there was a significant risk I would try to escape justice. I was sent to the remand section of Edinburgh prison while the repercussions of what we'd done washed through the Scottish police service. While Jimmy's network of contacts did their best to cut themselves off from their worst nightmare. I had my own room, with the door locked twenty three hours a day. The other hour I walked around a dusty yard with thirty guys in for everything from stealing cars to murder. They told me it got better when you actually got convicted.

I didn't know who to trust. Every time the police sat me down to ask questions I didn't know if they were Jimmy's guys or not. Sarah came to see me a few weeks after it all happened, she told me to tell them everything, that it didn't matter any more, I just had to do what I could to reduce my sentence. I'd already decided to talk anyway. The only people I would have protected were already dead. She told me to stay strong. I'd only get a few years. That I had to come and see her when I was out. I promised I would.

I wasn't allowed to use the internet. I couldn't check my emails to see if Jenny had tried to contact me, but I was allowed to write a letter to her, and a prison officer would type it in and send it on my behalf. I spent hours on that letter, trying to find a way to say what I wanted. But it was impossible, it was hopeless. Maybe I could get her to overlook me not telling her about the drugs, maybe I could even get her to think it was somehow exciting, it wouldn't matter. She wouldn't wait for me, not for years. A girl like her was going to get plenty of offers in the meantime. In the end I gave up. I didn't even have the email sent.

Instead I wrote this, waiting for my trial. Staring at the brick wall of my cell, painted prison grey, a locked door to my left, a high barred window to my right. The whole story of how I got into smuggling drugs, and got out again the other side.

EPILOGUE

THE TAXI PULLED up in the small square next to the inner harbour in George Town, the capital of Grand Cayman. A cluster of former colonial buildings crowded the waterfront, their paint faded and peeling in the hot sunshine. Amongst them a few modern steel and glass buildings tried to fit in, trying not to advertise how they sat on the hidden wealth of the world. A pontoon was crowded with glass bottom tourist boats, locals trying to make a living from the cruise ships that stopped here. Further out a few small yachts nodded up and down at anchor in the calm blue water. It looked a nice enough place to disappear.

I paid the taxi and looked around. There was a café there, a few tables outside where men smoked and drank, and an interior that looked dark in the midday sunshine. I went in and ordered a coffee, then added a rum as well. I pulled out my phone and sat looking at it.

It took nine months for the trial to be scheduled and organised. Nine fucking months. They told me at first it would be nine weeks. Then the trial took nearly two months. For what I'd done I should have been facing charges with a life sentence, but because I co-operated it was reduced to five years. With time served that meant maybe a year in prison.

And then what?

When I took stock of what I had left in life, it boiled down to one thing. It didn't make any sense but there it was. Not much in life makes sense when you stop to think about it.

I finished my drink and went back out into the sun, checking my watch. My eyes went once again to the bay outside the harbour. One yacht in particular caught my eye, its mast towering above all the others. There were people on deck, but it was too far away to see who, perhaps a head of blond hair?

I looked at my phone again, the screen hard to see in the brightness. I walked over to a palm tree and leaned against the trunk, using its brushy foliage to shield the sun. I scrolled through the contacts. There weren't many to choose from, but it still took me a while to select the name I wanted. My finger hovered over the button, my hand didn't feel my own when I finally pressed the call button. I saw it begin to ring.

I put the phone to my ear, still watching that figure on the foredeck of the yacht, a woman perhaps. It was too far away really but I fancied I could see her pulling out a phone, looking at the screen.

The phone rang, for a long time the figure didn't move. No one answered. Then I saw movement on the yacht. A voice answered.

"Are you here?"

"Yeah."

"I'd best come ashore then."

"OK."

"Come down to the landing slip."

"OK."

I didn't move at first. Just watched the yacht where the figure was now climbing into an inflatable dinghy tied onto the stern. Then I shouldered my backpack and walked the few metres down to the slip. It was too hot to sit in the sun so once again I sheltered under a palm. I watched the little grey inflatable buzzing through the water towards me. It was close enough now that I could see who it was. I was tempted to raise a hand in greeting, but the young woman driving the boat wasn't looking, she was concentrating on her task.

A few months into my remand, my lawyer suggested that he access my email account to deal with any outstanding issues which might have come up. Apparently that's fairly standard. One of those issues was the few people who had written to me since I'd been arrested, asking what was going on. My lawyer printed them out and delivered me the messages, so I could reply if I wanted to. Mostly I didn't want to. Except for a string of messages from one person.

The woman steered the boat expertly to the quayside and cut the engine a few meters short so that the rubber nose of the boat bumped the concrete. She reached out and caught hold of an iron ring, then threaded the painter through it, tying it off neatly. She looked around, not seeing me. Her hair shone in the sun. I pushed myself forward off the wall and stepped into the sunlight.

"Hello Jenny," I said.

For a long time she didn't move. Her lips were set thin, her expression not angry but unsure.

"So. You still want to buy that yacht?" I said.

She stared at me, trying to read my face, then she looked down at the water and shook her head. Then looked at me again. And smiled.

"I think you'd better buy me lunch first," she said, and reached out a hand for me to help her from the boat.

A Short Message from the Author

Thank you for reading *The Desert Run* and I really hope you enjoyed it.

It's the second novel I've published, following the (rather surprising) success of my debut novel *The Wave at Hanging Rock.* It actually started out as a short story, but as I enjoyed writing it, I just kept going. I hope something similar happened to you when you picked it up to read.

If you did enjoy the book it would be great if you could leave a short review on Amazon. It's easy to do, just visit the book's Amazon page and click the button saying "Write a Customer Review". If you're a reader you probably already know, but reviews are vitally important for new authors like myself. Each and every one helps to push a book that little bit higher up the rankings. Every review is greatly appreciated.

If you'd like to hear about any future books I write (and I'm particularly excited about book three as I write this), please do join my reader group. It's easy and free and I make all books I write available here first and at a significant discount (quite often free). It goes without saying I'll never sell your email address or send you spam or anything nasty like that, and you can unsubscribe at any time if my infrequent updates get on your nerves! To join, simply visit www.greggdunnett.co.uk and add your name at the bottom of the page.

Thanks again for reading!

Gregg Dunnett
May 2017

About the Author

Gregg Dunnett worked as Staff Writer and Photographer for the best-selling windsurfing magazine *Boards* for nearly ten years. He was sent around the world testing equipment and reporting on competitions and locations. Eventually *Boards* went bust, which wasn't entirely his fault, and he eventually turned to writing novels instead. His first to be released was *The Wave at Hanging Rock* in 2016 and in 2017 he released *The Desert Run.*
He lives on the UK's south coast with his partner Maria and their two young children.

Gregg on why he writes:
"I've always wanted to do two things in life, to write, and to have adventures. When I was a kid I imagined grand affairs. Kayaking across Canada, cycling to Australia. Whole summers in the Arctic. Did it happen? Well, partly.

I've been lucky, I spent some years abroad teaching English. I worked in sailing schools in Greece and Spain. I really lucked out with a job testing windsurfing boards for the magazine I grew up reading. I made a questionable decision (OK, a bad decision) to buy a windsurfing centre on the edge of the Sinai Desert. I've also done my fair share of less exciting jobs. Packing and stacking potatoes on a farm, which got me fitter than I've ever been in my life. A few years in local government which taught me that people really do have meetings that result only in the need for more meetings, and they really do take all afternoon. I spent a pleasant few months in a giant book warehouse, where I would deliberately get lost among the miles of shelves unpacking travel guides and daydreaming. I've done a bit of writing too, at least I learned how to write. *Boards* Magazine isn't well known (it doesn't even exist today) but it did have a reputation for being well written and I shoe-horned articles in my own gonzo journalism style on some topics with the most tenuous of links to windsurfing. But the real adventures never came. Nor did the real writing.

Then, in 2015, my brother announced he was going to become the first person to windsurf alone around Great Britain. I don't know why. Apparently it was something he'd always wanted to do (news to me.). It was a *proper* adventure. It was dangerous, it was exciting. Before he even set off he got on TV, in the papers. Some people thought he was reckless, some thought he was inspirational. Lots of people thought he'd fail.

But he didn't. He made it around. He even sailed solo from Wales to Ireland, the first to make the crossing without the aid of a safety boat. I was lucky enough to be involved in a superficial planning level, and take part in a few training sails, and the last leg of the trip. But he did ninety nine percent of it on his own. One step at a time, just getting on with it. That was quite inspiring.

In a way it inspired me to pull my finger out. I'd been writing novels - or trying to write novels - then for a few years. But it was touch and go as to whether I was going to be one of those 'writers' with a half-finished novel lost on a hard drive somewhere, rather than someone who might actually manage to finish the job.

I've now got two lovely, highly demanding children, so real adventures are hard right now. I still try to get away when I can for nights out in the wilds rough camping, surf trips sleeping in the van, windsurfing when the big storms come. I love adventures with the kids too.

I hope in time to get around to a few real adventures. I want to sail across an ocean. I want to bike across a continent. I definitely want to spend more time surfing empty waves.

But for me, for now at least, the real adventures take place in my mind. In my real life I'm too chained-down with the mortgage to travel the world at the drop of a hat. But when I'm writing I'm totally free. When I write, that's me having an adventure."

Also by Gregg Dunnett

What if your best friend was a psychopath…
And you didn't notice?

A psychological thriller with soul. Expat teenager Jesse forms a tight friendship with charismatic local surfer John, but as their bond grows, a darker side to John emerges. Will Jesse notice before it's too late?

Newly qualified psychologist Natalie's life falls apart when her husband Jim is lost at sea. Was it a tragic accident, or something more? A mysterious phone call sets Natalie on a path to discover the truth, but as she delves deeper her own demons may come back to haunt her. Get set for a page-turning ride as these stories crash together with a twist that's been described as mind-blowing, shocking, and unmissable.

The Wave at Hanging Rock is the debut novel from British writer Gregg Dunnett. Since publication in September 2016 it's collected more than 500 five star reviews across Amazon, been shortlisted for the Chanticleer Award for the best mystery/suspense novel of 2016/17 and is being translated into Russian and Spanish.

Available on Amazon and in all good book shops.

Made in the USA
San Bernardino, CA
30 September 2018